FOUR SCORE AND SEVEN YEARS FROM NOW . . .

In the 21st century, Planet Earth was in the grip of an orientalized, paternalistic World State that gave all—and took all. Only in the land that was once the United States were the principles of freedom paid so much as lip service, and even there liberty flickered toward extinction. In such a world as this the Jeffersonians were a band of hopeless visionaries, political cranks, a quixotic underground dreaming of the reinstitution of the American Constitution.

But then a star drive was developed and the Jeffersonians were sentenced to eternal exile. On a world twenty light years and a century from their homes they set out to create a society conceived in liberty and dedicated to the proposition that the individual is more important than the state. They are the New Americans. This is their story.

SPECIAL BONUS: The Hugo and Nebula Winning THE QUEEN OF AIR AND DARKNESS, and HOME.

New America

Poul Anderson

TOR

A TOM DOHERTY ASSOCIATES BOOK

Copyright© 1983 by Poul Anderson

A TOR Book

Published by Tom Doherty Associates, Inc., 8-10 West 36th Street, New York, New York 10018

First TOR printing: December 1982

ISBN: 48-553-0

Cover art by Tom Kidd

Printed in the United States of America

Distributed by:
Pinnacle Books
1430 Broadway
New York, New York 10018

Acknowledgements: The stories contained herein were first published and are copyright as follows:

"My Own, My Native Land:" *Continuum I,* copyright ©1974 by Roger Elwood

"Passing the Love of Women:" *Continuum II,* copyright ©1974 by Roger Elwood

"A Fair Exchange:" *Continuum III,* copyright© 1974 by Roger Elwood

"To Promote the General Welfare:" *Continuum IV,* copyright© 1975 by Roger Elwood

"The Queen of Air and Darkness:" *The Magazine of Fantasy and Science Fiction,* copyright ©1971 by Mercury Press, Inc.

"Home:" *Orbit I,* copyright ©1966 by Berkeley Publishing Corporation

"Our Many Roads to the Stars:" *Galaxy,* copyright© 1975 by Universal Publishing and Distributing Corporation.

TABLE OF CONTENTS

MY OWN, MY NATIVE LAND

The boy stood at sunrise on the edge of his world. Clouds torrented up along the gap which clove it. They burned in the light. Wind sang, cold and wholly pure.

A spearfowl broke from those mists to soar further aloft, magnificence upon wings the hue of steel. For an instant the boy did not move. He could not. Then he screamed, once, before he fled.

He took shelter in a thicket until he had mastered both tears and trembling. Boys do not tell anyone, least of all those who love them, that they are haunted.

"Coming in, now," said Jack O'Malley over the radio phone, and got to work at a difficult approach.

On its northeastern corner, that great tableland named High America did not slope in mountains and valleys, to reach at last the sea level which lay eight kilometers straight beneath. Here the rim fell in cliffs and talus until vapors drowned vision. Only at one place were the heights climbable: where a fault had driven them apart to make the Cleft. And the drafts which it channeled were treacherous.

As his aircar slanted toward ground, O'Malley had a clear view across the dropoff and its immense gash. At evening, the almost perpetual clouds that lapped around the plateau were sinking. Rock heaved dark and wet above the ocean, which billowed to the horizon. Their whiteness bore a fire-gold tinge and shadows were long upon them; for the Eridani sun was low in the west, barely above the sierra of the Centaurs. The illusion of its hugeness could well-nigh overwhelm a man who remembered Earth, since in fact its disc showed more than half again the width of Terrestrial Sol. Likewise the ruddier hue of its less ardent G5 surface was more plain to see than at high noon.

Further up, O'Malley's gaze had savored a sweep of country from Centaurs to Cleft, from Hercules Mountains to Lake Olympus, and all the grasslands, woodlands, farmlands in between, nourished by the streams out of yonder snowpeaks. Where the Swift and Smoky Rivers joined to form the Emperor, he should have been able to make out Anchortown. But the rays blazed too molten off their waters.

Instead, he had enjoyed infinite subtleties of color, the emerald of man's plantings mingled in patchwork with the softer blue greens of native growth. Spring was coming as explosively as always on Rustum.

Raksh, the larger moon, stood at half phase in a sky turning royal purple. About midway between the farthest and nearest points of its eccentric orbit, it showed a Lunar size, but coppery rather than silver. O'Malley scowled at the beautiful sight. It was headed in closer, to raise tides in the dense lowland air which could make for even heavier equinoctial storms than usual. And that was just when he wanted to go down there.

His pilot board beeped a warning and he gave his whole attention back to flight. It was tricky at best, in this changeable atmosphere, under a fourth more weight then Earth gives to things: Earth, where this vehicle was designed and made. He wondered if he'd ever see the day when the colony manufactured craft of its own, incorporating the results of experience. Three thousand people, isolated on a world for which nature had never intended them, couldn't produce much industrial plant very soon.

Nearing ground, he saw Joshua Coffin's farmstead outlined black against sky and some upsurgings from the cloud deck. The buildings stood low, but they looked as massive as they must be to withstand hurricanes. Gim trees and plume oak, left uncut for both shade and windbreak, were likewise silhouetted, save where the nest of a bower phoenix phosphoresced in one of them.

O'Malley landed, set his brakes, and sprang out: a big, freckle-faced man, athletic in spite of middle age grizzling his red hair and thickening his waist. He wore a rather gaudy coverall which contrasted with the plainness of Coffin's. The latter was already, courteously, securing the aircar's safety cable to a bollard. He was himself tall, as well as gaunt and crag-featured, sun-leathered and iron-gray. "Welcome," he said. They gripped hands. "What brings you here that you didn't want to discuss on the phone?"

"I need help," O'Malley answered. "The matter may or may not be confidential." He sighed. "Lord, when'll we get proper laser beams, not these damn 'casts that every neighborhood gossip can listen in on?"

"I don't believe our household needs to keep secrets," said Coffin a bit sharply. Though he'd mellowed over the years, O'Malley was reminded that his host stayed a puritanical sort. Circumstance had forced this space captain to settle on Rustum—not any strong need to escape crowding, corruption, poverty, pollution, and the tyranny on Earth. He'd never been part of the Constitutionalist movement. In fact, its rationalism, libertarianism, tendency toward hedonism, to this day doubtless jarred on his own austere religiousness.

"No, I didn't mean that," O'Malley said in haste. "The thing is—Well, could you and I talk alone for a few minutes?"

Coffin peered at him through the gathering dusk before he nodded. They walked from the parking strip, down a graveled path between ornamental bushes. The stellas were starting to flower, breathing a scent like mingled cinnamon and—something else, perhaps new hay—into coolness. O'Malley saw that Teresa Coffin had finally gotten her roses to flourish, too. How long had she worked on that, in what time she could spare from survival and raising their children and laying the groundwork of a future less stark than what she had known of Rustum? Besides science and ingenuity, you needed patience to make Terrestrial things grow. Life here might be basically the same kind as yours, but that didn't mean it, or its ecology, or the soil that that ecology had formed, were identical.

The small stones scrunched underfoot. "This is new, this graveling," O'Malley remarked.

"We laid it two years ago," Coffin said.

O'Malley felt embarrassed. Was it that long since he'd had any contact with these people? But what had he in common with farmers like them, he, the professional adventurer? It struck him that the last time he'd trodden such a path was on an estate on Earth, in Ireland, an enclave of lawns and blossoms amidst rural bondage and megalopolitan misery. Memory spiraled backward. The sound of pebbles hadn't been so loud, had it? Of course not. His feet had come down upon them with only four-fifths the weight they did here. And even on High America, the air was thicker than it was along the seashore of Earth, carried sound better, made as simple an act as brewing a pot of tea into a different art—

A volant swooped across Raksh, warm-blooded,

feathered, egg-laying, yet with too many strange-nesses to be a bird in anything than name. Some-where a singing "lizard" trilled.

"Well," said Coffin, "what is this business of yours?"

O'Malley reflected on how rude it would be to make Teresa wait, or the youngsters for that mat-ter. He drew breath and plunged:

"Phil Herskowitz and I were running scientific survey in the deep lowlands, around the Gulf of Ardashir. Besides mapping and such, we were col-lecting instrument packages that completed their programs, laying down fresh ones elsewhere—oh, you know the routine. Except this trip didn't stay routine. A cyclops wind caught us at the interme-diate altitude where that kind of thing can happen. Our car spun out of control. I was piloting, and tried for a pontoon landing on the sea but couldn't manage it. The best I could do was crash us in coastal jungle. At least that gave us some treetops to soften impact. Even so, Phil has a couple of broken ribs where the fuselage got stove in against his chair.

"We didn't shear off much growth. It closed in again above the wreck. Nobody can land nearby. We put through a distress call, then had to struggle a good fifty kilometers on foot before we reached a meadow where a rescue car could safely settle.

"That was five days ago. In spite of not being hurt myself, I didn't recover from the shock and exhaustion overnight."

"Hm." Coffin tugged his chin and glanced sideways. "Why hasn't the accident been on the news?"

"My request. You see, it occurred to me—what I mean to ask of you."

"Which is?"

"I don't think a lot of the wreckage can be salvaged, damn it, but I'd like to try. You know what it'd be worth to the colony, just to recover a motor or something. Salvagers can't feasibly clear a landing area; they'd have no way of removing the felled trees, which'd pose too much of a hazard. But they can construct a wagon and slash a path for it. That'd at least enable them to bring out the instruments and tapes more readily—I think—than by trudging back and forth that long distance carrying them in packs."

"Instruments and tapes," Coffin said thoughtfully. "You consider that, whether or not repairable parts of the car can be recovered, the instruments and tapes must be?"

"Oh, heavens, yes." O'Malley replied. "Think how much skilled time was spent in the manufacture, then in planting and gathering the packages —in this labor-short, machine-poor economy of ours. The information's tremendously valuable in its own right, too. Stuff on soil bacteria, essential to further improvement of agriculture. Meteorology, seismology—Well, I needn't sell you on it, Josh. You know how little we know, how much we need to know, about Rustum. An entire *world*!"

"True. How can I help?"

"You can let your stepson Danny come along with me."

Coffin halted. O'Malley did the same. They stared at each other. The slow dusking proceeded.

"Why him?" Coffin asked at last, most low. "He's only a boy. We celebrated his nineteenth . . . anniversary . . . two tendays ago. If he were on Earth, that'd have been barely a couple of months past his fifteenth."

"You know why, Josh. He's young, sure, but he's the oldest of the exogenes—"

Coffin stiffened. "I don't like that word."

"I'm sorry. I didn't mean—"

"Just because he was grown artificially instead of in a uterus, from donated cells instead of his parents coming here in person, he's not inferior."

"Sure! Understood! How would three thousand people be a big enough gene pool for the future, cut off in an environment like this, if they didn't bring along—"

"—a potential million extra parents. When you marry, you'll also be required to have one of them brought to term for you to adopt."

O'Malley winced. His Norah had died in the Year of Sickness. Somehow he'd never since had more than fleeting liaisons. Probably that was because he'd never stayed put long at a time. There was too much discovery to be made, by too few persons who were capable of it, if man on Rustum was to endure.

Yet he was still, in one way, shirking a duty to wed. Man in his billions was a blight on Earth, but on Rustum a very lonely creature whose hold on existence was precarious at best. His numbers must be expanded as fast as possible—and not merely to provide hands or even brains. There is a more subtle kind of underpopulation, that can be deadly to a species. Given too few parents, too much of their biological heredity will be lost, as it fails to find embodiment in the children they can beget during their lifetimes. In the course of generations, individuals will become more and more like each other. And variability is the key to adaptability, which is the key to survival.

A partial, though vital solution to the problem lay in adoption. Spaceships had been overburdened with colonists; they would certainly not add a load of plants and animals. It sufficed to carry seeds—of both. Cold-stored, sperm and ovum could be kept indefinitely, until at last it was convenient to unite them and grow a new organism an an exogenetic tank. As easily as for dogs or cattle, it could be done for humans. Grown up, marrying and reproducing in normal fashion—for they would be perfectly normal people—they would contribute their own diverse chromosomes to the race.

This was, however, only a partial measure. The original settlers and their descendants must also do their part.

Coffin saw O'Malley's distress, and said more gently: "Never mind. I get your point. You remembered how Danny can tolerate lowland conditions."

The other man braced himself. "Yes," he replied. "I realize the original cell donors were chosen with that in mind. Still, the way we lucked out with him, this early in the game—Look. The trip does involve a certain hazard. It always does, when you go down where everything's so unearthly and most of it unknown. That's why I've kept my idea secret, that Danny would be the best possible partner on this expedition. I don't think the risk is unduly great. Nevertheless, a lot of busybodies would object to exposing a boy to it, if they heard in advance. I thought, rather than create a public uproar . . . I thought I'd leave the decision to you. And Teresa, naturally."

Again Coffin bridled. "Why not Danny?"

"Huh?" O'Malley was startled. "Why, I, well, I took for granted he'd want to go. The adventure—a *real* springtime vacation from school . . . After all, when he was a tyke, he wandered down the Cleft by himself—"

"And got lost," Coffin said bleakly. "Almost died. Was barely saved, found hanging onto the talons of a giant spearfowl that aimed to tear him apart."

"But he *was* saved. And that was what proved he was, is, the first real Rustumite, a human who can live anywhere on the planet. I've not forgotten what a celebrity it made him."

"We've gone back to a decent obscurity, him and the rest of us," Coffin said. "I've seen no reason to publicize the fact that he's never since cared to go below the clouds. He's a good boy, no coward or sluggard, but whenever he's been offered a chance to join some excursion down, even a little ways, he's found an excuse to stay home. Teresa and I haven't pushed him. That was a terrible experience for a small child. In spite of being a ninety days' wonder, he had nightmares for a year afterward. I wouldn't be surprised if he does yet, now and then."

"I see." O'Malley bit his lip. They stood a while beneath a Raksh whose mottled brightness seemed to wax as heaven darkened. The evening star trembled forth. A breeze, the least bit chilly, made leaves sough. It was not bedtime; this close to equinox, better than thirty-one hours of night stretched before High America. But the men stood as if long-trained muscles, guts, blood vessels, bones felt anew the drag upon them.

"Well, he's got to outgrow his fears," burst from O'Malley. "He has a career ahead of him in the lowlands."

"Why should he?" Coffin retorted. "We'll take generations to fully settle this one plateau. Danny can find plenty of work. We could even argue that he ought to protect those valuable chromosomes of his, stay safe at home and found a large family. His descendants can move downward."

O'Malley shook his head. "You know that isn't true, Josh. We won't ever be safe up here on our little bit of lofty real estate—not till we understand a hell of a lot more about the continent, the entire planet that it's part of. Remember? We could've stopped the Sickness at its beginning, if we'd known the virus is carried from below by one kind of nebulo-plankton. We'll never get proper storm or quake warnings till we have adequate information about the general environment. And what other surprises is Rustum waiting to spring on us?"

"Yes—"

"Then there's the social importance of the lowlands. We came because it was our last hope of establishing a free society. In those several generations you speak of, High America can get as crowded as Earth. Freedom needs elbow room. We've got to start expanding our frontiers right away."

"I'm not convinced that a political theory is worth a single human life," Coffin said. His tone softened. "However, the practical necessities you mention, you're right about those. Why do you need Danny?"

"Isn't it obvious? Well, maybe it isn't unless you've seen the territory. Take my word for it, men who have to wear reduction helmets are too handicapped to accomplish much in that wilderness. I told you, Phil and I barely made it to rendezvous with our rescue craft, and we had nothing more to do than hike. Salvagers will have to work harder."

"Who'll accompany him?"

"Me. We haven't got anybody else who can be spared before weather ruins the stuff. I figure my experience and Danny's capabilities will mesh together pretty well.

"I've arranged about the wage, plus a nice payment for whatever we bring back. The College will be delighted to fill his pockets with gold. That equipment, that information represents too many manhours invested, maybe so many lives saved in future, that anybody would want to write it off."

Coffin was quiet for another space, until he said,

"Let's go inside," squared his shoulders and trudged toward the house.

Within lay firelit cheeriness, books and pictures, more room than any but the mightiest enjoyed on Earth. Teresa had tea and snacks ready; this household did not use alcohol or tobacco. (The latter was no loss, O'Malley reflected wryly. Grown in local soil, it got fierce!) Seven well-mannered youngsters greeted the visitor and settled back to listen to adult talk. (On Earth, they'd probably have been out in street gangs—or enslaved, unless barracked on some commune.) Six of them were slender, brown-haired, and fair-skinned where the sun had not scorched.

Danny differed in more than being the oldest. He was stocky, of medium height. Though his features were essentially caucasoid — straight nose, wide narrow mouth, rust-colored eyes—still, the high cheekbones, blue-black hair, and dark complexion bespoke more than a touch of Oriental. O'Malley wondered briefly, uselessly, what his gene-parents had been like, and what induced them to give cells for storage on a spaceship they would never board, and whether or not they had ever met. By now they were almost certainly dead.

Small talk bounced around the room. There was no lack of material. Three thousand pioneers didn't constitute a hamlet where everybody knew day by day what everybody else was doing, especially when they were scattered across an area the size of Mindanao. To be sure, some were concentrated in Anchor; but on the whole, High

American agriculture could not yet support a denser settlement.

Nonetheless, an underlying tension was undisguisable. O'Malley felt grateful when Teresa suddenly asked him why he had come. He told them. Their eyes swung about and locked upon Danny.

The boy did not cringe, he grew rigid, in the manner of his stepfather. But his answer could scarcely be heard: "I'd rather not."

"I admit we'll face a bit of risk," O'Malley said. "However"—he grinned—"you tell me what isn't risky. I'm mighty fond of this battered hide of mine, son, and I'll be right beside you."

Teresa strained her fingers together.

Danny's voice lifted and cracked. "I don't *like* it down there!"

Coffin hardened his lips. "Is that all?" he demanded. "When you can carry out a duty?"

The boy stared at him, and away, and hunched in his chair. Finally he whispered, "If you insist, Father."

Hours passed before O'Malley left the house, to go home and prepare himself. Meanwhile full night had come upon the highland. The air was cold, silent, and altogether clear. Raksh, visibly grown in both size and phase, stood low above the cloud-sea, while tiny Sohrab hastened in pursuit; both moons crossed the sky widdershins. Elsewhere, darkness was thronged with stars. Their constellations weren't much changed by a score of light-years' remove. And though it was a trifle more tilted, Rustum's axis did not point far from Earth's. He could know the Bears, the Dragon —and near Bootes, a dim spark which was Sol—

More than forty years away by spaceship, he thought—human cargo cold-sleeping like the cells of their animals and plants and foster children, for four decades till they arrived and were wakened back to life. But did the spaceships still fare? It had been a nearly last-gasp effort which assembled the fleet that carried the pioneers here: an effort by which the government, with their own consent, rid itself of Constitutionalist trouble-makers who kept muttering about foolishnesses like freedom. Had any of those vessels ever gone anywhere else again? Radio had not had time to bring an answer to questions beamed at Earth. Nor would man on Rustum be prepared to build ships which could leave it for a much longer time to come. Quite possibly never . . . O'Malley shivered and hastened to his car.

Roxana was a large continent, and this trip was from its middle to the southern edge. Time dragged for Danny. They were flying high, for the most part very little below the normal cloud deck. Hence transient nimbuses, further down, often cut them off from sight of land. But then they would pass over the patch of weather and come back into clear vision—as clear as vision ever got, here.

O'Malley made several attempts at cheerful conversation. Danny tried to respond, but words wouldn't come. At last talk died altogether. Only the hum of jets filled the cabin, or a hoot of wind and cannonade of thunder, borne by the thick atmosphere across enormous distances.

O'Malley puffed his pipe, whistled an occasional tune, sat alertly by to take over from the autopilot if there was any trouble. Danny squired in the seat beside him. *Why didn't I at least bring a book?* the boy thought, over and over. *Then I wouldn't have to just sit here and stare out at that.*

"Grand, isn't it?" O'Malley had said once. Danny barely kept from yelling back, "No, it's horrible, can't you see how awful it is?"

Above, it was pearl-gray, except in the east where a blur of light marked the morning sun. Mountains reared beneath: so tall, as they climbed toward the homes of men, that their heads were lost in the skyroof. They tumbled sharply downward, though, in cliffs and crags and canyons, vast misty valleys, gorges where rivers gleamed dagger bright, steeps whose black rock was slashed by waterfalls. Ahead were their foothills, and off to the west began a prairie which sprawled around the curve of the world. A storm raged there, swart bulks of cloud where lightning flared and glared, remorseless rains driven by the great slow winds of the lowlands. Hues were infinite, for vegetation crowded all but the stoniest heights. Yet those shades of blue-green, tawny, russet were as somber in Danny's eyes as the endless overcast above them; and the wings which passed by in million-membered flocks only drove into him how alien was the life that overswarmed these lands.

O'Malley's glance lingered upon him. "What a shame you don't like it here," he murmured. "It's your kind of country, you know. You're fitted for it in a way I'll never be."

"I don't, that's all," Danny forced out. "Let's not talk about it. Please, sir."

If we talk, I won't be able to hide the truth from him, I'll start shaking. I'll stammer, the sweat that's already cold in my hands and armpits, already sharp in my nose, it'll break out so he can see, and he'll know I'm afraid. Oh, God, how afraid! Maybe I'll cry. And Father will be ashamed of me.

Father, who followed me down into yonder horror and plucked me free of death.

Fear didn't make sense, Danny told himself. His mind had stated the same thing year after year, whenever a dream or a telepicture or a word in someone's mouth brought him back to the jungle. That was what had branded him. Not heat and wet and gloom. Not hunger and thirst (once his belly had lashed him into trying fruits which were unlike those he had been warned were poisonous). Not rustlings, croakings, chatterings, roar and howl and maniacal cackle, his sole changes from a monstrous silence. Not the tusked beast which pursued him, or even—entirely—the gigantic bird of prey whose beak had gaped at him. It was the endlessness of jungle, through which he stumbled lost for hours that stretched into days and nights, nights.

Sometimes he thought a part of him had never come back again, would always grope weeping among the trees.

No, I'm being morbid, his mind scolded him before it sought shelter at home on High America.

Skies unutterably blue and clear by day, brilliant after dark with stars or aurora, the quick clean rains which washed them or the heart-shaking, somehow heart-uplifting might of a storm, the white peace which descended in winter. Grainfields rippling gold in the wind; flowers ablaze amidst birdsong. Wild hills to climb, and woods which were open to the sun. Rivers to swim in—a thousand cool caresses—or to row a boat on before drifting downstream in delicious laziness. The reach of Lake Olympus, two hours' airbus ride whenever he could get some free time from school or farm work, but worth it because of the sloop he and Toshiro Hirayama had built; and the dangers, when a couple of gales nearly brought them to grief, those were good too, a challenge, afterward a proof of being a skilled sailor and well on the way to manhood, though naturally it wouldn't be wise to let parents know how close the shave had been . . .

This I've had to leave. Because I've never had the courage to admit I'm haunted.

Am I really, anymore? That wasn't too bad a nightmare last sleep-time, and my first in years.

The eon ahead of him needn't be unbearable, he told himself. Honestly, it needn't. This trip, he had a strong, experienced boss, radio links to the human world, proper food and clothing and gear; a quick flit home as soon as the job was done, the promise of good pay and the chance of an even better bonus. *All I've got to do is get through some strenuous, uncomfortable days. No more than that. No more. Why, the experience ought to help me shake off what's left of my old terrors.*

Not that I'll ever return!

He settled into his chair and harness, and fought to relax.

The vehicle, a bulky cargo bus, almost filled the open space on which it had set down. Tall, finely fronded blue-green stalks—plants of that varied and ubiquitous family which the colonists misnamed "grass"—hid the wheels and much of the pontoons. Trees made a wall around. They were mostly ruddy-barked goldwood, but among them stood slim feathery soartop, murky fake-pine, crouched ant thorny gnome. Between the trunks, brush and vines crowded like a mob waiting to attack. A few meters inward, the lightlessness amidst all those leaves seemed total, as if to make up for the lack of any noticeable shadows elsewhere. Insectoids glittered across that dusk. Wings beat overhead, some huge in this upbearing pressure. None of life closely resembled what dwelt on High America, and much was altogether unlike it. Those environments were too foreign to each other.

The air hung windless, hot and heavy. It was full of odors, pungent, sweet, rank, bitter, none recalling home. Sounds came loud—a background of trills, whispers, buzzes, rustles, purling water; footfalls; above everything else, the first incautious words of human speech.

Danny took a breath, and another. His neck felt stiff, but he made himself stare around. *No matter how horrible a bush looks, it won't jump out and bite me. I've got to remember that.* It helped a little that they'd let their craft pressurize gradually before venturing forth. Danny had had a chance to get used to the feel of it in lungs and bloodstream.

Jack O'Malley had not. He could endure the gas concentration for a while if he must, with no consequences afterward worse than a bad headache. But let him breathe the stuff too long and carbon dioxide acidosis would make him ill, nitrogen narcosis blur his brain, over-much oxygen begin slowly searing his tissues. Above his coverall, sealed at the neck, rose a glassite helmet with a reduction pump, an awkward water tube and chowlock for his nourishment, a heavy desiccator unit to prevent fogging from the sweat which already studded his face.

And yet he's spent his years on Rustum exploring the lowlands, Danny thought. *What could make a man waste that much life?*

"Okay, let's unload our stuff and saddle up." O'Malley's voice boomed from a speaker, across the mutterings. "At best, we won't get where we're bound before dark."

"Won't we?" Danny asked, surprised. "But you said it was about fifty kilometers, along a hard-packed game trail. And we must have, uh, twenty hours of daylight left. Even stopping to sleep, there shouldn't be any problem."

O'Malley's smile flickered, wistful. "Not for you maybe. I'm not young anymore. Worse, I've got this thing on my head and torso. The pump's powered by my chest expansion when I breathe, you know. You'd be surprised how the work in that adds up, if you weren't so lucky you'll never need the gadget yourself."

Lucky!

"However." O'Malley continued, "we can hike on after nightfall, and I guess we'll arrive with plenty of time for preliminary jobs before daybreak."

Danny nodded. Sometimes he wondered if men wouldn't do best to adapt to the slow turning of Rustum. Whatever the medics said, he felt it should be possible to learn to stay active for forty hours, then sleep for twenty. Could it be that efficient electric lanterns were the single reason the effort had never been made?

"Come dawn, then, we can start constructing what we need to haul the salvage back here," O'Malley said.

"If we can," Danny mumbled.

He hadn't intended to be heard, but was. Blast the dense atmosphere! O'Malley frowned disapproval.

After a moment the man shrugged. "Maybe we will have to give up on the heaviest stuff, like the engine," he conceded. "Maybe even on the biggest, bulkiest instruments, if my idea about the wagon doesn't work out. At a minimum, though, we are going to bring back those tapes—Huh? What's wrong?"

Danny hugged the metal of a pontoon to himself. "N-n-nothing," he pushed forth, around the shriek

that still struggled to escape him. He couldn't halt
the shudders of his body.

Above the meadow soared a spearfowl, not the
big raptor of the highlands but its truly immense
cousin, eight meters from wingtip to wingtip, with
power to carry a little boy off and devour him.

Yet boughs overarched the trail. Nothing flew
beneath that high, high ceiling of bronze, amber,
and turquoise except multitudinous small volants
like living rainbows. And when a flock of tarzans
went by, leaping from branch to branch, chatter-
ing and posturing, Danny found himself joining
O'Malley in laughter.

Astonishing, too, was the airiness of the forest.
"Jungle" was a false word. Roxana wasn't in the
tropics, and no matter how much energy Rustum
got from its nearby sun, the Ardashir coast was
cooled by sea breezes. The weather was not so
much hot as warm, actually: a dry warmth, at that.
Brush grew riotously only where openings in the
woods provided ample light. Elsewhere, between
the boles, were simply occasional shrubs. The
ground was soft with humus; it smelled rich.

Nor was the forest gloomy. That appearance
had merely been due to contrast. Pupils expanded,
the human eye saw a kind of gentle brightness
which brought out infinite tones and shadings of
foliage, then faded away into mysterious cathedral distances.

Cathedral? Danny had seen pictures and read
descriptions from Earth. He'd always thought of a
big church as hushed. If so, that didn't qualify this

wilderness, which hummed and sang and gurgled —breezes in the leaves, wings and paws, eager streams, a call, a carol. Where was the brooding cruelty he remembered?

Maybe the difference was that he wasn't lost; he had both a friend and a gun at his side. Or maybe his dread had not been so deep-rooted after all; maybe, even what he had feared was not the thing in itself, but only memories and bad dreams which for some years had plagued a child who no longer existed.

The trail was easy, broad, beaten almost into a pavement. He scarcely felt the considerable load on his back. His feet moved themselves, they carried him afloat, until he must stop to let a panting O'Malley catch up.

Higher oxygen intake, of course. What an appetite he was building, and wouldn't dinner taste good? What separated him from his chief, besides age, was that for him this atmosphere was natural. Not that he was some kind of mutant: no such nonsense. If that had been the case, he couldn't have stood the highlands. But his genes did put him at the far end of a distribution curve with respect to certain biochemical details.

I don't have to like this country, he told himself. *It's just that, well, Mother used to say we should always listen to the other fellow twice.*

When they camped, he had no need to follow O'Malley into sleep immediately after eating. He lay in his bag, watched, listened, breathed. They had established themselves off the trail, though in sight of it. The man's decision proved right, because a herd of the pathmaking animals came by.

Danny grabbed for his rifle. The plan was to do pothunting, wild meat being abundant. Rustumite life didn't have all the nutrients that humans required, but supplemental pills weighed a lot less than even freeze-dried rations—

He let the weapon sink, unused. It wouldn't be possible to carry off more than a fraction of one of those bodies; and it would be a mortal sin to waste so towering-horned a splendor.

After a while he slept. He fell back into a tomb silence of trees and trees, where the spearfowl hovered on high. He woke strangling on a scream. Although he soon mastered the terror, for the rest of his journey to the wreck he walked amidst ghastliness.

The last several kilometers went slowly. Not only did compass, metal detector, and blaze marks guide the travelers off the game path, while a starless night had fallen, but many patches were less thickly wooded than elsewhere, thus more heavily brushcovered. None were sufficiently big or clear for a safe landing. O'Malley showed Danny how to wield the machetes they carried, and the boy got a savage pleasure from it. *Take that, you devil! Take that!* When they reached the goal, he too could barely stay on his feet long enough to make camp, and this time his rest was not broken.

Later they studied the situation. The slender shape of the car lay crumpled and canted between massive trees. Flashbeams picked out a torn-off wing still caught among the limbs above. There went a deep, changeable pulsing through the odorous warmth. It came from the south, where the ground sloped evenly, almost like a ramp, four or five kilometers to the sea.

Danny had studied aerial photographs taken from the rescue car. In his troubled state, he had not until now given them much thought. Now he asked, "Sir, uh, why'd you head inland, you and Mr. Herskowitz? Why not just out onto the beach to get picked up?"

"Haven't got a beach here," O'Malley explained. "I know; went and looked. The bush continues right to the edge of a whacking great salt marsh, flooded at high tide and otherwise mucky. Wheels or pontoons would too damn likely stick fast in that gumbo. If you waited for flood, you'd find the water churned, mean and tricky, way out to the reefs at the bay mouth—nothing that a pilot would want to risk his car on, let alone his carcass."

"I see." Danny pondered a while. "And with Mr. Herskowitz injured, you couldn't swim out to where it'd be safe to meet you. . . . But can't we raft this stuff to calm water, you and me?"

"Go see for yourself, come morning, and tell me."

Danny had to force himself to do so. Alone again in the wilderness! But O'Malley still slept, and would want to start work immediately upon awakening. This might be Danny's one chance to scout a quicker way of getting the cursed job done.

He set teeth and fists, and loped through the thin fog of sunrise.

At the coast he found what O'Malley had described. Of the two moons, Raksh alone raised significant tides; but those could rise to several times the deep-sea height of Earth's. (Earth, pictures, stories, legends, unattainable, one tiny star at night and otherwise never real.) Nor was the pull of the sun negligible.

From a treetop he squinted across a sheet of glistening mud. Beyond it, the incoming waters brawled gunmetal, white-streaked, furious. Rocks reared amidst spume and thunder. The low light picked out traces of cross-currents, rips, sinister eddies where sharpness lurked already submerged. Afar, the bay widened out in a chop of waves and finally reached a line of skerries whereon breakers exploded in steady rage. Past these, the Gulf of Ardashir glimmered more peaceful.

No doubt at slack water and ebb the passage would be less dangerous than now. But nothing would be guaranteed. Certainly two men couldn't row a sizeable, heavily laden raft or hull through such chaos. And who'd want to spend the fuel and cargo space to bring a motorboat here, or even an outboard motor? The potential gain in salvage wasn't worth the risk of losing still another of Rustum's scarce machines.

Nor was there any use reconnoitering elsewhere. The photographs had shown that eastward and westward, kilometer after kilometer, the coastline was worse yet: cliffs, bluffs, and banks where the savage erosive forces of this atmosphere had crumbled land away.

Above, the sky arched colorless, except where the sun made it brilliant or patches where the upper clouds had drifted apart for a while. Those showed so blue that homesickness grabbed Danny by the throat.

He made his way back. Since he'd gotten a proper rest, again the country did not seem out and out demonic. But Lord, how he wanted to leave!

O'Malley was up, had the teakettle on a fire and was climbing about the wreck making more detailed investigations. "Satisfied?" he called. "Okay, you can rustle us some breakfast. Did you enjoy the view?"

"Terrible," Danny grumbled.

"Oh? I thought it was kind of impressive, even beautiful in its way. But frustrating, I admit. As frustrating as wanting to scratch my head in my helmet.

"—I'm afraid we'll accomplish less than I hoped."

Danny's heart leaped to think they might simply make a few trips between here and the bus, backpacking data tapes and small instruments. The voice dashed him:

"It's bound to be such slow going at best, you see, especially when I'm as handicapped as I am. We won't finish our wagon in a hurry. Look how much work space we'll have to clear before we can start carpentering." They had toted in lightweight wheels and brackets, as well as tools for building the rest of the vehicle from local timber and cannibalized metal. "Then it'll be harder cutting a road back to our game trail than I guessed from what I remembered. And the uphill gradient is stiffer, too. We'll spend some days pushing and hauling our loot along."

"Wh-what do you expect we'll be able to carry on the wagon?"

"Probably no more than the scientific stuff. Damn! I really did hope we could at least cut the jets and powerplant free, and block-and-tackle them onto the cart. They're in perfectly good shape."

Danny felt puzzled. "Why didn't we bring more men? Or a small tractor, or a team of mules?"

"The College couldn't afford that, especially now in planting season. Besides, a big enough bus would cost more to rent than the salvage is worth, there's such a shortage of that kind and such a demand elsewhere. What we have here is valuable, all right, but not that valuable." O'Malley paused. "Anyway, I doubt the owner of a really big vehicle would agree to risk it down here for any price."

"It's only okay to risk us," Dannny muttered. *I'm not afraid,* he told himself. *I'm not! However... all the reward I could win doesn't counterbalance the chance of my dying this young in this hell.*

O'Malley heard and, unexpectedly, laughed. "That's right. You and I are the most society can afford to gamble for these stakes. God never promised man a free ride."

And Father always says, "The laborer is worthy of his hire," came to Danny. *In his mind, it means the laborer* must *be.*

Day crept onward. The work was harsh—with machete, ax, cutting and welding torches, drill, wrench, hammer, saw, and tools less familiar to the boy. Nevertheless he found himself quite fascinated. O'Malley was a good instructor. More: the fact that they were moving ahead, that they were on their way to winning even a partial victory over the low country, was heart-lifting, healing.

Danny did object to being stuck with trail clearance while the other went off to bag them some meat. He kept quiet, but O'Malley read it on his face and said, "Hunting hereabouts isn't like on High America. Different species; whole different ecology, in fact. You'd learn the basic tricks fast, I suppose. But we don't want to spend any extra time, do we?"

"No," Danny replied, though it cost him an effort.

And yet the man was right. Wasn't he? The more efficiently they organized, the sooner they'd be home. It was just that—well, a hunt would have been more fun than this toil. *Anything* would be.

Slash, chop, hew, haul the cut brush aside and attack what stood beyond, in a rain and mist of sweat, till knees grew shaky and every muscle yelled forth its separate aches. It was hard to believe that this involved less total effort than simply clearing a landing space for the cargo bus. That was true, however. A field safe to descend on, in so thick a forest, would have been impossible to make without a lot of heavy equipment, from a bulldozer onward. A roadway need not be more than passable. It could snake about to avoid trees, logs, boulders, any important obstacle. When it meant a major saving of labor, Danny allowed himself to set off a small charge of fulgurite.

Returning, O'Malley was gratified at the progress. "I couldn't have gotten this far," he said. "You couldn't yourself, up in thinner air." He estimated that in two days and nights they would link their path to the game trail. Then remained the slogging, brutal forcing of the loaded wagon upward to the bus.

At midday dinner, O'Malley called his superiors in Anchor. The communicator in that distant cargo carrier had been set to amplify and relay signals from his little transceiver. Atmospherics were bad; you couldn't very well use FM across those reaches. But what words straggled through squeals, buzzes, and whines were like the touch of a friendly hand. *Wherever we go on Rustum,* Danny thought, *we'll belong,* and was wearily surprised that he should think this.

Rain fell shortly after he and his companion awoke at midafternoon, one of the cataracting lowland rains which left them no choice but to relax in their tent, listen to the roar outside, snack off cold rations, and talk. O'Malley had endless yarns to spin about his years of exploration, not simply deeds and escapes but comedies and sudden, startling lovelinesses. Danny realized for the first time how he had avoided, practically deliberately, learning more than he must about this planet which was his.

The downpour ended toward evening and they crawled out of the shelter. Danny drew a breath of amazement. It was likewise a breath of coolness, and an overwhelming fragrance of flowers abruptly come to bloom. Everywhere the forest glistened with raindrops, which chimed as they fell onto wet grass and eastward splintered the light into diamond shards. For heaven had opened, lay clear and dizzyingly high save where a few cloudbanks like snowpeaks flung back the rays of the great golden sun. Under that radiance, leaf colors were no longer sober, they flamed and glowed. In treetops a million creatures jubilated.

O'Malley regarded the boy, started to say something but decided on a prosaic: "I'd better check the instruments." They were still in the wreck and, though boxed, might have been soaked through rents in the fuselage.

He climbed up a sort of ladder he had made, a section of young treetrunk with lopped-off branches leaned against a door which gaped among the lower boughs. Foliage hid just what happened. Danny thought later that besides making things slippery, the torrent had by sheer force loosened them in their places. He heard a yell, saw the ladder twist and topple, saw O'Malley crash to the ground under the full power of weight upon Rustum.

Night deepened. The upper clouds had not yet returned; stars and small hurtling Sohrab glimmered yonder, less sharply than on High America but all the more remote-looking and incomprehensible. The tent was hot, and O'Malley wanted breezes on his sweating skin. So he lay outside in his bag, half propped against a backpack. Light from a pair of lanterns glared upon him, picked out leaves, boles, glimmer of metal, and vanished down the throat of croaking darkness.

"Yes." Though his voice came hoarse, it had regained a measure of strength. "Let me rest till dawn, and I can hike to the bus." He glanced down at his left arm, splinted, swathed, and slung. Fortune had guarded him. The fracture was a clean one, and his only serious injury; the rest were bruises and shock. Danny had done well in the paramedical training which was part of every education on Rustum, and surgical supplies went in every traveling kit.

"Are you sure?" the boy fretted. "If we called for help—a couple of stretcher bearers—"

"No, I tell you! Their work is needed elsewhere. It was harder for Phil Herskowitz to walk with those ribs of his, than it'll be for me." Pride as well as conscience stiffened O'Malley's tone. Bitterness followed: "Bad enough that we've failed here."

"Have we, sir? I can come back with somebody else and finish the job."

"Sorry." The man set his teeth against more than pain. "I didn't mean you, my son. *I've* failed." He turned his face away. "Lower me, will you? I'd like to try to sleep some more."

"Sure." Suddenly awkward, Danny hunkered down to help his chief. "Uh, please, what should I do? I can push our roadway further."

"If you want. Do what you like." O'Malley closed his eyes.

Danny rose. For a long while he gazed down at the stubbled, pale, exhausted countenance. Before, O'Malley could take off his helmet temporarily to wash, shave, comb his hair. Danny hadn't dared allow that extra stress on the body. Dried perspiration made runnels across furrows which agony had plowed. It was terrible to see this big, genial, powerful man so beaten.

Was he asleep already, or hiding from his shame under a pretense of it?

What was disgraceful, anyway, about a run of bad luck?

Danny scuffed boot in dirt and groped after understanding. Jack O'Malley, admired surveyor-explorer, had finally miscalculated and crashed in an aircar. He could make up for that—it could have happened to anybody, after all—by arranging to recover the most important things. But first it turned out that there was no way to haul back the motor, the heart of the vehicle. And then, maybe because he had actually continued to be a little careless, he fell and got disabled. . . . *All right. His pride, or vanity or whatever, is suffering. Why should it—this much? He's not a petty man. What's wrong with another person completing his project? Certainly not a mere chunk of salvage money. He's well off.*

It must be pretty crucial to him, this. But why?

Danny looked around, to the stars which were relentlessly blinking out as vapors rose from sea and soil, to the shadowiness which hemmed him in. Trees stood half-seen like trolls. They mumbled in the slow, booming wind, and clawed the air. Across the years, his fear and aloneness rushed toward him.

But I can beat that! he cried, almost aloud. *I'm doing it!*

O'Malley groaned. His eyelids fluttered, then squeezed shut again. He threw hale arm across helmet as if to shield off the night.

Realization came like a blow: *He's been afraid too. It's that alien down here, that threatening. More than it ever can be to me. . . . He won his victory over himself, long ago. But a single bad defeat can undo it inside him—*

Jack O'Malley, alone and mortal as any small boy?

Danny shook his fist at the forest. *You won't beat him! I won't let you!*

A minute later he thought how melodramatic that had been. His ears smoldered. Yet, blast, blast, blast, there had to be a way! The wagon was built. The few remaining kilometers of brush could be cleared in some hours. True, no one person could manhandle the thing, loaded, the whole way to the bus; and O'Malley lacked strength to help on that uphill drag. . . .

"Do what you like," the man had whispered in his crushed state, his breaking more of soul than bones.

Uphill?

Danny yelled.

O'Malley started, opened his eyes, fumbled after his pistol. "What is it?"

"Nothing," Danny chattered. "Nothing, sir. Go back to sleep." *Nothing—or everything!*

Roadmaking was a good deal easier between

camp and sea than in the opposite direction.
Besides the ground sloping downward, salt
intrusions made it less fertile. Still, there was
ample brush to lay on muddy spots where wheels
might otherwise get stuck. By the brilliance of a
lantern harnessed on his shoulders, Danny got the
path done before he must likewise sleep.

"You're the busy bee, aren't you?" O'Malley
said drowsily on one of his companion's returns to
see him. "What're you up to?"

"Working, sir," Danny answered correctly, if
evasively. O'Malley didn't pursue the question. He
soon dropped again into the slumber, half natural,
half drugged, whereby his body was starting to
heal itself.

Later, Danny took the wagon to the shore. It
went easily, aside from his occasional need for the
brake. Unladen, it was light enough for him to
bring back alone. But it would require more free-
board—he grinned—especially if it was to bear a
heavier burden than planned. With power tools he
quickly made ribs, to which he secured sheet metal
torched out of the wreck. Rigging would be
difficult. Well—tent and bags could be slashed for
their fabric.

He labored on the far side of the site, beyond
view of the hurt man. Toward morning, O'Malley
regained the alertness to insist on knowing what
was afoot. When Danny told him, he exclaimed,
"No! Have you gone kilters?"

"We can try, sir," the boy pleaded. "Look, I'll
make several practice runs, empty, get the feel of
it, learn the way, make what changes I find we

need before I stow her full. And you, you can pilot
the bus one-handed, can't you? I mean, what can
we lose?"

"Your fool life, if nothing else."

"Sir, I'm an expert swimmer, and—"

Shamelessly, Danny used his vigor to wear
O'Malley down.

Preparation took another pair of days. This
included interruptions when Danny had to go
hunting. He found O'Malley's advice about that
easy to follow, game being plentiful and unafraid.
Though he didn't actually enjoy the shooting, it
didn't weigh on his conscience; and the ranging
around became relaxation and finally a joy.

Once a giant spearfowl passed within reach of
his rifle. He got the creature in his sights and
followed it till it was gone. Only then did he
understand that he had not killed it because he no
longer needed to. How majestic it was!

O'Malley managed camp, in spite of the clumsi-
ness and the occasional need for pain-killer
forced on him by his broken arm. With renewed
cockiness, he refused to return to High America
for medical attention, or even talk to a doctor on
the radio. "I'm coming along okay. You did a first-
class job on me. If it turns out my flipper isn't set
quite right, why, they can soon repair that at the
hospital. Meanwhile, if I did call in, some officious
idiot would be sure to come bustling out. If he
didn't order us home, he'd cram his alleged help
onto us, so he could claim a share in the salvage
money—your money."

"You really will go through with it, then, sir?"

"Yes. I'm doubtless as crazy as you are. No. Crazier, because at my age I should know better. But if the two of us can lick this country—Say, my name is Jack."

Filled with aircraft motor and all, the wagon moved more sluggishly than on its trial trips . . . at first. Then the downgrade steepened, the brake began to smoke, and for a time Danny was terrified that his load would run out of control and smash to ruin. But he tethered it safely above high-water mark. Thereafter he had to keep watch while O'Malley walked back to the bus carrying the data tapes, which must not be risked. Danny could have done this faster, but the man said it was best if he spent the time studying the waters and how they behaved.

He also found chances to get to know the plants better, and the beasts, odors and winds and well-springs, the whole forest wonderland.

Wavelets lapped further and still further above the place to which he had let the wheels roll. He felt a rocking and knew they were upborne. Into the portable transceiver he said: "I'm afloat."

"Let's go, then." O'Malley's was the voice drawn more taut.

Not that excitement didn't leap within Danny. He recalled a remark of his comrade's—"You're too young to know you can fail, you can die"—but the words felt distant, unreal. Reality was raising the sail, securing the lift, taking sheet and tiller in hand, catching the breeze and standing out into the bay.

No matter how many modifications and rehearsals had gone in advance, the cart-turned-boat was cranky. It could not be otherwise. Danny knew sailing craft too well to imagine he would ever have taken something as jerry-built as this out upon Lake Olympus. The cat rig was an aerodynamic farce; the hull was fragile, ill-balanced, and overloaded; instead of a proper keel were merely leeboards and what lateral resistance the wheels provided.

Yet this was not High America. The set of mind which had decided, automatically, that here was water too hazardous for aircar or motorboat, had failed to see that a windjammer—built on the spot, involving no investment of machinery—possessed capabilities which would not exist in the uplands.

Here air masses thrust powerfully but slowly, too ponderous for high speed or sudden flaws, gusts, squalls. Here tide at its peak raised a hull above every rock and shoal except the highest-reaching; and, the period of Raksh being what it was, that tide would not change fast. An enormous steadiness surrounded the boat, enfolded it and bore it outward.

Not that there were no dangers! Regardless of how firm a control he had, it took a sailor who was better than good to work his way past reefs, fight clear of eddies and riptides, beat around regions against which the hovering man warned him.

Heaven was not leaden, it was silver. Lively little weather clouds caught the light of a half-hidden sun in flashes which gleamed off steel and violet hues beneath. The land that fell away aft was a many-colored lavishness of life; over the forest passed uncountable wings and a wander-song to answer the drumbeat of breakers ahead. The air blew full of salt and strength, it lulled, it whistled, it frolicked and kissed. To sail was to dance with the world.

Now came the barrier. Surf spouted blinding white. Its roar shook the bones. "Bear right!" O'Malley's voice screamed from the transceiver. "You'll miss the channel—bear right!" *Starboard*, Danny grinned, and put his helm down. He could see the passage, clear and inviting ahead. It was good to have counsel from above, but not really needed, in this place that was his.

He passed through, out onto the Gulf of Ardashir, which gives on the Uranian Ocean and thence on a world. Waves ran easily. The boat swayed in the long swell of them. So did the airbus, after O'Malley settled it down onto its pontoons. Still, this could be the trickiest part of the whole business, laying alongside and trans-ferring freight. Danny gave himself the challenge.

When both vessels were linked, the man leaned out of his open cargo hatch and cried in glory, "We've done it!" After a moment, with no less joy; "I'm sorry. You have."

"We have, Jack," Danny said. "Now let me give you the instruments first. The motor's going to be the very devil to shift across. We could lose it."

"I think not. Once the chains are made fast, this winch can snatch along three times that load. But sure, let's start with the lesser-weight items."

Danny braced feet against the rolling and began to pass boxes over. O'Malley received them with some difficulty. Nevertheless, he received them. Once he remarked through wind and wave noise: "What a shame we can't also take that remarkable boat back."

Danny gazed at this work of his hands, then landward, and answered softly, "That's all right. *We'll* be back—here."

PASSING THE LOVE
OF WOMEN

After three hours of troubled sleep, Dan Coffin awoke to the same knowing: *They haven't called in.*

Or, have they? his mind asked, and answered: *Unlikely. I gave strict orders I be told whenever word came, whatever it was.*

So Mary's voice has not reached us since dusk. She's lost, in danger. He forced himself to add: *Or she's dead.*

Forever stilled, that joyousness that ran from the radio to him especially? "Remember, Dan, we've got a date exacty three tendays from now. 'Bye till then. I'll be waiting." No!

Understanding it was useless, and thinking that he ought to get more rest, he left his bunk. The rug, a cerothere hide, felt scratchy under his bare feet, and the clay floor beyond was cold. The

53

air did surround him with warmth and sound —trillings, croakings, the lapping of waves, and once from the woods a carnivore's scream —but he hardly noticed. Paleness filled the windows. Otherwise his cabin was dark. He didn't turn on a light to help him dress. When you spend a lot of time in the wilderness, you learn how to do things after sunset without a fluoropanel over your head.

Weariness ached in him, as if his very bones felt the drag of a fourth again Earth's gravity. *But that's nonsense*, he thought. His entire life had been spent on Rustum. No part of him had ever known Earth—except his chromosomes and the memories they bore of billionfold years of another evolution—*I'm simply worn out from worrying.*

When he trod outside, a breeze ruffled his hair (as Mary's fingers had done) and its coolness seemed to renew his strength. Or maybe that came from the odors it brought, fragrances of soil and water and hastening growth. He filled his lungs, leaned back against the rough solidity of walls, and tried to inhale serenity from this, his homeland. A few thousand human beings, isolated on a world that had not bred their race, must needs be wary. Yet did they sometimes make such a habit of it that there could be no peace for them ever?

The two dozen buildings of the station, not only the log shelters like his own but the newer metal-and-plastic prefabs, seemed a part of the landscape, unless they were simply lost in its immensity. Behind them, pastures and grainfields reached wanly to a towering black wall of forest. Before them, Lake Moondance murmured and sheened to a half-seen horizon; and above that world-edge soared mountains, climbing and climbing until their tiers were lost in the cloud deck.

The middle of heaven was clear, though, as often happened on summer nights. Both satellites were aloft there. Raksh was nearly at maximum distance, a tiny copper sickle, while Sohrab never showed much more than a spark. The light thus came chiefly from natural sky-glow and stars. Those last were more sharp and multitudinous than was usual when you looked up through the thick lowland air. Dan could even pick out Sol among them. Two sister planets glowed bright enough to cast glades on the lake, and Sohrab's image skipped upon it as swiftly as the moonlet flew.

It's almost like a night on High America, Dan thought. The memory of walking beneath upland skies, Mary Lochaber at his side, stabbed him. He hurried toward the radio shack.

No one ordinarily stood watch there, but whoever was on patrol—against catlings, genghis ants, or less foreseeable emergency makers —checked it from time to time to see if any messages had come in. Dan stared at the register dial. Yes! Half an hour ago! His finger stabbed the playback button. "Weather Center calling," said a voice from Anchor. "Hello, Moondance. Look, we've got indications of a storm front building off the Uranian coast, but we need to check a wider area. Can you take some local readings for us?" He didn't hear the rest. Sickness rose in his throat.

A footfall pulled him back to here and now. He whirled rather than turned. Startled, Eva Spain stepped from the threshold. For a moment, in the dim illumination of its interior, they confronted each other.

"Oh!" She tried to laugh. "I'm not an urso hunting his dinner, Dan. Honest, I'm not."

"What are you after, then?" he snapped.

If that were Mary, tall and slim, hair like sunlight, standing against the darkness in the door—It was only Eva. In the same coarse coveralls as him, with the same knife and pistol—tools—at her belt, she likewise needed no reduction helmet on her red-tressed, snub-nosed, freckle-faced head. Also like him, she was of stocky build, though she lacked the share of Oriental genes that made his locks dark, cheekbones high, skin tawny. And she had a few years less than he did, whereas Mary was of his age. That didn't matter; they were all young. What mattered was that this was not Mary.

Now don't blame Eva for that, Dan told himself. *She's good people.* He recalled that for a long while, practically since they met, everybody seemed to take for granted that in due course they would marry. He couldn't ask for a better wife, from a practical viewpoint.

Practicality be damned.

Her eyes, large and green, blinked; he saw light reflected off tears. Yet she answered him stiffly: "I could inquire the same of you. Except I'd be more polite about it."

Dan swallowed. "I'm sorry. Didn't mean to be rude."

She eased a little, stepped close and patted his hand. Her palm was not as hard as his; she was a biologist, not an explorer who had lately begun farming on the side. Nevertheless he felt callouses left by the gear and animal harness that every lowlander must use.

(Mary's touch was soft. Not that she was an idler. Even on High America, survival required that every healthy adult work, and she did a competent job of keeping the hospital records. But she never had to cut brush, midwife a cow, cook on a wood fire for a campful of loggers, dress an animal she herself had shot and cure its hide. Such was lowlander labor, and it would be death for Highland Mary to try, even as it was death for her to be long marooned in the wilderness around Lake Moondance.)

"Sure," Eva said gently, "I understand. You've fretted your nerves raw."

"What does bring you here at this hour?"

"The same as you." She frowned. "Do you think I'm not concerned? Bill Svoboda and the Lochabers, they're my friends as well as yours."

Dan struck fist in palm, again and again. "What can we *do*?"

"Start a search."

"Yes. One wretched little aircar available, to scout over how many thousands of square kilometers? It'd take days to assemble a fleet of vehicles. They haven't got days. Bill does, maybe, but Mary and Ralph . . . very possibly don't."

"Why not? If their helmets are intact——"

"You haven't seen as many cases as I have. It takes a pretty strong man, with considerable training, to wear one of those rigs almost constantly. When your own chest expansion has to power the reduction pump—the ordinary person can't sleep in one of them. That, and sheer muscular exhaustion, make the body extra vulnerable to pressure intoxication, when the victim takes the helmet off so he can rest."

Dan had spoken in a quick, harsh monotone. Eva replied less grimly: "They can't be any old where. They were homebound, after all."

"But you know they, the Lochabers, they wanted to see more of the countryside, and Bill promised he'd cruise them around. They'd've been zigzagging the whole way. They could have landed at random, as far as we're concerned, for a closer look at something, and come to grief. Even if we pass near, treetops or crags or mists can hide their vehicle from us."

"I'm aware that this is a rather large and not especially mapped country." Eva's response was dry. It broke into anger. She stamped her foot. "Why are you moping around like this? Dan Coffin, the great discoverer! Won't you *try*?"

He hit back indignation of his own. "I intend to start at dawn. I assure you it's no use flying at night, it's a waste of fuel. Light-amplifier systems lose too much detail, in that complicated viewfield where the smallest trace may be the one that counts. The odds are astronomical against chancing in sight of a beacon fire or in metal-detector range or——" He slumped. "Oh, God, Eva, why am I being sarcastic? You've flown more than I have. It's so huge a territory, that's all. If I had the slightest clue——"

Once more her manner mildened. "Of course." Slowly: "Could we maybe have such a lead? Some faint indication that they might have headed one way rather than another? Did Mary—did Mary tell you she was especially interested in seeing some particular sight?"

"Well, the geysers at Ahriman," he said in his wretchedness. "But the last call-in we got from them was that they'd visited this and were about to proceed elsewhere."

"True. I've played back that tape a few times myself."

"Maybe you put an idea into their heads. Eva? You saw considerable of them, too, while they were here."

"So I did. I chatted about a lot of our natural wonders. Ralph's fascinated by the giant species." She sighed. "I offered to find him a herd of tera-saur. We flew to Ironwood where one had been reported, but it had moved on northward, the trail was clear but there was a thunderstorm ahead. I had trouble convincing Ralph how foolish we'd be to fly near that weather. Just because lowland air currents are slow, those High Americans always seem to think they lack force. . . . No, Ralph's bright, he knows better; but he does have a reckless streak. Why am I rambling? We——"

She broke off. Dan had stiffened where he stood. "What is it?" she whispered.

"That could be the clue we need." The night
wind boomed under his words.

"What?" She seized him by the wrist. Only afterward did he notice that her nails had broken his
skin.

"Terasaur—they migrate upward in summer,
you know. Bill could've promised to locate a herd
for the Lochabers, maybe the same herd you failed
to see. Their tracks are easy enough to spot from
above——" He grabbed her to him. "You're
wonderful! It may turn out to be a false lead, but
right now it is a lead and that's plenty. Come
daybreak, I'm on my way!"

Tears broke from her, though her voice stayed
level. "I'm coming along. You may need help."

"What? I'll take a partner, certainly——"

"The partner will be me. I can pilot a car, shoot
a gun, or treat an injury as well as anybody else.
And haven't I earned the right?"

In the several years of his career as an explorer,
Dan Coffin had often returned to High America.
Not only did the scientists and planners want the
information he gathered about this planet that
they hoped to people with their descendants; but
he himself must discuss further expeditions and
arrange for equipping them. Moreover, he had
family and friends there.

Additionally, at first, he found refreshment of
both body and spirit in the land. High America
rose above the cloud deck that covered most of
Rustum most of the time; its skies were usually
clear, its winters knew snow and its summers cool

breezes through their warmth. Compared to the low country, it was almost like Earth.

Or so he imagined, until gradually he began to wonder. He had gotten a standard teaching about the variations. The sun was smaller in Earth's sky though somewhat more intense, its light more yellowish than orangy. Earth took one-point-seven years to complete a circuit around Sol, but spun on its axis in a mere twenty-four hours. There was a single moon, gigantic but sufficiently far off that it showed half the disc that Raksh did and took about eleven days (about thirty Earth-days) for a cycle of phases. Dan Coffin, who weighed a hundred kilos here, would weigh eighty on Earth. The basic biologies of the two worlds were similar but not identical, for instance, leaves yonder were pure green, no blue tinge in their color, and never brown or yellow except when dying. . . .

Searching his memories, then asking questions carefully framed, he came to realize how poorly the older people—even those who had grown to adulthood on Earth, and even when helped by books and films—were able to convey to him some sense of what the mother globe really was like. Did the differences add up to such alienness that they themselves could no longer quite imagine it? And if this was true, what about the younger folk, the Rustumites born? And what about the children whom they in turn were starting to have?

So did Dan Coffin really need High America?

Most humans absolutely did, of course. The air pressure at lower altitudes was too much for them, made them ill if they were exposed more than very briefly, eventually killed them. But his body could take it, actually thrive on it. In fact, on each return he missed more keenly the high-metabolism vigor that was his down below, the clarity of sound and richness of smells. Besides, High America was too damn cramped. Oh, there was still a lot of fallow real estate; but the future belonged to those who could settle the lowlands. Already the whole wild, beautiful, mysterious, limitlessly beckoning surface of the world was theirs.

He continued to enjoy his visits as a change of pace, a chance to meet people, savor the civilized amenities, roister a bit in what few establishments Anchor supported for that purpose. Yet it was always good to get back to Moondance. This became especially true after Eva Spain arrived there.

Like him, she had been an exogenetic baby, her parentage selected with a view to tolerance of dense air. The result was equally satisfactory for her. He and she could both descend to sea level in comfort, which made them natural partners. Most of those who were beginning to settle the lowlands did not care to go that far down; Moondance station was at two kilometers altitude. Eventually, man as a whole would be able to live anywhere on the planet. That evolution wouldn't take a dreadfully long time, either: because the few who *now* had full freedom were sure to have a disproportionate share in the heredity.

Dan and Eva . . . they worked well together, liked each other, there was no burning romance but there was a growing attraction and certainly a marriage would make excellent sense from every standpoint. But then, for the first time since school days, he encountered Mary Lochaber.

This near summer solstice, at this middle latitude, daylight would endure for about forty-two hours. The searchers intended to lose none of them. Their aircar was aloft before the first eastward paling of the clouds.

Those had again covered the sky. Dan remembered Mary wondering how he could endure such almost perpetual gloom. "It's not like that at all," he answered. "Still another thing you ought to experience for yourself."

Finally she had come, and—His knuckles stood white on the controls.

Eva turned her eyes from the forest. Beneath silver-bright heaven, in the absence of clear shadows, its treetop hues were an infinitely subtle and changeable intermingling. Their endlessness was broken by the upheaval of a plutonic tor, the flash of a waterfall and a great river, the splendid northward climbing of the entire land. Kilometers away, uncountable birds moved like a storm.

"You really are suffering, aren't you?" she asked quietly.

He heard his own voice, rough and uneven: "I used to revel in the sheer bigness of the country. Now, when we have to find one speck that's gotten lost somewhere, it's horrible."

"Don't let it get to you that way, Dan. Either we learn to live with the fact of death—here—or we can never be happy."

He recalled the tidal cross-chop that had capsized their boat when they were taking biological samples off the Hephaestian coast. Half-stunned, he might have drowned if she hadn't come to his aid. Toshiro Hirayama, who had been like a brother to both of them, was indeed lost. The rest of the crew clung to the keel for hours before a rescue flyer found them. She got back her merriment as fast as any of the others. Nevertheless she still laid a wreath now and then before Toshiro's little cenotaph.

"You're a fine girl, Eva," Dan said.

"Thanks," she answered low. "However, it's another girl on your mind, isn't it?"

"And Ralph. And Bill."

"Mainly her. Right?"

Brought up in his stepfather's tradition that a man should not reveal his private feelings to the world, Dan had to struggle for a moment before he could nod and say: "Yes."

"Well, she is beautiful." Eva spoke without tone. "And a very charming, gracious person. But a wife for you?"

"We . . . haven't discussed that . . . yet."

"You've been giving it some mighty serious thought. And so has she."

His heart stumbled. "I don't know about her."

"I do. The way her look dwells on you, the voice she speaks in when you are there—it's obvious." Eva bit her lip. "Is either of you in earnest, though? Truly?"

He thought of long talks, of hikes and horseback rides across her father's lands, of dances in Wolfe Hall and afterward walking her home under frosty stars and hasty Sohrab and the bronze light of Raksh upon a clangorous river. There had been kisses, no more; there had been words like, "Hey, you know, I like you," no more. Yet he had felt that when he came to dinner, her parents (and Ralph, her brother, who shared her blond good looks and sunny temperament) were studying him with a certain amiable intensity.

She herself? "I'm not sure," he sighed. "They've got such a . . . a different style on High America."

Eva nodded. "It might not count as a decent-sized village on earth," she said, "but Anchor is where most of the population on Rustum centers, and where the industry and wealth and culture are. The alpine hinterland may be sparsely settled, but essentially it's been tamed. People have leisure for fine manners. They may even be overcultivating that kind of thing, as a reaction against the early hardships. Meanwhile, we're the raw frontier folk."

"You're hinting at a social gap? No, the Lochabers aren't snobs. Nor are we yokels. We're scientists, carrying out research that is both interesting and necessary."

"Granted. I don't want to exaggerate. Still, it was getting to know those friends of yours—a sort of overnight intimacy that never quite happens in their own safe environment—that drove home to me the fact that there is a difference."

He could not kiss Mary at Moondance. A glassite bulb sealed off her head, maintaining an air pressure that was normal for her. The same pressure was kept in the station's one small guesthouse; but it took discouragingly long to go through its decompression chamber when one's own lungs were full of lowland atmosphere. Anyway, she shared it with her brother.

But there were rich compensations. At last he could show her something of his world, that overwhelmingly greatest part of the planet she had known only from reading, pictures, a few stereotyped tours, and his words. During five magical days, she and Ralph could wander with him and Eva through the templelike vastness, intricacy, and serenity of the woods, or go ahorseback on a laughing breakneck hunt, or see how biological engineering joined slowly with hard work and patience to make the soil bear fruit for man, or. . . .

Rakshlight glimmered on the curve of her helmet and the long fair tresses within. It made a rocking bridge across the waters, which lapped against the boat louder and more chucklingly clear than ever waves did in the highlands. Wind had died, though coolness still breathed through the summer air, and the sail stood ghostly. That didn't matter. Neither he nor she were in any hurry to return.

She asked him: "Where does the name Moondance come from?"

"Well," he said, "the lake's big enough to show tides when Raksh is as close as now; and then the reflections gleam and flash around the way you see."

She caught his hand. "I was thinking," she murmured, "it ought to be Moon-Dan's. Yours. To me it always will be. What you're doing is so great."

"Oh, really," he stammered. "I'm just a servant. I mean, the scientists give me instrument packages to plant and collect, experiments and observations to carry out, and I follow orders. That's all."

"That is not all, as you perfectly well know. You're the one who has to cope and improvise and invent, in the face of unending surprises. Without your kind of people, we'd forever be prisoners on a few narrow mountaintops. How I wish I could be one of you!"

"Me too," he blurted.

Was she suddenly as half-frightened as he? She was quick to ask: "Where did Ralph and Eva go?"

He retreated likewise into the casual: "I'm not sure. Wherever, I'd guess their flit will pass over the Cyrus Valley. She's mighty taken by your car. She's been faunching to try it out under rough conditions. The updrafts there——"

Her tone grew anxious. "Is that safe?"

"Sure, yes. Eva's an expert pilot, qualified to fly any vehicle at any air density. This model of yours can't handle much unlike the H-17, can it? It's only a modification." Because there was around him the splendor of his country, he had to add: "You know, Mary, what worries me is not how well the craft performs, but what its engine may signify. I've read books about what fossil fuels did to the environment on Earth, and here you're reintroducing the petroleum burner."

She was briefly taken aback. "Haven't you heard?" A laugh. "I guess not. You seem to have other things on your mind when you visit us. Well, the idea is not to replace the hydrogen engine permanently. But petroleum systems are easier to build, with far fewer man-hours; mainly because of fuel storage, you know. Dad thinks he can manufacture and sell them for the rest of his lifetime. By then, there should be enough industrial plants on Rustum that it'll be feasible to go back to a hydrogen economy. A few hunded oil-fired power plants, operating for thirty or forty years, won't do measurable harm."

"I see. Good. Not that I'm too surprised. Your brother was telling me yesterday about the work he does in his spare time, drilling into children how they must not repeat the old mistakes. . . ." Again he skirted too near the thing that was uppermost in his heart. "Uh, by the way, you mentioned wanting to see more of the lowlands on your way home, if you could get a pilot who can safely take you off the mapped and beaconed route. Well, I may have found one."

She leaned close. Her gaze filled with moonlight. "You, Dan?"

He shook his head ruefully. "No. I wish it were, but I'm afraid I've taken too much time off from work as is. Like Eva. However, Bill Svoboda is about due for a vacation and——"

The three of them had flown away into silence.

Eva's yell cut like a sword. *"There!"*

She swung the car around so the chassis groaned and brought it to hover on autopilot, a hundred meters aloft and jets angled outward. Dan strained against the cabin canopy, flattening his nose till tears blurred vision and he noticed the pain that had brought them forth. His heart slugged.

"They're alive," he uttered. "They don't seem hurt." Mutely, his companion passed him his binoculars. He mastered the shaking of his hands and focused on the survivors below him and the scene around them.

Mountains made a rim of russet-and-buff woods, darkling palisades, around a valley shaped like a wide bowl. Save for isolated trees, it was open ground, its turquoise grass rippling and shimmering in wind. A pool near the middle threw back cloud images. That must have been what first attracted the terasaur.

They numbered some thirty adults, five meters or more of dark-green scaliness from blunt snouts to heavy tails, the barrels of their bodies so thick that they looked merely grotesque until you saw one of them break into a run and felt the earthquake shudder it made. Calves and yearlings accompanied them; further developed than Terrestrial reptiles, they cared for their young. The swathe they had grazed through the woods ran plain to see from the south. Doubtless Bill Svoboda had identified and followed it just as Eva had been doing.

A hill lifted out of the meadowland. On its grassy lower sloper the other vehicle had landed, in order to observe the herd at a respectful distance. Not that terasaur were quick to attack. Except for bulls in rut, they had no need to be aggressive. But neither had they reason to be careful of pygmies who stood in their way.

"What's happening?" Eva breathed. "They never act like this—in summer, anyhow."

"They're doing it, though." Dan's words were as jerky as hers.

The car from Anchor was not totally beyond recognition. Tough alloys and synthetics went into any machine built for Rustum. But nothing in the crumpled, smashed, shattered, and scattered ruin was worth salvage. Fuel still oozed from one tank not altogether beaten apart. The liquid added darkness to a ground that huge feet had trampled into mud. Now and then a beast would cross that slipperiness, fall, rise besmeared and roaring to fling itself still more violently into the chaos.

The hillcrest around which the herd ramped was naked stone, thrusting several meters up like a gray cockscomb. There the three humans had scrambled for refuge. The berserk animals couldn't follow them, though often a bull would try, thunder-bawling as he flung himself at the steeps, craned his great wattled neck and snapped his jaws loud enough for Dan to hear through all the distance and tumult. Otherwise the terasaur milled about, bellowed, fought each other with tushes, forelegs, battering tails, lurched away exhausted and bleeding till strength came back to seek a fresh enemy. Several lay dead, or dying with dreadful red slowness, in clouds of carrion bugs.

Females seemed less crazed. They hung about on the fringes of the rioting giants and from time to time galloped clamoring in circles. Terrified and forgotten, the calves huddled by the pool.

High overhead, light seeping through clouds burnished the wings of two spearfowl that waited for their own chance to feast.

"I'd guess—well, this has got to be the way it was," Dan said. "Bill set down where you see. The herd, or some individual members, wandered close. That seemed interesting, no cause for alarm. Probably all three were well away from the car, looking for a good camera angle. Then suddenly came the charge. It was a complete surprise; and you know what speed a terasaur can put on when it wants. They had no time to reach the car and get airborne. They were lucky to make it up onto the rock, where they've been trapped ever since."

"How are they, do you think?" Eva asked.

"Alive, at least. What a nightmare, clinging to those little handholds in darkness, hearing the roars and screams, feeling the rock shiver underneath them! And no air helmets. I wonder why that."

"I daresay they figured they could dispense with apparatus for the short time they planned to be here."

"Still, they'd've had the nuisance of cycling through pressure change." Dan spoke absently, nearly his whole attention on the scene that filled the lenses. At the back of his mind flickered the thought that, if this had gone on for as many hours as evidently was the case, the herd would have

wiped itself out by now had it not been handicapped by darkness.

"Well," Eva was saying, "Ralph told me more
than once how he longed to really experience the
lowlands, if only for a few breaths." Her fist
struck the control panel, a soft repeated thud.
"Oh, God, the barrier between us!"

"Yes. Mary remarked the same to me. Except I
always had too much else to show her and try to
make her see the beauty of——"

Bill Svoboda was on his feet, waving. The
glasses were powerful; Dan saw how haggard,
grimed, and unkempt the man was. Mary looked
better. But then, he thought, she would forever.
She must in fact be worse off, that bright head
whirling and ready to split with pain, that breast a
kettle of fire . . . together with hunger, thirst,
weariness, terror. She kept seated on her perch,
sometimes feebly waving an arm. Her brother
stayed sprawled.

"Ralph's the sickest, seems like," Dan went on.
"He must be the one most liable to pressure
intoxication."

"Let me see!" Eva ripped the binoculars from
him.

"Ouch," he said. "Can I have my fingers back,
please?"

"This is no time for jokes, Dan Coffin."

"No. I guess not. Although——" He gusted a
sigh. "They are alive. No permanent harm done,
I'm sure." Relief went through him in such a wave
of weakness that he must sit down.

"There will be, if we don't get them to a proper

atmosphere in . . . how long? A few hours?" Eva lowered the binoculars. "Well, doubtless a vehicle can arrive from High America before then, if we radio and somebody there acts promptly."

Dan glanced up at her. Sweat glistened on her face, she breathed hard, and he had rarely seen her this pale. But her jaw was firm and she spoke on a rising note of joy.

"Huh?" he said. "What kind of vehicle would that be?"

"We'd better take a minute to think about it." She jackknifed herself into the chair beside his. Her smile was bleak. "Ironic, hm? This colony's had no problems of war or crime—and now, what I'd give for a fighter jet!"

"I don't understand—No, wait. You mean to kill the terasaur?"

"What else? A laser cannon fired from above . . . Aw, no use daydreaming about military apparatus that doesn't exist on Rustum. What do you think about dropping a lot of fulgurite sticks? Bill's dad can supply them from his iron mine." She grimaced and lifted a hand. "I know. A cruel method of slaughter. Most of the beasts'll be disabled only. Well, though, suppose as soon as our friends have been taken off, suppose a couple of agile men go afoot and put the creatures out of their misery with some such tool as a shaped-charge drill gun."

Shocked, he exclaimed: "You'd destroy the entire herd?"

"I'm afraid we must," she sighed. "After all, it's gone crazy."

"*Why* has it? We've got to find that out, Eva.
Otherwise somebody else'll get caught by the
same thing, and might not survive."

She nodded.

"I doubt if we can learn the cause from a lot of
mangled dead meat," he told her.

"We can arrange experiments on other herds,
later."

"To what effect? Look at the damage here. We
could wipe out the terasaur in this entire region.
They aren't common; nothing so big can be. But it
appears they're mighty damn important to the
ecology. Have you seen Joe de Smet's paper on
how they control firebrush? That's a single item.
It'd be strange if there aren't more that we haven't
discovered yet." Dan gulped. "Besides, they're, oh,
wonderful," he said through the tumult below.
"I've seen them pass by in dawn mists, more silent
than sunrise. . . ."

Eva regarded him unbelievingly, until she whispered: "Are you serious? Would you risk Mary
Lochaber's life, and two more, to save a few
animals?"

"Oh, no. Of course not."

"Then what do you propose?"

"Isn't it obvious? We carry field gear, including
a winch and plenty of rope. Lower a line, make
them fast, and we'll crank them right up into this
car."

She sat for an instant, examining his idea with a
fair-mindedness he well knew, before the red head
shook. "No," she said. "We can't hover close, or
our jet turbulence may knock them right off that

precarious perch. Then we'd have to drop the line from our present altitude. This is a windy day; the hill's causing updrafts. I don't expect the end of a rope could come anywhere near—unless we weight it. But then we've made a pendulum for the wind to toss around, and very possibly to brain someone or knock him loose. See what tiny slanty spaces they've got to cling to, and think how weakened they are by now."

"Right," he answered, "except for one factor. That weight isn't going to be any unmanageable lump. It's going to be me."

She nearly screamed. One hand flew to her opened mouth. "Dan, no! *Please*!"

Lowland air need not move fast to have a mighty thrust. And the topography here made for more flaws, gusts, and whirlings than was common. To control the winch, Eva had to leave the car on autopilot, which meant it lurched about worse than when hovering under her skilled hands. Dan swung, spun, was yanked savagely up and let drop again, scythed through dizzy arcs, like the clapper of a bell tolled by a lunatic.

The winds thundered and shrilled. Through his skull beat the brawl of jets aimed to slant past him, groundward. Below him the terasaur bellowed and trampled a drumfire out of the earth. Knotted around his waist, the line wouldn't let him fall, but with every motion it dug bruisingly into his belly muscles. He grasped it above his head, to exert some control, and the shivers along it tore at his palms and thrummed in his shoulders. An animal rankness boiled up from the herd, into his nostrils and lungs. He didn't know if that or the gyring made him giddy.

Here came the rock!

Two meters above, he swept through a quarter circle. "Lower away!" he cried futilely. His partner understood, however, and let out some extra rope. His boots reached for solidity. All at once the car stumbled in an air pocket. He fell, snapped to a halt, and saw the cliff face rush toward him. He was about to be dashed against it.

He heaved himself around the cord till he stretched horizontally outward. The curve of his passage whistled him centimeters above bone-shattering impact. He caught a glimpse of Bill Svoboda, wildly staring, and folded his legs in bare time to keep from striking the man.

Then he was past, and swarming up the rope. On the return arc, the soles of his boots made contact with the stone. He let them brake by friction. It rattled his teeth, but it practically stopped his swinging. The next touch, on the next sway of the pendulum bob—which was himself—came slow and easy. He got his footing and stood among his friends.

Immediately, Eva released more rope. Hanging loosely now, it couldn't haul him back if the car should suddenly rise. He sank to the rock and spent a minute sweating, panting, and shuddering.

He noticed Bill crouched at his side. "Are you all right?" the other man babbled. "Lord, what a thing! You might've been killed! Why'd you do it? We could've held out till—"

"You're okay?" Dan croaked.

"Y-yes. That is, the Lochabers are sick, but they ought to recover fast."

Dan crawled on hands and knees to Mary. "I came for you," he said, and held her close. Dazed, she responded only with a mumble. He let her go, rose, and conferred with Bill.

Taking in still more line, they secured bights around bodies at five-meter intervals. Bill would go first, he being in condition to help Eva; next came Ralph; then Mary (as he made her fast, Dan thought what an odd and deep intimacy this was); finally Dan himself, who could best endure the maximum oscillation.

The remnant of the task proved simple. Eva raised the car, at the lowest possible rate, until one by one the four on the rope dangled free in the sky. She continued to rise till they were in calm air. Thereafter she left the vehicle again at hover and winched them in.

Though reduction helmets were always on hand, she depressurized the cabin on the way back to Moondance. The Lochabers sat half asleep, half in a faint. Eva called the station medic. He said the highlanders should stay in the guesthouse till they had regained enough strength for a flight home; but on the basis of Bill's account, he didn't think that would take long, nor that treatment need consist of more than bed rest and nourishment.

Dan spoke little. He was sunk in thought. Directly after landing, he prepared to take off again.

When he had cycled through the lock, he found

Eva on hand. The quarters were a dormitory with kitchenette and mini-bath—cramped, austere, and relieved only by windows that gave on a view of lake and forest, but they could never be opened to the breeze that sang outside. Eva had drawn a chair into the narrow aisle between rows of bunks. Ralph lay at her left, Mary at her right. The siblings were in pajamas, propped up on pillows. Nearby stood a vase of triskele that the visitor must have brought. The room had grown vivid with the goldenness of the blossoms, pungent with their summery odor.

Dan halted. Eva had been crying! She'd washed her face afterward, but even though she seldom wept, he knew the traces of it upon her.

"Why hello, stranger," Ralph greeted. His tone was a little mechanical. Both the Lochabers already seemed well on their way back to health —and less than happy. "How did your expedition go?"

"Successful, I think." Dan's gaze went to Mary and would not let itself be hauled away. Her hair was molten amber across the pillows and her eyes like the heavens about High America. She smiled at him; but the smile was uncertain, even timid.

"How are you doing?" he said, 99 percent to her.

"We're coming along fine." She spoke so low that he had to strain to hear her in this thin air. "Thanks to you."

"Oh, that wasn't much." Curiously, he didn't blush. Rather, he felt the ghost of a chill.

"It was plenty." Ralph's words came firm. He, too, was a leader. "Damn few men could have done what you did, or would have dared to risk their necks like that."

"I did try to talk him out of it," Eva said in a dulled voice.

"A heroic action," Ralph went on. "You saved us several extra hours of suffering. Please don't think we're ungrateful. Still, we can't help wondering. Why?"

"Your lives," Dan answered. "Or, maybe, worse, brain damage."

Mary shook her head. "That wasn't at stake, dear, once you'd located us," she said gently. "We could have waited awhile more."

"I couldn't be sure of that," he said, with a slight upstirring of anger that she should be thus withdrawn. "I didn't know how long you'd been marooned, and you just might have been among those people whose pressure tolerance is abnormally low." *As low as mine is high.*

"We aren't," Ralph said. "But anyway, it was quite an exploit, and we owe you our sincerest thanks." He paused. "And then you flew back at once, not even stopping to rest. I stand in awe." He chuckled, though his heart wasn't in it. "Or, I will stand in awe as soon as the doctor lets me out of bed."

Dan was glad to shift the subject. "My job, after all." He drew up a chair to face Eva and them. It was good to sit. Hour upon hour had drained him. (The flight from here to the valley again, through air that in places had gotten heavily turbulent; the hovering above the rampage; the squinting and studying, while the agony of the herd tore in him

almost as if it had been his own; the final thing he
did; and not even his triumph able to lift the weariness off his bones, during the long flight back.)
Maybe he should have caught some sleep after his
return, before coming here.

"Was it the terasaur you were concerned
about?" Mary asked. "Eva told us you were going
back to them, but she didn't know more than that
herself."

He nodded. "Uh-huh. They're an important part
of the environment. I couldn't pass up this chance
to learn more about them, and try to save what
was left."

Eva half rose. Something of the woe behind her
eyes disappeared. "Did you?" she cried.

"I think so." A measure of joy woke likewise in
him. "Frankly, I feel more like bragging about that
than about a bit of athletics at a rope's end."

"What happened? What'd you do?" Eva reached
toward him.

He grinned. The tide of his pleasure continued
to flow. "Well, you see, terasaur do go rather wild
in rutting season. The cause must be a change in
body chemistry, whether hormonal or pher-
omonal we don't know—but we do know how
micro amounts of such substances will affect
animal behavior, humans included. Now, this herd
wasn't mating and its antics were crazy even for
that time of year. However, there were certain
basic similarities. I wondered what new factor
might have triggered the madness."

He stopped for breath. "Go on!" Eva urged.

Dan sought Ralph's gaze. "Petroleum is complicated stuff," he said. "Besides long-chain

hydrocarbons, it contains all sorts of aromatics and the chemists alone know what else. In addition, your jet fuel probably has polymers or whatever, produced in the course of refining. My idea was that in among those molecules is one, or a set, that happens to resemble the terasaurian sex agent." Mary drew a gasp. "Not your fault," Dan added hastily. "Nobody could have known. But it does underline the necessity of learning everything we can about this planet, doesn't it?"

The blond young man scowled. "You mean . . . wait a minute," he said. "A few bulls drifted near our car, probably just curious. They got a whiff of unburned fuel dissipating in the exhaust; we'd left the motor idling as a precaution—what we thought was a precaution. That whiff was enough to make them charge, cutting us off from the car. Then, when the first tank was ruptured and fuel spilled out by the hundreds of liters, it drove the entire herd into a frenzy. Is that what you mean?"

Dan nodded again. "Correct. Though of course the total situation was wrong, unbalanced, for the poor beasts. The molecules involved must have similarities but no doubt aren't identical with their natural gonad stimulator. Besides, it's the wrong time of year and so forth. No wonder they ran amok. Suppose someone injected you with an overdose of any important hormone!"

"It's an interesting guess. Are you certain, though?"

"The biochemists will have to check out the details. But, yes, I am certain in a general way. You see, I flitted back to the site, where they were still rampaging. I ignited the spilled fuel with a

thermite bomb. It went up fast, in this
atmosphere. Almost immediately, the herd started
to calm down. By the time I left, the survivors had
returned to their calves."

"M-m-m—"

"I know why you're glum, Ralph. Your family
business is getting set to produce oil-fired motors.
And now it'll have to do a lot more research first.
What's at stake isn't merely the terasaur, you
realize. It's every related species, maybe the entire
lowland ecology."

"That's why you were so anxious to save the
herd," Mary said low. "Eva's told us how you
insisted."

"Oh, I didn't have any definite ideas at that
time," Dan replied. "Only a—general principle."
His mood drooped. Trying to lift it, he said, "This
doesn't mean your father's project has to be can-
celled. Once the chemicals have been identified,
I'm sure they can be taken out of the fuel."

"Indeed." Ralph forced a smile. "You've done us
a considerable favor, actually. Besides the rescue,
you've saved us a number of further losses like
this."

"But you didn't know!" tore from Mary.

Dan started half out of his seat. "What's that?"

"You didn't know—then—and anyway, even if
you had known, there are other herds—" She
began to weep.

Appalled, he went to her, knelt by her bunk, and
gripped her hand. It lay cold and moveless in his.
"Mary, what's wrong?"

"I was afraid of this . . . what Ralph and Eva
were getting at . . . before you came . . . don't you

see? You, you care so greatly about this land . . . that to save a part of it . . . you'd risk—"

"Not your life, ever!" he exclaimed.

"No, I s-s-suppose not . . . but your own!"

"Why shouldn't I, if I want to?" he asked in his bewilderment.

Her look was desperate upon him. "I thought—I hoped—All the years we might have had! You risked those!"

"But . . . but Mary, my duty—"

In long, shuddering breaths, she mastered herself enough to say, with even the ghost of a smile: " 'I could not love thee (Dear) so much, Lov'd I not honour more.' Dan, I never really sympathized with that attitude. Or, at least, I think two people have to share the same, well, the same honor, if they really want to, to share each other. We belong to different countries, you and I. Can you understand?"

He shook his head as he spoke, harshly. "No. I'm afraid I don't." He rose to go. "But you're still exhausted, Mary. I'd better not keep after you about this, or anything. Let's talk later, shall we?"

He stooped above her bed, and their lips touched, carefully, as if they were strangers.

Though the air outside was hot and damp, a rising wind roared in treetops; and over the lake came striding the blue-black wall of a rainstorm that would cleanse and cool.

Nobody else was in sight when Dan and Eva left the guesthouse. Nonetheless they did not continue on among the neighbor buildings, but went down to the shore. The water chopped at their feet. Afar, lightning flashes were reflected off its steeliness, and thunder rolled around heaven.

"Well," he said at last, into the wind, "I guess that's that."

"You'll get over it," said Eva, no louder or livelier than he. "You both will, and be friends when you happen to meet."

"Except why couldn't she *see*—?"

"She could, Dan. That's precisely the trouble, or the salvation. She sees far too clearly."

"You mean, because I care about the land, she doesn't imagine I care about her? No! She's not that petty."

"I didn't say she is, Dan. In fact, she's very large, very wise and kind. Look, she *can* live here, never going outside of cages like a house and a helmet. But to make you stay all your days, or more than a bare fragment of them, where she can be—that'd cage you. You, who now have the whole world before you. Better to say goodbye at once, while you're still fond of each other."

And you, Eva, inherit me, he thought in bitterness. He glanced down at her, but her head was averted from him and he saw only flying cinnabar locks.

Wind skirled, thunder cannonaded. He barely heard, after a minute: "That's what I had to tell Ralph before you arrived. When he asked me to marry him."

The breath went from Dan. The first stinging drops of rain smote him in the face.

Then she turned back and took both his hands. In her eyes he saw—not a plea, not an invitation—the challenge to make a new beginning.

A FAIR EXCHANGE

Nowhere on Rustum was autumn like that season anywhere on Earth. But on the plateau of High America it did recall, a little, the falls and Indian summers of the land whence this one had its name—if only because many plants from another mother planet now grew there. Or so the oldest colonists said. They had become very few. Daniel Coffin knew Earth from books and pictures and a dim star near Boötes, which his foster father had pointed out as Sol.

Red leaves of maple, yellow leaves of birch, gold-streaked scarlet leaves of gim tree, scrittled on the wind, while overhead tossed the blue featheriness of plume oak that does not shed for winter. The founders of Anchor were forethoughtful men and women, who laid out broad streets lined with saplings when they were huddling in tents or sod huts. The timber grew with the town. In summer it gave shade, today it gave radiance to pavement, to walls of brick and tinted concrete and what frame buildings remained from earlier times, to groundcars and trucks—and an occasional horse-drawn wagon, likewise a souvenir of the pioneers—that bustled along the ways.

Children bound for school dodged in and out among elder pedestrians. Their shouts rang. Coffin remembered the toil and poverty he had lived with, like everyone else, and smiled a bit. *Yes, there is such a thing as progress,* he thought.

Air flowed and murmured, cool on his face, crisp in his nostrils. The sky arched altogether clear, pale blue, full of southbound wings. Eastward, the early morning sun stood ruddy-orange at the end of street and town, above the snowpeaks of the distant Hercules range. Though Anchor's hinterland was an entire planet, it was itself not large: about ten thousand permanent residents, more than half of them children. To be sure, this was a fourth of the world's humanity.

Glancing the opposite way, Coffin saw a tattered drift of smoke above the mostly low roofs. A flaw of wind brought a rotten-egg stench. He scowled. *Progress can get overdone.* Though he had never seen it in person, writings, films, and the tales of witnesses had driven into his bones what too much population and industry had done to Earth.

And as for children—the cheerfulness of the weather departed. Here was the hospital. His heart knocked and he mounted the steps more slowly than was his wont.

"Good morning, Mr. Coffin." The nurse on desk duty was quite young. She addressed him with an awe which hitherto he had found wryly amusing. Him, plain Dan Coffin, lowland farmer?

Well, of course he'd made a name for himself as a young man, one of the few who could explore the immensities down yonder and gain the knowledge of Rustum that all men must have. And, yes, he'd had experiences that made sensational stories. But he'd always winced at those, recollecting the ancient saying that adventure happens only to the incompetent—then excusing himself with the fact that in so much unknownness, it was impossible to foresee every working of Murphy's Law.

And anyhow, that was long behind him. He'd been settled down at Lake Moondance for—was it thirty-five years? (*Which'd be about twenty Terrestrial,* said an echo from his childhood, when people were still trying to keep up traditions like Christmas.) Oh yes, he did have by far the biggest plantation in those parts, or anywhere in the lowlands. He could be reckoned as well-off. His neighbors for three or four hundred kilometers around considered him a sort of leader, and had informally commissioned him to speak for them in High America. Nevertheless!

"Good morning, Miss Herskowitz," he said, bowing as was expected in Anchor, where they went in more for mannerly gestures than folk did on the frontier. "Uh, I wonder, I know it's early but I have an appointment soon and—"

The sudden compassion on her face struck him with terror. "Yes, by all means, Mr. Coffin. Your wife's awake. Go right on in."

That gaze followed him as he strode: a stocky, muscular man, roughly clad for his field trip later today, his features broad and weathered, his black hair streaked with gray. He felt it on his back, in his heart.

The door was open to Eva's room. He closed it behind him. For a moment he stood mute. Against propped-up pillows, sunlight through a window gave her mane back the redness it had had when first they knew each other. She was nursing their baby. On a table stood a vase of roses. He hadn't brought them, hadn't even known the town now boasted a conservatory. The hospital staff must have given them. That meant—

She raised her eyes to him. Their green was faded by weariness and (he could tell) recent crying. For the same reason, the freckles stood forth sharply on her snub-nosed countenance. And yet she was making a recovery from childbirth that would have been fast and good in a much younger woman.

"Dan—" He had long had a little trouble hearing, in the High American air that was scarcely thicker than Earth's. Now he must almost read her lips. "We can't keep him."

He clamped his fists. "Oh, no."

She spoke a bit louder, word by word. "It's final. They've made every clinical test and there is no doubt. If we bring Charlie to the lowlands, he'll die."

He slumped on a chair at the bedside and groped for her hand. She didn't give it to him. Holding the infant close in both arms, she stared at the wall before her and said, flat-voiced: "That was twelve or thirteen hours ago. They tried to get hold of you, but you weren't to be found."

"No, I—I had business, urgent business."

"You've had a lot of that, the whole while I was here."

"Oh, God, darling, don't I know it!" He barely, lightly grasped her shoulder. His hand shook. "Don't you know it, too?" he begged. "I've explained—"

"Yes. Of course." She turned to him with the resolution he knew. She even tried to smile, though that failed. "I've just . . . been lonely. I've missed you. . . ." Then she could hold out no longer, and she bent her head and wept.

He rose, stooped over her, gathered clumsily to his bosom her and the last child the doctors said she could ever have. "I know half a dozen fine homes that'd be happy to foster him," he said. "That's one thing that kept me busy, looking into this matter, in case. We can come see him whenever we want. It's not like him being dead, is it? And, sure, we'll adopt an exogene as soon as possible. Sweetheart, we both knew our luck couldn't hold out forever. Three children of our own that we could keep may actually have bucked the odds. We've a lot to be glad of. Really we do."

"Y-yes. It, it's only that . . . little Charlie, here at my breast, m-m-milking me this minute—Could we move here, Dan?"

He stiffened before answering slowly: "No. Wouldn't work. You've got to realize that. We'd lose everything we and—the rest of our kids—ever hoped and worked for. We'd be too homesick—"

—for soaring mountains, rivers gleaming and belling down their cliffs; for boundless forests, turquoise, russet, and gold, spilling out to boundless prairies darkened by herds of beautiful beasts; for seas made wild by sun and outer moon, challenging men to sail around the curve of the world; for skies argent with cloud deck, or bright and changeable when that broke apart, or ablaze with lightning till the mighty rains came cataracting; for air so dense and rich with odors of soil and water and life, that the life in humans who could breathe it burned doubly bright, ran doubly strong; for the house that had grown under their hands from cabin to graciousness, the gardens and arbors and enormous fields that were theirs, the lake like a sea before them and wildwoods elsewhere around it; for friends with whom roots had intertwined over the years until they were more than friends and a daughter of theirs became the first love of a boy called Joshua Coffin—

"You're right," Eva said. "It wouldn't work. I, I, I'll be okay . . . later on. . . . But hold me for a while, Dan, darling. Stay near me."

He let her go and stood up. "I can't, Eva. Not yet."

She stared as if in horror.

"The whole community depends on, well, on me," he said wretchedly. "The negotiations. We've discussed them often enough, you and I."

"But—" She shifted the gurgling baby, in order to hold out one arm in beseeching. "Can't that wait for a while? It's waited plenty long already."

"That's part of the point. Everything I've been working for is coming to a head. I dare not hesitate. The time's as good as it'll ever be. I *feel* that. I can't let . . . my man . . . cool off; he'll back away from the commitment he's close to making. I've gotten to know him, believe me. In politics, you either grab the chance when it comes, or—"

"Politics!"

He consoled her for the short span he was able. At least, she accepted his farewell kiss and his promise to come back soon, bearing his triumph and their people's for a gift. He did not tell her that the triumph was not guaranteed. Doubtless she understood that. Her brain and will had been half of his throughout the years. In this hour she was worn down, she needed him, and he had never done anything harder than to leave her alone, crying, while he went to do his damned duty.

Or try to. Nothing is certain, on a world never meant for man.

Consider that world, its manifold strangeness, and the fact that no help could possibly come from an Earth which a handful of freedom-lovers had left behind them. Consider, especially, a gravity one-fourth again as great as that under which our species, and its ancestors back to the first half-alive mote, evolved.

Hardy folk adapted to the weight. Children who grew up under it became still better fitted. But the bearing of those children had not been easy. It would never be easy for most women, until natural selection had created an entire new race.

Worse, that gravity held down immensely more atmosphere than did Earth's. Because this was more compressed, men could breathe comfortably near the tops of the loftiest mountains. As they descended, however, the gas concentration rose sharply, until it became too much for most of them. Carbon dioxide acidosis, nitrogen narcosis, the slower but equally deadly effects of excess oxygen: these made the average adult sick, and killed him if he was exposed overly long. Babies died sooner.

Now the human species is infinitely varied. One man's meat can quite literally be another man's poison. Such variability requires a gene pool big enough to contain it. The original colonists of Rustum were too few—had too few different chromosomes between them—to assure long-range survival in an alien environment. But they could take with them the sperm and ova of donors, preserved in the same fashion as were those of animals. These could be united and brought to full fetal development in exogenetic "tanks," on whatever schedule circumstances might allow. Thus man on Rustum had a million future parents.

And: as far as practicable, the donors back on Earth had been chosen with a view to air-pressure tolerance.

Some of the original settlers could stand the conditions at intermediate altitudes; some could actually thrive. But exogenes like Daniel Coffin and Eva Spain could live well throughout the entire range, from ocean to alp. To them and their descendants, and whoever else happened to be born equally lucky, the whole planet stood open.

The human species is infinitely varied. A type on the far end of a distribution curve will not always breed true. There will be throwbacks to the median —perfectly normal, healthy children, perfectly well suited to live on Earth. Certain among them will be so vulnerable to unearthliness that they die already in the womb.

Because of that possibility, every woman who could manage it spent the latter halves of her pregnancies on High America. In earlier years, Coffin had often been able to visit Eva there. During this final wait she had seen little of him, in spite of all the time he spent on the plateau.

Thomas de Smet was a fairly young man; the accidental death of his father had early put him in charge of the Smithy. He ran it well, producing most of the heavy machinery on Rustum, and planned to diversify. Thus far, businesses were small, family affairs. They were, that is, with respect to number of employees. Since machines had started to beget machines, the volume of production—given the resources of an entire unravaged world—was becoming impressive. Manpower was the worst bottleneck, and the settlers were doing their lusty best to deal with that.

Coffin had known de Smet since their youth, albeit slightly. On Rustum, everybody of the least importance knew everybody else of the same. When the first glimmerings of his scheme came to

him, Coffin decided that this was the man to zero
in on. He had spent as much of the past year as he
could, cultivating his friendship.

The worst of it is, Coffin thought, *I like the
fellow. I like him a lot, and feel like a hound for
what I hope to do.*

"Hi, Tom," he said. "Sorry I'm late."

"Who cares?" de Smet replied. "This is my day
off."

"Not quite."

"Dan, you don't mean to propagandize me again,
do you? I thought we were going fishing."

"First I want to show you something. It'll
interest you."

De Smet, a lanky towhead, studied Coffin for a
second. Nothing in the lowlander's squint-eyed
smile, relaxed stance, and easy drawl suggested a
serious intent. However, that was Coffin's way at
the poker table. "As you wish. Shall we flit?"

They entered the aircar. Since Coffin would be
guide on the first stage of the outing, de Smet
waved him to the pilot's seat. The vehicle quivered
and murmured up from the lot behind the Smithy.
Anchor became a collection of dollhouses, where
the Swift and Smoky rivers ran together to form
the Emperor and all three gleamed like drawn
swords. The countryside spread brown in plow-
land and stubblefields, amber in late-ripen-
ing crops, fading green in Terrestrial grasses
and clovers, blue-green in their native equivalents,
multihued in timberlots and woods, one vast
subtle chessboard. Dirt roads meandered between
widely spaced farmsteads. Far to the north, where

the tableland dropped off, a white sea of cloud deck shone above the low country. Eastward reared the Hercules; southward, the yet mightier Centaur Mountains came into sight above the horizon; westward, cultivation presently gave way to wilderness.

Coffin aimed in that last direction, set the auto-pilot, leaned back, drew forth a pipe and tobacco pouch. He hadn't commanded a high speed of the machine. Equinox was barely past; daylight pre-vailed for better than thirty hours.

"How's Eva?" de Smet asked.

"Herself healthy." Coffin was silent for a heart-beat. "As we feared, we can't take the kid home."

De Smet winced. "That's hard." His fingers stole forth to touch his companion's arm. "I'm awfully damn sorry."

Coffin grew busy charging his pipe. "We've seen it happen to neighbors of ours. Eva feels bad, but she's tough. We'll get us another exogene baby who can live with us." They had long since added to their brood the one that law required every family to adopt. "I reminded her of how she, and I for that matter, how we're as fond of Betty as of those we made ourselves. Which is true."

"Naturally. Uh, have you made any arrange-ments for . . . yours?"

"Not yet. We couldn't, before we got the verdict." Coffin hesitated. "Don't be afraid to say no, I realize this is none of my business and we do have ample opportunities. But what might you and Jane think about taking our Charlie in?"

"Huh? Why, mmm—"

"You haven't taken your exogene yet. Well, we'll be adopting a second. The rules allow a family to do that on another's behalf, you know. Eva and I would be mighty glad to have you raise Charlie. Then you'd be free to order an exogene later on, or not, whichever you chose."

"This is rather sudden, Dan." De Smet sat awhile in thought. "I'll have to discuss it with Jane, of course. Frankly, though, to me it looks like a very attractive proposition. Instead of getting some doubtless nice kid, but one whose parentage is a total blank, we'd get one that we're certain comes of high-grade stock." After a moment: "And, hmm, it'd create a tie between two influential houses, in highlands and lowlands."

Coffin chuckled. "In effect," he said, "we'd swap babies. You'd have to adopt a tank-orphan—except that now Eva *must* take a second. So you gain freedom of choice, we gain a proper home for Charlie, both families gain, as you say, a kind of alliance . . . and, well, the babies gain, too. Mind you, this is my own notion. I'll have to talk it over with Eva also. I'm sure she'll agree if Jane does."

He kindled his pipe. De Smet, though a non-smoker, didn't object. Among numerous achievements on his plantation, Coffin had, with the help of a consulting agronomist, developed tobacco that could grow in Rustumite soil without becoming utterly vile.

He puffed for a bit before he added, "It's what you've kept insisting, Tom, as we argued. A fair exchange is no robbery."

De Smet had first quoted that proverb of economists to Coffin on the first occasion that the two men seriously discussed business. This was several lunations after they began to be well acquainted. They amused themselves by calculating precisely how many, since only a short while before, the lunation—the time it took for both moons to return to the same position in the sky—had been defined officially, if not quite truthfully, as five Rustumite days.

Coffin had returned from one of his frequent expeditions into the highland wilds, returned to Anchor and Eva. The de Smets invited him to dinner. Later the men sat far into the night, talking.

That meant less on Rustum than it did on Earth. Here, folk were regularly active through part of each long darkness. Nevertheless, most of the town was abed when Coffin asked: "*Why* won't you? I tell you, and I'd expect you and your experts to check me out beforehand, I tell you, it'll pay. The Smithy will turn a profit."

De Smet was slow to respond. They sat side by side in companionable wise, whisky and soda to hand, pipe in the fist of the guest, out on a balcony. The air was warm; somewhere a fiddlebug stridulated, and rivers boomed and clucked; the windows of Anchor were lightless, and it had no street lamps, but it glowed coppery-silver beneath a sky full of stars, in which the moons were aloft, gibbous Raksh and tiny hurtling Shorab.

"I hate to sound like a Scrooge," de Smet said at length. "You leave me no choice, though. The profit's too small."

"Really? The resources we've got—"

De Smet drew breath. "Let me make a speech at you, Dan. I sympathize with you lowlanders, especially your own Moondance community, which is the largest. You want industries, too, besides agriculture and timber and suchlike nature-dependent enterprises. Currently, the machines that make machines are all here, because that's where colonization started and High America is where the great majority of people still live. You want me to bring down a lot of expensive apparatus and technical personnel, and build you facilities that'll belong to you, not me."

"True. True. Except we're not asking for any handouts. We have money from the sale of what we produce—"

De Smet raised a palm. "Please. Let me continue. I'm going to get a little abstract, if you don't mind.

"Money is nothing but a symbol. It gives the owner a certain call on the labor and property of others. One can play many different games with money, until at last one loses sight of what the stuff *is* and ends by wrecking its value. Luckily, that's no danger on Rustum, yet. First, we're too few to maintain elaborate fiscal schemes. Second, we have a free-market economy with a strictly gold-standard currency.

"Why do we have that? First, because the founders of the colony wanted to be free, free as individuals; and the right to buy, sell, or trade as one chooses is an important part of this. Second, they'd read their history. They knew what funny money leads to, always, as inevitably as fire will burn if you stick your bare hand in it. Therefore the Covenant ties the currency to gold, whose supply grows too slowly to outrun the growth of real wealth. This causes most transactions to be in cash. One can borrow, of course, if one can find a willing lender; but the lender had better have that claim-on-wealth in his personal pocket.

"As a result, now that the hard early days are behind us, now that production is expanding faster than the money supply, the price of nearly everything is falling."

"I know that," Coffin protested. "What I got for my wheat last year barely paid the cost of raising it."

De Smet nodded. "That was bound to happen. Fertile soil, new varieties of grain suited to local conditions—how easily we get surpluses that drive prices down! Meanwhile machinery and human labor are in shorter supply, with more call on them. Hence their price gets bid up; or, to be exact, it doesn't fall in proportion to the price of natural products."

"Easy for you to say."

"You aren't starving, are you? One advantage of tight money is that it discourages speculation, especially by an individual. He can't have a mortgage foreclosed on his land because he was never able to get a mortgage on it in the first place, valuable though it is." In haste: "I don't mean to insult your intelligence, Dan. This is the same elementary economics you and I both learned in school. I'm simply recapitulating. I want to spell out that I have better reasons than greed for saying no to you."

"Well, but look, Tom, I'm better off than most of my friends down there, and I often feel the pinch."

"What you mean is, you'd like to do certain things, and can't do them without High American help. You might wish for an up-to-date flour mill, for instance, instead of a waterwheel or windmill— or instead of selling your wheat here and buying back part of it, as bread, at a considerable markup. Yes, surely. The fact is, however, I regret it very much, but the fact is you will simply have to do without until there's enough machinery available to bring its rental or purchase price down. Meanwhile, you can be self-sufficient. And nobody is pointing a gun at your head forcing you to overproduce."

De Smet filled his lungs afresh before he continued: "You see, if we gave you a subsidy, the cost of that would have to be met either through taxation or inflation. No matter which way, it'd amount to taking earnings from the highlander for the benefit of the lowlander, who gives nothing in return. Price controls would have the same effect. In fact, any kind of official intervention would distort the economy. Instead of meeting our difficulties head-on and solving them once and for all, we'd hide them behind a screen of paper, where they'd grow worse and breed new troubles to boot.

"Machinery and labor are costly because there's a demand for them—they're *wanted*, in both senses of the word—and at the same time, for the nonce, they remain scarce. In a free market, the price of a commodity is nothing more nor less than an index of how much people are prepared to exchange for it."

"You High Americans, though"—Coffin chopped the air with his hand—"you've got more than your share of machines. Even per capita you do. Which means, yours is the way the money flows, no matter what we lowlanders do. It isn't right!"

De Smet took a sip of whisky before he shook his head and sighed, "Dan, Dan, you're a frontiersman. You know better than I, from experience, no two people ever have identical luck.

"It isn't as if your folk were in dire want. If they were, I'd be the first to bring them relief. The free market doesn't forbid helping your fellow man. It only makes such acts voluntary—and so in the long run, I believe, encourages altruism, though I admit that's just my opinion.

"Your folk aren't suffering, except in their own minds. The poorest of them eats well, dresses decently, his adequate shelter. You yourself, to judge from the pictures you've shown me, you live in a bigger and better house than mine, live like a medieval baron. All you lowlanders enjoy many things we don't, such as unlimited room to move around. And . . . whoever can't stand it is welcome here. We have this chronic labor shortage; he can earn excellent wages."

"We want to be our own men," Coffin growled, albeit not hostilely.

"I admire you for that," de Smet said in a mild tone. "Still, recall your origins. Individuals who could live in the low country went there first to study it, paid by High America because the knowledge they could get was essential. They fell in love with the land and settled. And this was right. Mankind ought to take over the whole planet.

"That'll be slow, however. Meanwhile, most of us are confined to the uplands. We have the same right as you to improve our standards of living, don't we? Since you lowlanders can come join us but would rather not, why should we sacrifice to support you in your own free choice—a much freer choice than we have?

"That's where the social utility of the supply-demand law shows itself, Dan. High America is also still young, has plenty left to do. Plenty that must be done, because we'll be crowded long before the typical lowlander can see his neighbor's chimney smoke. The quicker return— the effectively higher profit—to be made here, simply reflects that urgency, as well as the fact that here, today, are far more persons needing to be served.

"Please don't take this wrong; but honestly, it looks to me as if your community is the one asking for more than is fair, not ours."

"I told you, we don't want a handout," Coffin answered with somewhat strained patience. "I can prove to you that the return on any investment you make among us will be good. Okay, granted, maybe not as good as equal investment made on High America. Still, you'll gain, and gain well."

"We already have considerable investments in the lowlands," de Smet pointed out.

Coffin nodded violently. "Yes! Mines, power stations, transport lines that you own, you High Americans. You employ lowlanders to work in them, but they're your property, and the profits go to you."

He leaned over. His pipestem jabbed, stopping barely short of the other man's chest. "Now let me explain some home truths," he said. "Believe it or not, I understand your economics. I know that I'm asking, on behalf of my community, I'm asking you to use part of the stuff and staff you command, part of it to come build us—oh, that flour mill, or a factory producing machine tools, or whatever—come build that for us, instead of building something like it for High America.

"Well, I tell you, my friend, economics is not all there is to life. Rightly or wrongly, the lowlanders are starting to feel slighted. After a while they'll come to feel neglected, and then go on to feeling exploited. I'm not saying that makes sense, but I am saying it's true."

"I know," de Smet replied as if half-apologetic. "I've been down there myself, inside an air helmet, remember. You're not the first lowlander I've talked to at length. Yes, you're already beginning to think of yourselves as a separate breed, rough, tough, bluff frontiersmen opposed to us dandified, calculating uplanders. That notion hasn't developed far yet—"

"It will. Unless you come help us. If you do, maybe this will stay a unified planet. Or don't you care about your grandchildren?" Coffin waited before he added, gravely, "This is not a threat. But do bear in mind, Tom, several generations from tonight the highlanders will be an enclave. The population will nearly all be down yonder. And so will the power. Man, win their good will before it's too late."

"I've thought about that. I genuinely have. I'm aware that this isn't a problem with any neat either-or solution. If some arrangement could be made, an economically sensible arrangement, so it'd endure. . . . But why should the lowlands be industrialized? In time, and not such a terribly long time, the prices of food and timber will soar, as High America fills up. Wouldn't it be wiser to wait for that day? Meanwhile you'd keep your attractive surroundings."

"They're not that attractive, when we have to overwork our kids for lack of equipment we know could be built. Anyway, nobody wants to found an industrial slum. Of course not. We just want a few specific items. We've ample space to locate them properly, ample resources to treat the wastes so they don't poison the land."

"We haven't. At least, we don't have that kind of chance much longer, at the rate we're going." De Smet locked eyes with his guest and said in a voice tautened by intensity: "That's my main reason for wanting to get rich fast. I mean to buy up as much virgin highland as possible and make a preserve of it."

Coffin smiled in fellow feeling. De Smet's outdoorsmanship was what had originally brought them together. It is hard not to like a man with whom you have been hiking, boating, camping for days on end.

"Maybe we can work something out," de Smet finished. "However, it has got to involve a quid pro quo, or it's no good. As the saying goes, a fair exchange is no robbery."

Lake Royal, where they planned to fish, gleamed remotely on the right. Still the car whined ahead. A ways further came a break in the forest, an ugly scar where the ground had been ripped open across several kilometers. No life save a few weeds had returned to heal it.

Coffin gestured with his pipestem. "How old is that thing, anyway?"

De Smet peered out the canopy. "Oh, the strip mine?" He grimaced. "Seventy, eighty years, I guess. From the early days."

"Industrialization," Coffin grunted.

De Smet stared at him. "What're you talking about? Necessity. They had to have fuel. Their nuclear generator was broken down, couldn't be fixed soon, and winter was coming on. Here was a surface seam of coal which they could easily quarry and airlift out."

"Nevertheless, industry, huh? Earlier this morning, I caught a knock-you-over stink from the refinery."

"That'll have to be corrected. I'm leaning on the owners. So are others. Mainly, Dan, you know as well as I do, we've had to take temporary measures, but we're almost back to a clean hydrogen-fueled technology."

"Then why do you worry about industrialization? Why do you want to set aside parts of High America?"

De Smet seemed bewildered. "Isn't it obvious? Because . . . I, highlanders who feel like me, we can never really belong in your unspoiled lowland nature. Shouldn't we too have a few places to be, well, alone with our souls?" He uttered a nervous laugh. "Sorry. Didn't mean to get pompous."

"No matter." Coffin blew a smoke ring. "As population grows, won't there be more and more pressure to turn this whole plateau into a big loose city? Do you really think your wilderness areas won't be bought out, or simply seized? Unless ample goods are coming from the lowlands. Then High Americans will be able to afford letting plenty of land lie fallow. . . . Well, that can't happen without trade, which can't happen unless the lowlanders have something—not only raw materials but finished products—to trade with.

"Don't you think, even today, even at the cost of some profit, it makes better sense to spread the industry more thin?"

De Smet leaned back and regarded Coffin for a while before he said, "You promised me, no further arguments on our holiday."

"Nor've I broken my promise, Tom. I just reminded you about what I'd said before, to help you appreciate the interesting thing I also promised to show you."

The autopilot beeped. Coffin switched it off, took the controls, checked landmarks, and slanted the car downward. Below was a rough and lovely upthrust of hills. A lake gleamed among them like a star, and overhead circled uncountably many waterfowl. Sunlight made rainbow iridescences on their wings.

"You recall, several close friends and I have been around here quite a bit," Coffin said. "We gave out that we were investigating botanical matters, to try to get a line on a problem we're having in our home ecology. It wasn't altogether false—we did even get the information we wanted—and nobody paid much attention anyhow."

De Smet waited, braced.

"In addition," Coffin said, "we prospected."

Air whistled around the hull. Ground leaped dizzyingly upward.

"You see," Coffin went on, "if we lowlanders don't have the wherewithal to develop our country as we'd like, and if nobody'll help us get it, why, we'd better go help ourselves. If we could stake out a claim in *your* country, then transportation to Anchor would be fast and cheap, giving us a competitive break. Or we might sell out to a highland combine, or maybe take a royalty. In any case, we'd have the money we need to bid for the equipment and personnel we need."

"Nobody's prospected these parts to speak of," de Smet said slowly.

"That's why we did. You think of this section as being far from home, but to us, it's no further than Anchor."

The car came to a halt, then descended straight into a meadow. Coffin opened the door on his side. A thousand songs and soughings flowed in, autumn crispness and the fragrance of that forest which stood everywhere around, ripe. Grasses rippled, trees tossed their myraid colors, not far off blinked the lake.

"Marvelous spot," Coffin said. "You're lucky to

own it."

"Not lucky." De Smet smiled, however worried he perhaps was. "Smart. I decided this ought to be the heart of my preserve, and claimed the maximum which the Homestead Rule allows."

"You don't mind that my gang and I camped here for a bit?"

"Oh, no, certainly not. You'd leave the place clean."

"You see, in searching for clues to minerals on unclaimed land, we needed an idea of the whole region. So we checked here too. We made quite a discovery. Congratulations, Tom."

De Smet grew less eager than alarmed. "What'd you find?" he snapped.

"Gold. Lots and lots of gold."

"Hoy?"

"Mighty useful industrial metal, like for electrical conductors and chemically durable plating. Making it available ought to be a real social service." Coffin's thumb gestured aft. "You'll want to see for yourself, no doubt. I brought the equipment. I knew you know how to use it, otherwise I'd've invited along any technician you named. Go ahead. Inspect the quartz veins in the boulders. Put samples through the crusher and assayer. Pan that brook, sift the lakeshore sands. My friend, you'll find every indication that you're sitting on a mother lode."

De Smet shook his head like a man stunned. "Industry can't use a lot of gold. Not for decades to come. The currency—"

"Yeh. That should be exciting, what happens to

this hard currency you're so proud of. Not to mention what happens to the wilderness, the majority of it that you don't own, when the rush starts. And it'll be tough to get labor for producing things we can merely eat and wear. You, though, Tom, you'll become the richest man on Rustum."

Coffin knocked the dottle from his pipe, stretched, and rose. "Go ahead, look around," he suggested. "I'll make camp. I've brought a collapsible canoe, and the fishing's even better here than at Lake Royal."

De Smet's look searched him. "Do you . . . plan . . . to join the gold rush?"

Coffin shrugged. "Under the circumstances, we lowlanders won't have much choice, will we?"

"I—See here, Dan—"

"Go on, Tom. Do your checking around, and your thinking. I'll have lunch ready when you come back. Afterward we can go out on the water, and maybe dicker while we fish."

He stroke into the hospital room, grabbed Eva from her bed to him, and bestowed upon her a mighty kiss.

"Dan!" she cried low. "I didn't expect—"

"Nor I," he said, and laughed. "I never dared hope things'd go this fast or this well." The sun stood at noon. "But they did, and it's done, and from this minute forward, sweetheart, I am yours altogether and forever."

"What-what—Dan, let me go! I love you, too, but you're strangling me."

"Sorry." He released her, except to lower her

most gently, bent over her, and kissed her again with unending tenderness. Afterward he sat down and took her hand.

"What's happened?" she demanded. "Speak up, Daniel Coffin, or before heaven, I'll personally wring the truth out of you." She was half weeping, half aglow.

He glanced at the door, to make doubly sure he had closed it, and dropped his voice. "We've got our contract, Eva. Tom de Smet called in his counselor as soon as we returned, a couple hours ago, and we wrote a contract for the Smithy to come do work at Moondance, and you know Tom never goes back on his word. That's one reason I was after him particularly."

"You finally persuaded him? Oh, wonderful!"

"I s'pose you could call it persuasion. I—Okay, I've told you before, strictly confidentially, how my gang and I weren't just doing research in the High American backwoods, we were trying for a mineral strike."

"Yes. I couldn't understand why the hurry." Her tone did not accuse. Nor did it forgive. It said that now she saw nothing which needed forgiving, and merely asked for reasons. "I kept telling you, the minerals would wait, and the ecological trouble wasn't that urgent."

"But getting the contract I was after was." He stared downward, and his free hand knotted into a fist. "I had to leave you mostly alone, and I knew it hurt you, and yet I didn't dare explain even to you."

She leaned over to kiss him afresh. When he

could talk again, he said: "You see, machinery and engineers are scarce. The Smithy itself has none too big a supply. Any day, someone else might've instigated a project which'd tie everything up for years to come. And in fact, if word should leak out that we lowlanders might seriously bid, why, then chances were that somebody else *would* tie the Smithy up, and invent a project afterward. Not to suppress us or anything, but because it's true that profits are higher here than amongst us.

"It wouldn't've mattered if you, under anesthesia or whatever, if you let slip that I was quietly prospecting. I knew there'd be suspicion of that in Anchor; and what the hell, plenty of people go on such ventures, even if not quite that far afield. This other thing, though, this real aim of mine—"

"I see, I see. And you did succeed? You're a marvel."

"According to Tom de Smet, I'm a bastard." He grinned. "Then after we'd talked awhile, he said I was a damn fine bastard who he was proud to call a friend, and we shook on it and have a date later today to go out and get roaring drunk."

Puzzlement darkened her eyes. "What do you mean, Dan? First you talk about prospecting, but evidently you didn't find your mine. Then you talk about getting this contract that you were actually after all the while. Didn't you simply, finally, persuade Tom to give it to you?"

He shook his head. "No. I tried and tried, for lunations, and he wouldn't agree. I grew sure he wanted to, down inside. But his silly social economic conscience insisted he stick by the dictates of economic theory. In the end, I told him I knew I'd gotten to be a bore on the subject, and I'd dog my hatch, and why not go fishing?''

"And—" she said like a word of love.

"This is a secret you and I take to our graves with us. Promise? Fine, your nod is worth more than most people's oaths.

"I took him to a mother lode of gold I'd found on land of his. I explained that I hated, the same as him, how a gold rush would destroy the wilderness, let alone the currency, and draw effort away from things more useful. But I had a duty to my own community, I said, to my friends who'd asked me to speak for them. I offered my silence, and my fellow prospectors'—I'd picked them very carefully—I offered him that in return for his contract with us. We could write that in, as a provision not made public unless our blabbing gave him cause to cancel the deal. Take it or leave it, I said. A fair exchange is no robbery.

"He took it, and I really am convinced he was personally glad to have that excuse for helping us. Say, how about letting him and Jane foster Charlie? They're more than willing."

"Dan, Dan, Dan! Come here—"

He knelt by the bed and they held each other for a long while.

Eventually, calmed a little, he took his chair and she lowered herself back onto her pillows. Eyes remained with eyes.

One of hers closed in a wink. "You don't fool me, Dan Coffin," she said.

"What do you mean?"

"That act of yours. The simple, hearty rural squire. Nobody gets to lead as many people as you do without being bloody damn shrewd."

"Well. . . ." He looked a trifle smug.

"My love," she said, barely audible, "this may be the first time in history that anyone salted a mine which the victim already owned."

"I have my contract, which Tom de Smet will honor in word and spirit both. Further than that, deponent saith not."

Eva cocked her head. "Have you considered, Dan, that the possibility may have occurred to Tom, and he decided not to check the facts too closely?"

"Huh?" Seldom before had she seen or enjoyed seeing her husband rocked back hard.

But when at last he left her—for a while, only a while—he walked again like a young buccaneer. The wind outside had strengthened, a trumpet voice beneath heaven, and every autumn leaf was a banner flying in challenge.

TO PROMOTE THE
GENERAL WELFARE

The Constitutional Convention had recessed for the midwinter holidays, and Daniel Coffin returned to his house at Lake Moondance. In this part of the lowlands the season brought roaring, chill rains, winds which streaked along mountains to make forests creak and sough, dazzlements of light and hasty shadow as the cloud deck swirled apart, re-formed, and broke open again upon sun, moons, or stars. To travel by aircar was not predictably safe; thus custom was for folk to stay home, visit only near neighbors, in revelry draw closer to their kindred.

Last year he had not done so, but had been the guest of Tom and Jane de Smet in Anchor. His place had felt too big and hollow, and at the same time too full of ghosts. Soon afterward, though, his eldest granddaughter Teresa and her husband Leo

Svoboda had suggested they move in with him. It was partly kindness to an old man they loved; their dwelling was no mansion like his, but it was comfortable and they were prospering. Yet there were enough mutual practical advantages—such as centralizing control over the vast family holdings, now that improved transportation made it possible—that they were not offending him with charity. He was glad to agree.

Pioneers marry young. However well tamed this region might be, the frontier was not far off, that entire planet which beckoned every lowlander on Rustum. Leo and Teresa already had two children, and a third on the way. Again the house resounded to joyous voices, again the lawns knew fleet little bodies of his own blood; and Daniel Coffin regained the happiness which is peace.

Today his household had been trimming the tree. Afterward he felt tired. He wasn't played out, he knew. His hair might be thin and white, the broad face seamed, but his eyes needed no contacts, his stocky frame was erect as ever, and he could walk many a man half his age into the ground. Still, he had overdone it a trifle in romping with the kids. A quiet couple of hours before dinner would let him take full part in its ceremonies and cheer.

He passed slowly through rooms and halls. Much of their serene proportions, blue-gray plastering, gleaming-grained wood floors, furniture and fireplaces, had grown beneath his hands; much of the drapery was Eva's work. Later, when the plantation commanded a large staff and most of their attention, they had hired professionals to enlarge the building. But the heart of it, he thought, would always be the heart that Eva and he had shared.

Upstairs was their suite, bedchamber, bath, and a separate study for each. At first, after she died, he had wanted to close hers off, or make a kind of shrine of it. Later he came to understand how she would have scorned that, she who always looked outward and lived in the overflowingness of tomorrow. He gave it to Teresa for her use and she could make whatever changes she wished.

His private room stayed as it had been, big desk, big leather armchair, walls lined with books as well as microtapes, book publishing having become a flourishing luxury industry well before anyone might have expected it to on an isolated colony world. French doors gave on a balcony. The panes were full of rain, wind hooted, lightning flared, thunder made drumfire which shuddered in the walls. He could barely see down a sweep of grass, trees, flowerbed-bordered paths to the great lake. Waves ran furious over its iron hue. Besides the storm, Raksh was at closest approach, raising tides across the tides of the sun.

The apartment was gloomy and a touch cold. He switched on the heater and a single fluoropanel, put Bach's Fifth Brandenburg on the player, poured himself a small whisky and settled down with his pipe and the *Federalist Papers*.

My duty to reread them, if we're trying to work out a government which'll stay libertarian, now that population's reached the point where Rustum

needs more than a mayor and council in Anchor,
he thought; then chuckling: *Duty, hell! I enjoy the
style. They could write in those days.*

*What'd you have said, Washington, Jefferson,
Hamilton, Madison, if you'd been told that someday some people would travel twenty light-years,
cut themselves off from the planet that begot mankind, just to keep alive the words you lived by?*

*I suspect you'd say, "Don't copy us. Learn from
us—from our mistakes, what we overlooked, as
well as what we got right."*

We're trying, gentlemen.

"The erection of a new government, whatever
care or wisdom may distinguish the work, cannot fail to originate questions of intricacy and
nicety—"

Bop, it said on the door. He knew that shy knock.
"Come in," he called.

His great-granddaughter entered. "Hi," she
said.

"I figured you'd be playing with the other kids,
Alice," he answered, referring more to those of the
staff than to her younger brother.

"I'm tired, too." The slight form in the crisp
white frock snuggled against his trousers.
"Story?"

"Calculating minx. Well, c'mon." He helped the
girl scramble to his lap. Her eyes were blue and
enormous, her curls and color and odor of sunlight—if memory served, exactly like those of
Mary Lochaber when she was young. No surprise,
considering that Mary was also an ancestor of
Alice. . . .

She gave him a happy sigh. "What kind of story do you want?" he asked.

" 'Bout you an' Eva-Granny."

For an instant he *knew* Eva was gone, no more than three years gone, and darkness went through him in a flood. It left; he could look at her picture on the desk and think how it was good to give this flesh of her flesh what he could of what she had been and done; for then, after he himself, and later the children they had gotten together, were likewise departed, a glow of her would live on.

And it was no longer pain for him, really, it was a special kind of pleasure to hark back.

"Hm-m-m, let me see," he murmured. He blew a series of smoke-rings, which made Alice giggle in delight and poke her finger through them as they went by. Images drifted before him, sharper and brighter than anything in this room except the girl and her warmth. Were they truly from so far in the past? That didn't seem believable. Of course, these days time went like the wind. . . .

"Ah, yes," he decided. "You recall I told you how we were explorers before we settled down, Eva-Granny and I."

"Yes. You tol' me 'bout when the t-t-t-TERA-SAURS," she got out triumphantly, "they went galloop, galloop 'roun' an' roun' the big rock till you made 'm stop."

"I couldn't have done that without Eva-Granny's help earlier, Alice. Okay, shortly afterward she got the idea of taking a boat out to some islands where nobody had ever landed, only flown over, but that looked wonderful from the air." (The fantastic cor-

aloid formations might give a clue to certain
puzzles concerning marine ecology, which in turn
were important if fisheries were to develop further. No need to throw these technicalities at the
youngster—nor, actually, any truth if he did, as
far as her viewpoint went; because Eva and he had
really wanted to explore the marvel for its own
sake. She was always seeking the new, the untried.
When she became a mother and the mistress of a
plantation, it had not taken the freshness from her
spirit; she originated more ideas, studies, under-
takings than he did, and half of his innovations
had been sparked by her eagerness.) "In those
days there weren't enough motors and things to go
around, no, not nearly enough. All the motorboats
were being used other places. We kept a sailboat
by the sea. It was the same kind, except bigger, as I
have on the lake, and, in case you don't know,
that's called a sloop."

"Becoss it goes sloop-sloop-sloop inna water?"

Coffin laughed. "Never thought of that! Anyhow—"

The phone bonged: its "urgent" tone. "'Scuse
me, sweetheart," Coffin said, and leaned over to
press the accept button.

The screen filled with the features of Dorcas
Hirayama, mayor of Anchor and thus president of
the Constitutional Convention. Her calm was
tightly held. "Why, hello," Coffin greeted. "Happy
holidays."

She smiled at the girl on his lap. "Happy holidays, Alice," she said. To Coffin: "I'm afraid you'd
better send her out."

He didn't ask the reason, knowing it would prove valid. He simply inquired, "For how long?"

"Shouldn't take more than five minutes to tell. Then I suppose you'll want to spend a while thinking."

"A moment, please." Coffin lowered Alice to the floor, rose, and clasped her hand. "Do you mind, dear?" He didn't see any public question as worth ignoring the dignity of a child. "My Lady Hirayama has a secret. Why don't you take this book—" she crowed in glee as he gave her a photo album from his roving days—"and go look at it in my bedroom? I'll call you as soon as I'm through."

When the door between was shut, he returned to the mayor. "Sorry, Dorcas."

"I'm sorry to interrupt you, Daniel. But this won't wait . . . in spite of going back about thirty-five years."

For several heartbeats he stood moveless. Chills chased along his spine and out to the ends of his nerves. Lightning glared, thunder exploded, rain dashed against the glass.

Thirty-five years. Rustum years. That's about twenty of Earth's. The time it takes light to go between Eridani and Sol.

He sat back down, crossed ankle on knee, tamped the coals in his pipe. "It's happening, then?" he said flatly.

"It has happened. The message was, they planed to launch a colonizing fleet toward us within five years—five of their years. Unless something interfered, and that doesn't seem likely, those ships are, at this moment, a third, maybe almost half of the way here. We may have as much as fifty years before they arrive, but no more and probably less."

"How many aboard?"

"It's a bigger fleet than carried our founders. The message gave an estimate of five thousand adult passengers."

In the little death of suspended animation, that they entered dreaming of a glorious resurrection on Rustum—

"What do people have to say about this?" Coffin asked.

"The man who read the tape had the sense to come straight to me, thank God. I swore him to silence. You're the first I've talked to."

"Why me?"

Hirayama smiled again, wryly this time. "False modesty never did become you, Daniel. You know how I respect your judgment, and I'm hardly alone in that. Besides, you're the convention delegate from the Moondance region, its leader at home and its spokesman in Anchor, and it's the largest and wealthiest in the lowlands, which makes you the most powerful person off High America and comparable in influence to anybody on it. Furthermore, you know your folk better than a highlander like me, who can't come down among them without a helmet, ever will. Must I continue spelling it out?"

"No need. I'd blush too hard. Okay, Dorcas, what can I do for you?"

"First, give me your opinion. We can't sit on the news more than a few days, but meanwhile we can lay plans and rally our forces. Offhand, what do you suppose the lowland reaction will be?"

Coffin shrugged. "Mildly favorable, because of glamour and excitement and the rest. No more than that. We're so busy overrunning the planet. Nor do five thousand immigrants mean a thing to us, as regards crowding or competition, when we don't yet total a lot more ourselves."

"You confirm my guess, then."

"Besides," Coffin said, not happily, "very few of the newcomers will be able to live down here anyway."

"Doubtless true. The devil's about to break loose on High America, you realize that, don't you?"

"Indeed I do."

"Suggestions?"

Coffin pondered before he said: "Let me think at leisure, as you predicted I'd want to. I'll call you back after sleeptime. Agreeable?"

"It's got to be. Well, happy holidays."

"Same to you. Don't let this spoil your fun, Dorcas. You and I won't have to cope with the arrival."

"No. That girl of yours will."

"Right. We'll have to decide on her account. I only hope we're able to. Good-bye."

Coffin switched off, crossed the room, and knocked on the inner door. "All done, Alice," he said. "Shall we continue our story?"

A calm spell, predicted to last a while, enabled Coffin to flit about by aircar, visiting chosen

households throughout that huge, loosely defined
territory which looked to him for guidance in its
common affairs. He could have phoned instead,
but the instrument made too many nuances impossible. Nobody objected to his breaking the
custom of the season. They were glad to return
some of the hospitality he and Eva had shown
them.

Thus he went for a horseback ride with George
Stein, who farmed part of the estate whereon he
lived but mainly was the owner of the single steel
mill in the lowlands, hence a man of weight. Stein
knew that Coffin's real desire was to speak
privately. Yet the outing was worthwhile in its
own right.

The Cyrus Valley was lower and warmer than
Lake Moondance. Here many trees and shrubs—
goldwood, soartop, fakepine, gnome—kept their
foliage the year around. The blue-green "grasses"
of summer had given way to russet muscoid,
whose softness muffled hoofbeats. This was open
woodland, where groves stood well apart.
Between them could be seen an upward leap of
mountains, which lost themselves in pearl-gray
cloud deck. The air was mild and damp, blowing a
little, laden with odors of humus. Afar whistled a
syrinx bird.

When Coffin had finished his tale, Stein was
quiet for a space. Saddle leather squeaked,
muscles moved soothingly between thighs. *A good
land*, Coffin thought, not for the first or the
hundredth time. *How glad I am that, having
conquered it, we made our peace with it. May there*

always be this kind of restraining wisdom on Rustum.

"Well, not altogether unexpected, hey?" Stein said at length. "I mean, ever since radio contact was established, it's seemed more and more as if this colony wasn't a dying-gasp attempt after all. Earth's made some resumption of a space effort. And they may have a few expeditions out looking for new habitable planets, as they claim; but they know for certain that ours is."

"On the highlands," Coffin answered redundantly. "I doubt that this lot they're shipping to us, I doubt it contains a bigger percentage than the original settlers had, of persons able to tolerate lowland air pressure. And . . . the highlands are pretty well filled up."

"What? You're not serious, Dan."

"Never more so, my friend. There isn't much real estate that far aloft, and High America contains nearly the whole of what's desirable. Most has been claimed, under the Homestead Rule, and you can bet your nose that the rest soon will be, after this news breaks."

"Why? Who has to worry about getting crowded? The lowlands can feed a hundred High Americas if we expand cultivation. Let them industrialize the whole plateau if need be." Stein lifted a hand. "Oh, yes, I remember past rivalry. But that was before you got some industry started down here. Now we don't have to fear economic domination. Anytime they overcharge us, we can build new facilities and undersell them. Therefore it makes perfectly good sense to specialize along geographical lines."

"The trouble is," Coffin said, "that prospect is exactly what's worrying the more thoughtful High Americans. Has been for quite a while. They've been raised in the same tradition of elbow room and ample unspoiled nature as we have, George. They want to keep it for their descendants; and the area available to those descendants will be limited for a long time, historically speaking, until at last the pressure-tolerant genes have crowded the older kind out of man on Rustum.

"For instance, take my sometime partner Tom de Smet. He's spent a fairish part of his life buying out land claims in the wilderness, as he got the money to do it. He's created a really gigantic preserve. He'll deed it to the public, *if* we write into the Constitution an article making its preservation perpetual, and certain other provisions he wants as regards the general environment. Failing that, his family intends to keep it. On a smaller scale, similar things have been happening— similar baronies have been growing—everywhere on High America. People have not forgotten what overpopulation did to Earth, and they don't aim to let their personal descendants get caught in the same bind."

"But—oh, Lord!" Stein exclaimed. "How many immigrants did you say? Five thousand? Well, I grant you even forty years hence, or whenever they arrive, even then they'll be a substantial addition. Nevertheless, a minority group. And no matter how they breed, they won't speed population increase enough to make any important difference."

"They will, though," Coffin replied, "having no land available to them for the reasons I just gave you—they will be a damned significant augmentation of one class of people we're already beginning to get a few of."

"Who?"

"The proletariat."

"What's that?"

"Not everybody on High America succeeded in becoming an independent farmer, a technical expert, or an entrepreneur. There are also those who, however worthy, have no special talents. Laborers, clerks, servants, routine maintenance men, et cetera. Those who have jobs, whatever jobs they happen to get, rather than careers. Those whose jobs get automated out from under them when employees acquire the means to build the machinery—unless they accept low wages and sink to the bottom of the social pyramid."

"What about them?" Stein asked.

"You've not been keeping in touch with developments on High America over the years. I have. Mind you, I'm not scoffing at the people I'm talking about. Mostly they're perfectly decent, conscientious human beings. They were absolutely vital in the early days.

"The point is, the early days are behind us. The frontier on High America is gone. We have a planetful of frontier in the lowlands, but that's no help to men and women who can't breathe here without getting sick.

"Anchor hasn't got a real city proletariat yet, nor has its countryside got a rural one. Nevertheless, the tendency exits. It's becoming noticeable, as increasing numbers of machines and workers end the chronic labor shortage we used to have.

"If something isn't done, Rustum will repeat Earth's miserable history. Poverty-stricken masses. Concentration on wealth and power. The growth of collectivism. Later, demagogues preaching revolution, and many of the well-off applauding, because they no longer have roots either, in a depersonalized society. Upheavals which can only lead to tyranny. Everything which we were supposed to escape by coming to Rustum!"

Stein frowned. "Sounds farfetched."

"Oh, it is farfetched in the lowlands," Coffin admitted. "A territory this big won't stifle in a hurry. But High America is a different case."

"What do they plan to do to head off this, uh, proletariat?"

Coffin smiled, not merrily. "That's a good question. Especially when the whole idea of the Constitutional Convention is to secure individual rights—close the loopholes through which they got shot down in the republics of Earth—limit the government strictly to keeping public order and protecting the general environment—because, thank God, we don't have to worry about foreign enemies." Somberly: "Unless we generate our own. Societies have been known to polarize themselves. Civil wars are common in history."

"On the one hand, then, you don't want a government able to take hold of things; on the other hand, you don't dare let things drift," Stein complained. "What do you propose, then?"

"Nobody has a neat solution," Coffin said. "Besides, we hope to avoid imposing any ideology, unless you count freedom itself. However—official policies could maybe encourage an organic development. For instance, under the 'public order' heading, government might create incentives for employers to treat their employees as human beings, *individual* human beings, not just interchangeable machines or a faceless organized mass. Better conditions could be maintained for the growth of small than big businesses; a strict hard-money rule ought to help there, if it includes some provision for persons down on their luck. On the larger scale, under 'environmental protection,' maybe agreements can be reached which'll distribute economic activity in such ways that everybody will have a chance to get ahead, no matter where he lives. Voluntary agreements, of course, with a profit motive behind them, but entered into under the advice of scholars who see more than just the immediate profit."

Coffin sighed. "Those are superficial examples," he finished. "We can't prescribe the behavior of future generations. All we can do is be aware of certain dilemmas, present and future, put forth ideas, and hammer into our successors that they will face the future ones and had better start preparing well in advance."

Stein rode sunk in thought. Wind lulled, leaves whispered. Two kilometers off, a herd of cerothere left a wood and started across the sward in graceful bounds.

Finally he said: "I guess I see what you're driving at, Daniel. Forty or fifty years from now, the proletariat problem should still be fairly small. Only a few people, at worst, should be in that uprooted condition. The economy will be expanding, jobs potentially plentiful, lots of surplus wealth which can be used to help the laid-off city worker get on his own feet. Nothing unmanageable, given common sense and good will.

"Except . . . then Earth dumps five thousand newcomers on us."

Coffin nodded. "Yes," he said.

"Who'll get no chance to become freeholders. Who'll have to adapt to the higher gravity, the longer day and shorter year, a million different matters before they can work. And then they aren't likely to have skills that're in demand, considering how even the simplest things must be done otherwise on Earth. Instead of occasional individuals who need a helping hand once in a while, High America gets an instant proletariat!"

"For which it won't be prepared, George, because it won't have had experience with the type. Shucks, I certainly wouldn't know how best to treat them, and doubt if the most sophisticated Anchor dweller could make a much better guess than mine."

"It'll hardly affect the lowlands."

"Oh, yes, it will, if we want to keep a unified planet." Coffin paused. "Or a free one. Elbow room doesn't guarantee liberty. Some of the harshest empires in Earth history had all kinds of wide-open spaces."

He straightened in the saddle, though he was becoming to feel weariness from a ride that he would once have considered short. "That's why I'm traveling around, talking to influential and respected persons like you," he said. "I've got to have the backing of this community—because I mean to make a damned radical proposal when the convention reopens."

Stein considered his friend for a while before he responded. "I may or may not agree with you, Daniel. Frankly, here is my country, the country I care about, not High America. But I'll hear you out, of course."

And if need be, Coffin thought, *I have reserves of my own to call on.* He began speaking.

The de Smet house, where Coffin stayed when he visited Anchor, lay well out from the center of town, in an area where most homes stood on broad grounds, amidst groves and gardens. Street lamps were infrequent, and trees broke the city's light haze. Thus, there was little to blur the sky when the man from Lake Moondance went for a walk.

Winter on the altiplano had turned silent and cold. The face stung, the body was glad of a thick coverall, breath felt liquid as it entered the nostrils and came back out in stiff white puffs. Where byways were unpaved, the ground rang underfoot. Elsewhere reached snow, frost-glittering until vision faded out in distance and shadowiness. The occasional yellow shining from windows looked infinitely tender but infinitely tiny. Far in the east, the peaks of the Hercules reared glacier-sharp.

Overhead stood heaven. One rarely saw such a wonder in the lowlands, however many other wonders they gave in exchange. Stars crowded the dark, sparks of frozen fire which melted into the Milky Way; tonight that great torrent gleamed like sea-glow. Three sister planets burned in copper, silver, and amber. Among them hastened pygmy Sohrab, while Raksh hung near the half, so low in the west that illusion made it huge, and cast the shadows of trees and drifts long across the land.

Eva had always loved this sight.

The path reached the Emperor River and followed its bank. It sheened hard frozen. On its opposite side, buried fields and pastures rose toward hills and wilderness. Against that remote murk glimmered a few lights, from one of the villages which were springing up across the plateau.

To Coffin, sound seemed muffled in this thin air; and in these his latter years he had grown hard of hearing. He wasn't aware of the skaters until he rounded a bend in the river, screened by a clump of plume oak, and saw them. Here a road was carried by a bridge. Around its piers and across the ice frolicked a score of boys and girls. They whizzed, they swooped, they laid arms about each other's waists and took wing. Their shouting and laughter crackled in the chill.

Coffin went onto the span to watch. Abruptly he noticed another already present. The lad was tall, but not only was he wearing a black outfit, the African share of his ancestry made his face almost invisible at a distance. The skates which he had removed caught the moonlight at his feet.

"Why, . . . hullo," Coffin said, peering.

"Oh." The youth turned. "Mr. Coffin. How do you do, sir?"

The man recognized him, Alex Burns, son of a neighbor of de Smet: a bright, well-mannered chap. "Taking a rest?"

"Not exactly, sir." Alex gripped the railing and stared away. "I got to thinking."

"On a night like this? Seems as if you're missing a lot of fun. Sure wish I could get in on it."

"Really? Sir, you're welcome to borrow my skates."

"Thanks, but at my age, a fall under Rustum gravity can be a serious matter. And I've got business ahead of me."

"Yes, sir. Everybody knows that."

Then Alex swung around again to confront him and said in a desperate voice, "Mr. Coffin, could I talk with you?"

"Certainly. Though I don't know what a rusticating gaffer like me has to say that'd be of use." *Yet I remember my sons at your age—how short a while ago!*

"This news . . . about the fleet coming from Sol —it's true?" Somehow the adolescent squeak in midquestion was not ridiculous.

"As far as we can tell. Twenty light-years between makes for slow communications. The Earth government may have changed its mind meanwhile. They were phasing out space travel when your ancestors left. Too costly, given a bloated population pressing on resources worn thin. Not quite in their world view, either. The culture was turning more and more from science and technology to mysticism and ceremony."

"Th-that's what my teachers say. Which is how come I'm scared this is a, a false alarm."

"Well, I don't think it'll turn out to be. Giving the Constitutionalists passage to Rustum was a gimmick to get rid of them. But those who elected to go weren't all the Constitutionalists by any means, nor was that the only kind of dissenter. Once we started sending messages back, our example seems to've had considerable psychological effect, roused a widespread desire to emulate. My suspicion is, the government has no choice except to resume a space effort—for several decades, at least, till the social climate changes again. They claim they're searching for other habitable planets. . . . No, I think this emigrant fleet is indeed under weigh."

"Why don't our people want it?"

The anguish startled Coffin. "Well, uh, well, some folks worry about the effects on society. That's not unanimous, Alex. I assure you, the average lowlander has nothing against receiving a few thousand newcomers."

"But the, the average High American—"

"Nobody's taken a poll. I'm not sure, myself, how a vote on the question would go."

Alex flung an arm skyward, pointing. The constellations of Rustum were scarcely different from those of Earth; in this universe, twenty light-years are the single stumbling step of an infant.

But just above Bootes flickered a wanness which was Sol.

"Th-they can come to us," the boy stammered. "Why can't we go to them?"

"We haven't the industry to build spacecraft. Won't for generations, maybe centuries."

"And meanwhile we have to stay here! Our whole lives!" Did tears catch the level moonbeams?

Now Coffin understood. "How does your pressure tolerance test out?" he asked softly.

"I can live . . . down to about . . . t-t-two kilometers below."

"That's not bad. Plenty of territory in that range. You can have an adventurous life if you want."

"Oh, yes, sir. I s'pose."

"As I recall, you aim to become a scientist. Well, there's no lack of field research left to do. And if you want to go further down, clear to sea level, why, the new-model air helmets are excellent."

"It's not the same." Alex gulped, knotted fists at sides, and after a while said rapidly: "Please don't think I'm whining, sir. Nor am I, uh, uh, looking down on anybody. But most lowlanders I've met—you're different, of course—most of them, I don't . . . well, we don't fight or anything, but we don't seem to have a lot to talk about."

Coffin nodded. "The frontier doesn't exactly breed intellectuals, does it? Do bear in mind, though, son: those scouts, lumberjacks, farmers, fishermen—they aren't stupid. They simply have different concerns from this tamed High America.

In fact, the well-established lowland communities, like my Lake Moondance, they no longer maintain frontier personality either."

No, instead it's a wealth-conscious squirearchy, a yeomanry settling down into folkways—not effete, not ossified . . . still, we've become rather ingrown and self-satisfied, haven't we? It hasn't been so on my plantation; Eva never allowed it to become so. She got the kids, and me, to lift our eyes from our daily concerns. Elsewhere, however—No, I hardly think Alex would find many of his own sort around Lake Moondance.

"The compromise for you," he suggested, "might be to do your field work in company with roughneck local guides—who can be top-notch company, remember, who *are* if you take them on the proper terms—and afterward you come back here and write up your findings, where people are cultured."

"Culture!" Alex fleered. "They think 'culture' means playing the same symphonies and reading the same books their grandfathers did!"

"That's not entirely fair. We have artists, authors, composers, not to mention scientists, doing original work."

"How original? The science is . . . using tried and true methods, never basic research . . . and the arts copy the old models, over and over—"

He speaks considerable truth, Coffin thought.

Alex's finger stabbed back at the stars. "If they really were original, sir," he cried, "they wouldn't want to wall us off from those. Would they?"

Coffin consoled him as well as might be.

It was doubtful if man would ever altogether outlive the heritage of the planet which bore him. He could train himself to some degree of change from the ancient rhythm of her turning, but not enough to become a fully diurnal creature on Rustum. In the middle latitude at which Anchor lay, a midwinter night lasted for forty-two hours. Of necessity, during two fourteen-hour segments of that darkness, indoor and outdoor illumination made the town a cluster of small suns.

Beneath this sky-hiding roof of light, delegates to the second session of the Constitutional Convention mounted the staircase into Wolfe Hall. They numbered about fifty men and women. Though all were dressed to show due respect for the occasion, the costumes were nearly as varied as the ages. (Daniel Coffin was the oldest, the youngest a male who probably didn't shave oftener than once a day.) Here a professor walked lean and dignified, in tunic and trousers as gray as his head but the academic cloak gorgeous on his shoulders. There an engineer had reverted to archaic styles and put upon herself a long skirt of formality. Yonder a sea captain, weathered and squint-eyed, rolled forward in billed cap and brass buttons, next to the blue uniform of an air pilot. A rancher from lowland North Persis, otherwise a sensible man, flaunted leather garments and a necklace of catling teeth. The physician with whom he talked had underlined her standing in the cut of her jacket. . . . Coffin felt drab among them. And yet, he thought, weren't they reaching a bit, weren't they being just a touch too studiedly picturesque?

Citizens crowded the pavement, watching, in an eerie hush. Anchor had grown used to seeing the congress assemble. But this time was different. This time its first order of business was light-years remote and terrifyingly immediate. Soon they would hasten home, to follow the proceedings on television. Afterward they would argue in their houses, fields, shops, laboratories, camps, schools, taverns, and who knew what passions might flare?

Coffin paused in the lobby to leave his coverall. Most others had omitted that garment, as being too unsolemn when they scrambled in or out of it, and walked in frozen dignity from their lodgings. Low-voiced talk buzzed around him. An ache throbbed in his left wrist; probably he needed an arthritis booster. He shoved the awareness aside and concentrated on his plan of action. He must get his licks in early, because he hadn't the stamina any longer for ten or twelve unbroken hours of debate. Well, he and Dorcas Hirayama had discussed this privately beforehand.

The building had been enlarged over the years, but the meeting place was the original whole of it, piously preserved birch wainscoting and rough rafters. Echoes boomed. Folding chairs spread across the floor. At the far end rose the platform, decorated in red-white-and-blue bunting, Freedom Flag on the wall behind—the platform where for three generations, speakers had spoken, actors performed, orchestras played, callers sounded the measures of square dances.

For an instant the assembly was gone from around Daniel Coffin. They were calling a new one, and he and Mary Lochaber ran hand in hand, laughterful like skaters, to join in, and afterward he would walk her home under stars and moons.

No. That was then. Mary married Bill Sandberg, and I married Eva Spain, and this was best for us both, and at last we were united in Alice and David. I'm sorry, Eva.

It was as if he heard her chuckle and felt her rumple his hair.

Well—The delegates were taking their seats, much scrapping and muttering back and forth. Hirayama was mounting the podium. The cameramen were making final adjustments. Coffin shivered. *Poor heating in here. Or else simply that old blood runs cold.* His head lifted. *They may find it can still run pretty hot when it wants to.*

The gavel slammed. How far back did that signal go, anyway? To the first cave patriarch whose stone hammer smote a log? There was strength in the thought, a sense of not being utterly adrift and alone in time. No wonder the colonists tried so hard to keep Earth ways alive, or actually to revive some which had been as obsolete on Earth as the liberty their ancestors came here to save. And when this failed on a world that was not Earth, no wonder they were so quick to develop rituals and taboos of their own.

"In the name of the people of Rustum, for whom we are gathered, I call this meeting to order," said the clear female voice. It continued through parliamentary formalities to which nobody really listened, not even those who took part.

Until:

"As you doubtless know, we've had a surprise dropped in our laps." Coffin felt his mouth twitch upward. Now Dorcas could start behaving like herself! She leaned forward, hands on the lectern, small in her gown but large in her presence. "Maybe it's best that it did occur at this precise time. In writing the basic law of our planet, we'll remember that a universe encloses it.

"At any rate, many persons, including many members of this assembly, feel we should take the matter up before going on to our regular agenda. I agree. By virtue of the powers vested in me, et cetera, I've appointed a couple of committees to study the implications of the immigrant fleet and make recommendations. This will be kept brief, ladies and gentlemen. No general discussion. The idea is to set forth different views as clearly as possible, then adjourn to consider them, then reconvene to exchange thoughts in detail.

"Will Dr. O'Malley's committee please report first?"

Only their chairman joined her. He'd probably domineered over everyone else, for he had inherited genes from his grandfather. *However, Jack O'Malley made his domineering fun,* Coffin remembered from boyhood. *Also, ... well, I'm not saying Morris O'Malley is inferior; but a lab administrator is not the same as an explorer who could drink his whole band under the table and wake in six hours, hound-dog eager to go discover some new miracle.*

The speaker rustled papers. "My lady and colleagues, perhaps it would be best if I commence by summarizing the situation as my group understands it," he said, and did at a length which caused Hirayama to drum nails on the arm of her chair.

"Well." Finally O'Malley's tone grew vigorous. "The question before us is twofold. Should we allow the travelers to join us? If not, can we prevent it?

"The second part is simple. We can. Presumably the fleet is already en route. Theron Svoboda, chief of interstellar communications, thinks we have a fair chance of intercepting it with a maser beam, getting a message through to the officers on watch. These can change course for a different star or, more likely, return to the Solar System.

"If this fails and the ships arrive, we—rather, the next generation of us—will nevertheless be in full control. A minority of your committee advocates constructing nuclear missiles to ensure it. The majority considers that would be a waste of effort. Fuel requirements being what they are, those are surely unarmed vessels. They will depend on us to help them refine reaction mass for the trip home. In no case can a few bewildered newcomers impose their will on a planet."

He paused for a sip of water. "Very well. The issue is, therefore, *should* we give entry to these self-invited strangers?

"They bring us no benefit. We'd have to nurse them through adjustment to Rustum; for certainly we could never let them suffer and die as horribly as did many among our forefathers, whom nobody helped. Later we'd have to take time we can ill afford to teach them the habits, technicalities, and tricks which generations on Rustum have painfully learned for themselves. And at the end, in reward, what would we get? Workers not especially desirable, being grossly limited in what they can do. Perhaps not workers at all, but mere parasites. I shall return to this point shortly.

"We are under no moral obligation to admit them. Your committee has reviewed every tape of every communication between Earth and Rustum. A few from our side may have waxed overenthusiastic. But no government of ours has ever issued any invitation or given any promises—if only because hitherto we have never possessed a very formally organized government.

"If they are turned back, none but their officers on watch will even have looked upon the Promised Land. The human cargo would remain in suspended animation until reawakened in Earth orbit or, conceivably, in orbit around some wholly new planet. If they feel disappointment, why, so must every human being, often in this life.

"We have the power to exclude them, and we have the right. Your committee finds that we have, in addition and ultimately, the duty to exclude them."

Coffin heard out the argument against allowing a proletariat to appear overnight. He wasn't surprised to find it almost identical with the position he'd outlined to George Stein and the others. O'Malley was an intelligent man in his way, and knew history. . . . Coffin felt his lips quirk afresh.

You've got a moderately good opinion of yourself, don't you, Daniel, my boy?

He tensed when O'Malley went on, because here he recognized, not an abstract sociological argument, but that which reached into the guts and grabbed.

"More vital, ladies and gentlemen, people of Rustum, far more vital is what I next have to say. Dare we open our gates to a gang of aliens?"

O'Malley let silence underline that before he continued. "Your committee does not necessarily denigrate anyone's human worth," he said; and Coffin thought that the measured syllables, the overtones of regret, were the best oratory he'd heard in years. "Assuredly we do not subscribe to any cruel and absurd doctrine of racial hierarchies." He bowed a little toward Hirayama, toward Gabriel Burns, toward the entire room and planet. "If we are of predominantly Caucasoid North American stock, we are not exclusively that, and we are proud that in us lives the entire human species.

"But"—he lifted a finger—"it would be equally absurd and, in the long run, equally cruel, to pretend that *cultures* do not differ in basic ways. And let us hear no bleat that there can be no value judgments between them. The freedom we enjoy is superior to the despotism on Earth; the rational judgment we cultivate is superior to, yes, more truly human than the blind obedience and blinder faith which have overwhelmed Earth.

"People of Rustum, it is all too easy for us to imagine that the thousands on their way here are just like our forebears—perhaps not the same in color of skin or shape of eyelids, but the same inside, where it counts. Were this true, we might hope to prevent them from becoming proles, difficult though that would be.

"But consider. Earth has not been static since our founding fathers made their weary pilgrimage hither. Study the transcribed communication tapes for yourselves, people of Rustum. Judge for yourselves how social evolution back there seems to have nearly obliterated the last shards of American—no, Western civilization—those shards which we mean to preserve and to make the foundation of a new and more enduring house of liberty.

"Today's emigrants are not in search of freedom. That notion is extinct on Earth. They are apparently dissenters, but their dissent is not that of the individual demanding a steelclad bill of rights. What they seek, that puts them in conflict with their authorities, is not certain. It appears to be a kind of neo-Confucianism, though with paradoxical ecstatic elements. Who can tell? When seventy years must pass between question asked and reply received, there can be no real understanding.

"The point is, they are alien.

"Shall we, who still dwell precariously on a world that is still full of deadly surprises, shall we take upon ourselves such a burden of unassimilable outsiders?"

O'Malley lowered his voice. Almost, it tolled into the hush: "Would that actually be a kindness to

the outsiders themselves? I have pointed out that
they are a potential poverty class. I will now point
out that since they are alien, since there are bound
to be offenses and clashes, they could become the
victims of hatred, even outright persecution. We
are not saints on Rustum. We are not immune to
the ancient diseases of xenophobia, callousness,
legalized robbery, and mob violence. Let us not
inflict upon our home the same unhealable wound
which was inflicted on Mother America.

"Lead us not into temptation."

He stepped down to such applause, from the
mostly highlander congress, that Hirayama could
barely be heard: "We will take a half hour's
recess."

Coffin stood with his pipe, though smoke had
scant taste in air this keen, on an upstairs balcony.
Anchor gleamed and murmured beneath, busy at
its work, its hopes. Its radiance dimmed, in his
vision, the ice on the river, the reaching snow-
lands, the peaks and the stars above them. *But I
only have to walk a few kilometers out,* he thought,
*and I'll be alone with the unhuman and its
eternity.*

I'm also close to them in time, of course, his
mind added. *Soon I'll be among them.* It was a
strange feeling.

A voice brought him around. "Ah, greetings,
Daniel. Did you want to escape the crowd?"

He saw Morris O'Malley's ascetic visage between the street lamps and the moons. "Yes," he
replied; the mist of his words fled away into night.

"Say, that was a fine speech you made. To be quite frank, better than I expected."

The other man smiled. "Thanks. I'm no Demosthenes. But when you speak from conviction, it gets easier."

"Those are your beliefs?"

"Of course. I have no personal ax to grind. I may live to see that fleet arrive, but before the trouble becomes acute, I'll be safe in my grave. It's my grandchildren I'm worried about."

"Do you really think they'll have that much grief from a bunch of well-meaning Asians or Africans or whatever those are? This is a whole planet, Morris."

O'Malley's voice turned bleak. "For your kind it is."

"It was for your granddad too, in spite of his having to wear a reduction helmet—one of those primitive muscle-powered jobs—every time he ventured below three kilometers."

"He helped map the lowlands. He didn't live in them. We, confined to High America—" The talk he had given made it less astonishing than it would formerly have been, that dry Dr. O'Malley laid a hand on Coffin's shoulder. "Daniel, I know I was oversimplifying. I know the issues are much more subtle and complicated, with far more ifs and maybes. That's precisely what scares me."

Coffin drank smoke and looked across rooftops. "Your granddad never let anything scare him, permanently anyway, that I know of."

"Things were different then. Simple issues of survival."

"I have a notion that, at bottom, all issues are alike. They turn on the same principles. And, for your information, survival wasn't always a simple either-or question."

O'Malley was mute for a while before he said low: "I'm told you're to speak just after recess."

Coffin dipped his head. "It won't take as long or be near as eloquent as yours, Morris."

How many of their faces he knew! There was the mother of Leo Svoboda, there the son of Mary Sandberg, there his old poker opponent Ray Gonzales, there young Tregennis who'd worked for him before seeking a fortune in the western islands, there his and Eva's son Charlie whom Tom and Jane de Smet had raised because he couldn't live in the lowlands, his own hair grizzled . . . . Rustum was mystery and immensity, to this day; but man on Rustum remained a world very small and close and dear to itself.

"This is not exactly a committee report," Coffin said. "I represent the Moondance area, and because we thereabouts have reached a sort of consensus, I asked leave of the president to set our views before you."

His throat felt rough. Like his predecessor, he took a drink. He recognized the water; its faint iron tang brought him back to springs near the farm on the Cleft edge when he was a child. How much of everything he had known could he hope to pass on?

"I'll try to be brief," he said, "because my esteemed colleague Dr. O'Malley has covered the generalities, leaving the practicalities to me. Mind you, philosophy and theory are essential. Without them, we blunder blind at best, we're brutes at worst. But they are not ends in themselves; that'd make them mere parlor games. They are guides to action. Life depends on what we *do*—or don't do.

"Shall we or shall we not receive strangers into our midst? I propose we answer the question fast, in practical terms, and get on with our proper business."

He had them, he saw. He was no longer an old man allowed to drone on a while out of respect for what he had been; suddenly he gripped reality in the sight of them all.

"As for the problem that'd be created for High America if we admit outsiders," he said, taking advantage of his lack of oratorical ability to convey a sense of unemotional confidence: "many of you have been assuming that the highlanders would have to cope with it alone. Why should we lowlanders care? If so, I can sympathize with highlanders who want to use the majority they still will have when the ships come, to forbid them to land any passengers.

"Well, I am here to tell you that Lake Moondance and environs, clear through the Cyrus Valley, does care and wants to help." He heard the breath sigh into fifty pairs of lungs. No doubt it was doing so around the planet. Inwardly, he grinned. Half his effort had gone toward keeping this revelation secret, that he might spring it tonight for top effect.

The other half had gone into argument, cajolery,

chicanery, and genteel bribery, to get the support that he must have.

"I expect our sister lowland communities will follow suit," he continued, thereby going a ways toward committing them. "Frontiersmen are generally pragmatists. They have ideals, but their first thought is what material measures will put those ideals to work.

"In this case, the practical problem is that High America would find it difficult, maybe impossible, from both an economic and a social viewpoint, to take in five thousand persons of exotic background, who can't scatter across the globe and get absorbed, but must stay here where they can breathe."

Coffin reached for pipe and tobacco pouch. He didn't really want a smoke this soon after the last; but the homely action of filling the bowl should help bring everything down to a less giddily exalted plane.

"Now that ought to be solvable," he drawled. "As for the cost, why, Moondance is ready to pay a fair share in money, materials, labor, whatever is needed that we can supply. I repeat, I'm sure the other lowland communities will join us in that. Shared, the expense won't fall hard on anybody.

"And you know, that'll be an important precedent, a symbol and function of our unity. I hate to contradict Dr. O'Malley's noble disclaimer, but the fact is, we do have basic differences among us, not only social but actually genetic, racial. Some of us can live down there, some cannot. We must find as much common human ground as we can, to transcend that. Don't you agree?"

After a wait: " 'Common human ground' includes the good old Homo sapiens habit of not meekly adapting to circumstances, but grabbing them by the ears and adapting them to us.

"Look, air helmets have improved beyond belief since I was young. Why, when I was a baby they didn't exist! Who says we must stop here? Who says we can't work out something better, a biochemical treatment maybe, which'll let every man, woman, and child on Rustum live anywhere that he or she likes?"

The assembly stirred and exclaimed. He cut through the noise:

"Moondance proposes a joint research effort, which will itself be another unifying element, an effort to discover means of overcoming the handicap that most of our children are born with. I know that's been daydreamed about for a long time. Part of the reason nothing's happened has been that close cooperation of both human breeds is obviously essential, and we lowlanders, at least, have had no motivation toward it, especially with so much else to keep us busy. Tonight we do urge moving from daydream to reality.

"If we succeed in that, the problems associated with admitting immigrants will become trivial. Furthermore, if we commit ourselves to an open-door policy, then the knowledge that yonder fleet is aimed at us will be one hell of a stimulus to solving this merely scientific problem!"

Again he drank, before he added mildly, "Of course, without that open-door policy, the lowlanders will have no reason to help in such a project, or to promise to help bear the burden if the project fails. If you vote to close the gates, then to hell with you. Stay up here in the isolation you like so much."

Uproar. Dorcas Hirayama hammered for odor. As the racket died, a voice from the middle of the room shouted, "Why do you want a lot of damn foreigners?"

Coffin lit his pipe. "I was coming to that," he said, "impolitely though the question may have been put.

"Whether or not we can crack the air-pressure barrier, we can't expect to assimilate the immigrants quickly or easily. To some extent, probably we can never assimilate them at all, in the sense of making them or their descendants identical with us. Besides the obstacles raised by their unfamiliarity with Rustum, why, they're coming here to preserve a way of life, not lose it in a melting pot.

"As said, I think with some sacrifice by both highlands and lowlands, whatever happens otherwise, we can avoid creating a proletariat. At worst, we'll have to tide over the older generation, and make some economic-industrial changes to accommodate the younger one.

"But as for that second aspect Dr. O'Malley discussed—the introduction of foreign philosophies, minds strange to our own—"

He laid down his pipe. He filled his lungs and roared across the hall, echoes thunderous even in his deaf ears:

"*God damn it, that's exactly what we need!*"

And afterward, into their shock, himself most gently:

"Not many hours ago, I stood on North Bridge and talked to a very puzzled and embittered young man. He couldn't comprehend why his elders wanted to cut us off from the stars. We ended by considering ways and means whereby Rustum might acquire those spaceships when they arrive.

"Unlikely, of course. The point is, the news had made him realize how suffocated he is in this smug backwater we've become. Oh, yes, we have big jobs ahead of us. But who will do them? People exactly like us? If so, what'll there be afterwards, except sitting back and admiring the achievements of the ancestors?

"I'll tell you what there'll be. Hell to pay!

"I've heard a great deal of worry expressed about creating a rootless, impoverished proletariat, with no stake or interest in continuing the society that bred it. Ladies and gentlemen, have you considered the danger in creating a proletariat of the soul?

"*Let* foreigners in. Welcome unexpected insights, weird ways, astonishing thoughts and feelings. We may not always like them—probably we often won't—but we'll experience them and they'll make us look to the foundations of our own beliefs. If there's anything at all to the idea of liberty and individual worth, which we're supposed to be keeping alive, then on the whole, we'll be the better for being challenged. And it works two ways, you know. They'll learn from us. Together, the old and the new dweller on Rustum will do and think what neither alone could dream."

Coffin drew breath. He had gotten a little dizzy from so much talking. Sweat was on his skin and his knees shook.

He finished hoarse-voiced: "As most of you know, seeing how I brag about them, I have a couple of great-grandchildren. I don't want to protect them from the cosmos, any more than that boy I met wants to be protected.

"No, they deserve better."

When, after lunations, the debates were ended, the hard bargains driven, the resolutions drawn and passed, the law established that Rustum would greet and help the offspring of Earth—

Daniel Coffin sat alone in his room in the de Smet house. He had turned off the fluoros. Moonlight streamed through an open window, icy as the air. Afar reached the taut silence of winter night, barely disturbed by a rumble from the river, whose hardness had begun to break into floes under a first faint flowing of spring.

The coldness touched Eva's portrait on a table. He picked it up. His hand trembled. He was very tired; it would be good to lie down and rest.

"Sweetheart," he whispered. "I wish you could have seen." He shook his head, ran fingers through his hair. *Maybe you did? I don't know.*

"You see," he told his memory of her, "I did what I did because that was what you'd have wanted. Only because of you."

Publisher's Note:

Here ends the story of High America. But other worlds than Rustum were to receive the seed of Earth. Each responded in its own way to the men and women who had fled their own ruined planet. . . .

THE QUEEN OF
AIR AND
DARKNESS

The last glow of the last sunset would linger almost until midwinter. But there would be no more day, and the northlands rejoiced. Blossoms opened, flamboyance on firethorn trees, steel-flowers rising blue from the brake and rainplant that cloaked all hills, shy whiteness of kiss-me-never down in the dales. Flitteries darted among them on iridescent wings; a crownbuck shook his horns and bugled. Between horizons the sky deepened from purple to sable. Both moons were aloft, nearly full, shining frosty on leaves and molten on waters. The shadows they made were blurred by an aurora, a great blowing curtain of light across half heaven. Behind it the earliest stars had come out.

A boy and a girl sat on Wolund's Barrow just under the dolmen it upbore. Their hair, which

streamed halfway down their backs, showed startlingly forth, bleached as it was by summer. Their
bodies, still dark from that season, merged with
earth and bush and rock, for they wore only garlands. He played on a bone flute and she sang.
They had lately become lovers. Their age was
about sixteen, but they did not know this, considering themselves Outlings and thus indifferent
to time, remembering little or nothing of how they
had once dwelt in the lands of men.

His notes piped cold around her voice:

> "Cast a spell,
> weave it well
> of dust and dew
> and night and you."

A brook by the grave mound, carrying moonlight down to a hill-hidden river, answered with its
rapids. A flock of hellbats passed black beneath
the aurora.

A shape came bounding over Cloudmoor. It had
two arms and two legs, but the legs were long and
claw-footed and feathers covered it to the end of a
tail and broad wings. The face was half human,
dominated by its eyes. Had Ayoch been able to
stand wholly erect, he would have reached to the
boy's shoulder.

The girl rose. "He carries a burden," she said.
Her vision was not meant for twilight like that of a
northland creature born, but she had learned how
to use every sign her senses gave her. Besides the
fact that ordinarily a pook would fly, there was a
heaviness to his haste.

"And he comes from the south." Excitment jumped in the boy, sudden as a green flame that went across the constellation Lyrth. He sped down the mound. "Ohoi, Ayoch!" he called. "Me here, Mistherd!"

"And Shadow-of-a-Dream," the girl laughed, following.

The pook halted. He breathed louder than the soughing in the growth around him. A smell of bruised yerba lifted where he stood.

"Well met in winterbirth," he whistled. "You can help me bring this to Carheddin."

He held out what he bore. His eyes were yellow lanterns above. It moved and whimpered.

"Why, a child," Mistherd said.

"Even as you were, my son, even as you were. Ho, ho, what a snatch!" Ayoch boasted. "They were a score in yon camp by Fallowwood, armed, and besides watcher engines they had big ugly dogs aprowl while they slept. I came from above, however, having spied on them till I knew that a handful of dazedust—"

"The poor thing." Shadow-of-a-Dream took the boy and held him to her small breasts. "So full of sleep yet, aren't you?" Blindly, he sought a nipple. She smiled through the veil of her hair. "No, I am still too young, and you already too old. But come, when you wake in Carheddin under the mountain, you shall feast."

"Yo-ah," said Ayoch very softly. "She is abroad and has heard and seen. She comes." He crouched down, wings folded. After a moment Mistherd knelt, and then Shadow-of-a-Dream, though she did not let go the child.

The Queen's tall form blocked off the moons. For a while she regarded the three and their booty. Hill and moor sounds withdrew from their awareness until it seemed they could hear the northlights hiss.

As last Ayoch whispered, "Have I done well, Starmother?"

"If you stole a babe from the camp full of engines," said the beautiful voice, "then they were folk out of the far south who may not endure it as meekly as yeomen."

"But what can they do, Snowmaker?" the pook asked. "How can they track us?"

Mistherd lifted his head and spoke in pride. "Also, now they too have felt the awe of us."

"And he is a cuddly dear," Shadow-of-a-Dream said. "And we need more like him, do we not, Lady Sky?"

"It had to happen in some twilight," agreed she who stood above. "Take him onward and care for him. By this sign," which she made, "is he claimed for the Dwellers."

Their joy was freed. Ayoch cartwheeled over the ground till he reached a shiverleaf. There he swarmed up the trunk and out on a limb, perched half hidden by unrestful pale foliage, and crowed. Boy and girl bore the child toward Carheddin at an easy distance-devouring lope which let him pipe and her sing:

> "Wahaii, wahaii!
> Wayala, iaii!
> Wing on the wind

high over heaven,
shrilly shrieking,
rush with the rainspears,
tumble through tumult,
drift to the moonhoar trees and the dream-
    heavy shadows beneath them,
and rock in, be one with the clinking wave-
    lets of lakes where the starbeams drown."

As she entered, Barbro Cullen felt, through all grief and fury, stabbed by dismay. The room was unkempt. Journals, tapes, reels, codices, file boxes, bescribbled papers were piled on every table. Dust filmed most shelves and corners. Against one wall stood a laboratory setup, microscope and analytical equipment. She recognized it as compact and efficient, but it was not what you would expect in an office, and it gave the air a faint chemical reek. The rug was threadbare, the furniture shabby.

This was her final chance?

Then Eric Sherrinford approached. "Good day, Mrs. Cullen," he said. His tone was crisp, his handclasp firm. His faded gripsuit didn't bother her. She wasn't inclined to fuss about her own appearance except on special occasions. (And would she ever again have one, unless she got back Jimmy?) What she observed was a cat's personal neatness.

A smile radiated in crow's feet from his eyes. "Forgive my bachelor housekeeping. On Beowulf we have—we had, at any rate, machines for that, so I never acquired the habit myself, and I don't want a hireling disarranging my tools. More convenient to work out of my apartment than keep a separate office. Won't you be seated?"

"No, thanks. I couldn't," she mumbled.

"I understand. But if you'll excuse me, I function best in a relaxed position."

He jackknifed into a lounger. One long shank crossed the other knee. He drew forth a pipe and stuffed it from a pouch. Barbro wondered why he took tobacco in so ancient a way. Wasn't Beowulf supposed to have the up-to-date equipment that they still couldn't afford to build on Roland? Well, of course old customs might survive anyhow. They generally did in colonies, she remembered reading. People had moved starward in the hope of preserving such outmoded things as their mother tongues or constitutional government or rational-technological civilization. . . .

Sherrinford pulled her up from the confusion of her weariness: "You must give me the details of your case, Mrs. Cullen. You've simply told me your son was kidnapped and your local constabulary did nothing. Otherwise, I know just a few obvious facts, such as your being widowed rather than divorced; and you're the daughter of out-wayers in Olga Ivanoff Land, who nevertheless kept in close telecommunication with Christmas Landing; and you're trained in one of the biological professions; and you had several years' hiatus in field work until recently you started again."

She gaped at the high-cheeked, beak-nosed, black-haired and gray-eyed countenance. His lighter made a *scrit* and a flare which seemed to fill the room. Quietness dwelt on this height above the city, and winter dusk was seeping through the windows. 'How in cosmos do you know that?" she heard herself exclaim.

He shrugged and fell into the lecturer's manner for which he was notorious. "My work depends on noticing details and fitting them together. In more than a hundred years on Roland, tending to cluster according to their origins and thought-habits, people have developed regional accents. You have a trace of the Olgan burr, but you nasalize your vowels in the style of this area, though you live in Portolondon. That suggests steady childhood exposure to metropolitan speech. You were part of Matsuyama's expedition, you told me, and took your boy along. They wouldn't have allowed any ordinary technician to do that; hence, you had to be valuable enough to get away with it. The team was conducting ecological research; therefore, you must be in the life sciences. For the same reason, you must have had previous field experience. But your skin is fair, showing none of the leatheriness one gets from prolonged exposure to this sun. Accordingly, you must have been mostly indoors for a good while before you went on your ill-fated trip. As for widowhood—you never mentioned a husband to me, but you have had a man whom you thought so highly of that you will wear both the wedding and the engagement ring he gave you."

Her sight blurred and stung. The last of those words had brought Tim back, huge, ruddy, laughterful and gentle. She must turn from this other person and stare outward. "Yes," she achieved saying, "you're right."

The apartment occupied a hilltop above Christmas Landing. Beneath it the city dropped away in walls, roofs, archaistic chimneys and lamplit streets, goblin lights of human-piloted vehicles, to the harbor, the sweep of Venture Bay, ships bound to and from the Sunward Islands and remoter regions of the Boreal Ocean, which glimmered like mercury in the afterglow of Charlemagne. Oliver was swinging rapidly higher, a mottled orange disc a full degree wide; closer to the zenith which it could never reach, it would shine the color of ice. Alde, half the seeming size, was a thin slow crescent near Sirius, which she remembered was near Sol, but you couldn't see Sol without a telescope—

"Yes," she said around the pain in her throat, "my husband is about four years dead. I was carrying our first child when he was killed by a stampeding monoceros. We'd been married three years before. Met while we were both at the University—'casts from School Central can only supply a basic education, you know— We founded our own team to do ecological studies under contract—you know, can a certain area be settled while maintaining a balance of nature, what crops will grow, what hazards, that sort of question— Well, afterward I did lab work for a fisher co-op in Portolondon. But the monotony, the . . . shut-in-ness . . . was eating me away. Professor Matsuyama offered me a position on the team he was organizing to examine Commissioner Hauch Land.

I thought, God help me, I thought Jimmy—Tim wanted him named James, once the tests showed it'd be a boy, after his own father and because of 'Timmy and Jimmy' and—oh, I thought Jimmy could safely come along. I couldn't bear to leave him behind for months, not at his age. We could make sure he'd never wander out of camp. What could hurt him inside it? *I* had never believed those stories about the Outlings stealing human children. I supposed parents were trying to hide from themselves the fact they'd been careless, they'd let a kid get lost in the woods or attacked by a pack of satans or—Well, I learned better, Mr. Sherrinford. The guard robots were evaded and the dogs were drugged, and when I woke, Jimmy was gone."

He regarded her through the smoke from his pipe. Barbro Engdahl Cullen was a big woman of thirty or so (Rolandic years, he reminded himself, ninety-five percent of Terrestrial, not the same as Beowulfan years), broad-shouldered, long-legged, full-breasted, supple of stride; her face was wide, straight nose, straightforward hazel eyes, heavy but mobile mouth; her hair was reddish brown, cropped below the ears, her voice husky, her garment a plain street robe. To still the writhing of her fingers, he asked skeptically, "Do you now believe in the Outlings?"

"No. I'm just not so sure as I was." She swung about with half a glare for him. "And we have found traces."

"Bits of fossils," he nodded. "A few artifacts of a neolithic sort. But apparently ancient, as if the makers died ages ago. Intensive search has failed to turn up any real evidence for their survival."

"How intensive can search be, in a summer-stormy, winter-gloomy wilderness around the North Pole?" she demanded. "When we are, how many, a million people on an entire planet, half of us crowded into this one city?"

"And the rest crowding this one habitable continent," he pointed out.

"Arctica covers five million square kilometers," she flung back. "The Arctic Zone proper covers a fourth of it. We haven't the industrial base to establish satellite monitor stations, build aircraft we can trust in those parts, drive roads through the damned darklands and establish permanent bases and get to know them and tame them. Good Christ, generations of lonely outwaymen told stories about Graymantle, and the beast was never seen by a proper scientist till last year."

"Still, you continue to doubt the reality of the Outlings?"

"Well, what about a secret cult among humans, born of isolation and ignorance, lairing in the wilderness, stealing children when they can for—" She swallowed. Her head drooped. "But you're supposed to be the expert."

"From what you told me over the visiphone, the Portolondon constabulary questions the accuracy of the report your group made, thinks the lot of you were hysterical, claims you must have omitted a due precaution, and the child toddled away and was lost beyond your finding."

His dry words pried the horror out of her. Flushing, she snapped, "Like any settler's kid? No. I didn't simply yell. I consulted Data Retrieval. A few too many such cases are recorded for accident to be a very plausible explanation. And shall we totally ignore the frightened stories about reappearances? But when I went back to the constabulary with my facts, they brushed me off. I suspect that was not entirely because they're undermanned. I think they're afriad too. They're recruited from country boys, and Portolondon lies near the edge of the unknown."

Her energy faded. "Roland hasn't got any central police force," she finished drably. "You're my last hope."

The man puffed smoke into twilight, with which it blent, before he said in a kindlier voice than hitherto: "Please don't make it a high hope, Mrs. Cullen. I'm the solitary private investigator on this world, having no resources beyond myself, and a newcomer to boot."

"How long have you been here?"

"Twelve years. Barely time to get a little familiarity with the relatively civilized coastlands. You settlers of a century or more—what do you, even, know about Arctica's interior?"

Sherrinford sighed. "I'll take the case, charging no more than I must, mainly for the sake of the experience," he said. "But only if you'll be my guide and assistant, however painful it will be for you."

"Of course! I dreaded waiting idle. Why me, though?"

"Hiring someone else as well qualified would be

prohibitively expensive on a pioneer planet where every hand has a thousand urgent tasks to do. Besides, you have a motive. And I'll need that. As one who was born on another world altogether strange to this one, itself altogether strange to Mother Earth, I am too dauntingly aware of how handicapped we are."

Night gathered upon Christmas Landing. The air stayed mild, but glimmer-lit tendrils of fog, sneaking through the streets, had a cold look, and colder yet was the aurora where it shuddered between the moons. The woman drew closer to the man in this darkening room, surely not aware that she did, until he switched on a fluoropanel. The same knowledge of Roland's aloneness was in both of them.

One light-year is not much as galactic distances go. You could walk it in about 270 million years, beginning at the middle of the Permian Era, when dinosaurs belonged to the remote future, and continuing to the present day when spaceships cross even greater reaches. But stars in our neighborhood average some nine light-years apart, and barely one percent of them have planets which are man-habitable, and speeds are limited to less than that of radiation. Scant help is given by relativistic time contraction and suspended animation en route. These made the journeys seem short, but history meanwhile does not stop at home.

Thus voyages from sun to sun will always be few. Colonists will be those who have extremely special reasons for going. They will take along germ plasm for exogenetic cultivation of domestic plants and animals—and of human infants, in order that population can grow fast enough to escape death through genetic drift. After all, they cannot rely on further immigration. Two or three times a century, a ship may call from some other colony. (Not from Earth. Earth has long ago sunk into alien concerns.) Its place of origin will be an old settlement. The young ones are in no position to build and man interstellar vessels.

Their very survival, let alone their eventual modernization, is in doubt. The founding fathers have had to take what they could get, in a universe not especially designed for man.

Consider, for example, Roland. It is among the rare happy finds, a world where humans can live, breathe, eat the food, drink the water, walk unclad if they choose, sow their crops, pasture their beasts, dig their mines, erect their homes, raise their children and grandchildren. It is worth crossing three quarters of a light-century to preserve certain dear values and strike new roots into the soil of Roland.

But the star Charlemagne is of type F_9, forty percent brighter than Sol, brighter still in the treacherous ultraviolet and wilder still in the wind of charged particles that seethes from it. The planet has an eccentric orbit. In the middle of the short but furious northern summer, which includes periaston, total insolation is more than double what Earth gets; in the depth of the long northern winter, it is barely less than Terrestrial average.

Native life is abundant everywhere. But lacking elaborate machinery, not yet economically possible to construct for more than a few specialists, man can only endure the high latitudes. A ten-degree axial tilt, together with the orbit, means that the northern part of the Arctican continent spends half its year in unbroken sunlessness. Around the South Pole lies an empty ocean.

Other differences from Earth might superficially seem more important. Roland has two moons, small but close, to evoke clashing tides. It rotates once in thirty-two hours, which is endlessly, subtly disturbing to organisms evolved through gigayears of a quicker rhythm. The weather patterns are altogether unterrestrial. The globe is a mere 9,500 kilometers in diameter; its surface gravity is 0.42×980 cm/sec^2, the sea level air pressure is slightly above one Earth atmosphere. (For actually, Earth is the freak, and man exists because a cosmic accident blew away most of the gas that a body its size ought to have kept, as Venus has done.)

However, Homo can truly be called sapiens when he practices his specialty of being unspecialized. His repeated attempts to freeze himself into an all-answering pattern or culture or ideology, or whatever he has named it, have repeatedly brought ruin. Give him the pragmatic business of making his living and he will usually do rather well. He adapts, within broad limits.

These limits are set by such factors as his need for sunlight and his being, necessarily and forever, a part of the life that surrounds him and a creature of the spirit within.

Portolondon thrust docks, boats, machinery, warehouses into the Gulf of Polaris. Behind them huddled the dwellings of its 5,000 permanent inhabitants: concrete walls, storm shutters, high-peaked tile roofs. The gaiety of their paint looked forlorn amidst lamps; this town lay past the Arctic Circle.

Nevertheless Sherrinford remarked, "Cheerful place, eh? The kind of thing I came to Roland looking for."

Barbro made no reply. The days in Christmas Landing, while he made his preparations, had drained her. Gazing out the dome of the taxi that was whirring them downtown from the hydrofoil that brought them, she supposed he meant the lushness of forest and meadows along the road, brilliant hues and phosphorescence of flowers in gardens, clamor of wings overhead. Unlike Terrestrial flora in cold climates, Arctican vegetation spends every daylit hour in frantic growth and energy storage. Not till summer's fever gives place to gentle winter does it bloom and fruit; and estivating animals rise from their dens and migratory birds come home.

The view was lovely, she had to admit: beyond the trees, a spaciousness climbing toward remote heights, silvery gray under a moon, an aurora, the diffuse radiance from a sun just below the horizon.

Beautiful as a hunting satan, she thought, and as terrible. That wilderness had stolen Jimmy. She wondered if she would at least be given to find his little bones and take them to his father.

Abruptly she realized that she and Sherrinford

were at their hotel and that he had been speaking of the town. Since it was next in size after the capital, he must have visited here often before. The streets were crowded and noisy; signs flickered, music blared from shops, taverns, restaurants, sports centers, dance halls; vehicles were jammed down to molasses speed; the several-stories-high office buildings stood aglow. Portolondon linked an enormous hinterland to the outside world. Down the Gloria River came timber rafts, ores, harvest of farms whose owners were slowly making Rolandic life serve them, meat and ivory and furs gathered by rangers in the mountains beyond Troll Scarp. In from the sea came coastwise freighters, the fishing fleet, produce of the Sunward Islands, plunder of whole continents farther south where bold men adventured. It clanged in Portolondon, laughed, blustered, connived, robbed, preached, guzzled, swilled, toiled, dreamed, lusted, built, destroyed, died, was born, was happy, angry, sorrowful, greedy, vulgar, loving, ambitious, human. Neither the sun's blaze elsewhere nor the half year's twilight here— wholly night around midwinter—was going to stay man's hand.

Or so everybody said.

Everybody except those who had settled in the darklands. Barbro used to take for granted that they were evolving curious customs, legends, and superstitions, which would die when the outway had been completely mapped and controlled. Of late, she had wondered. Perhaps Sherrinford's hints, about a change in his own attitude brought about by his preliminary research, were responsible.

Or perhaps she just needed something to think about besides how Jimmy, the day before he went, when she asked him whether he wanted rye or French bread for a sandwich, answered in great solemnity—he was becoming interested in the alphabet—"I'll have a slice of what we people call the F bread."

She scarcely noticed getting out of the taxi, registering, being conducted to a primitively furnished room. But after she unpacked, she remembered Sherrinford had suggested a confidential conference. She went down the hall and knocked on his door. Her knuckles sounded less loud than her heart.

He opened the door, finger on lips, and gestured her toward a corner. Her temper bristled until she saw the image of Chief Constable Dawson in the visiphone. Sherrinford must have chimed him up and must have a reason to keep her out of scanner range. She found a chair and watched, nails digging into knees.

The detective's lean length refolded itself. "Pardon the interruption," he said. "A man mistook the number. Drunk, by the indications."

Dawson chuckled. "We get plenty of those." Barbro recalled his fondness for gabbing. He tugged the beard which he affected, as if he were an outwayer instead of a townsman. "No harm in them as a rule. They only have a lot of voltage to discharge, after weeks or months in the backlands."

"I've gathered that that environment—foreign in a million major and minor ways to the one that created man—I've gathered that it does do odd things to the personality." Sherrinford tamped his pipe. "Of course, you know my practice has been confined to urban and suburban areas. Isolated garths seldom need private investigators. Now that situation appears to have changed. I called to ask you for advice."

"Glad to help," Dawson said. "I've not forgotten what you did for us in the de Tahoe murder case." Cautiously: "Better explain your problem first."

Sherrinford struck fire. The smoke that followed cut through the green odors—even here, a paved pair of kilometers from the nearest woods—that drifted past traffic rumble through a crepuscular window. "This is more a scientific mission than a search for an absconding debtor or an industrial spy," he drawled. "I'm looking into two possibilities: that an organization, criminal or religious or whatever, has long been active and steals infants; or that the Outlings of folklore are real."

"Huh?" On Dawson's face Barbro read as much dismay as surprise. "You can't be serious!"

"Can't I?" Sherrinford smiled. "Several generations' worth of reports shouldn't be dismissed out of hand. Especially not when they become more frequent and consistent in the course of time, not less. Nor can we ignore the documented loss of babies and small children, amounting by now to over a hundred, and never a trace found afterward. Nor the finds which demonstrate that an intelligent species once inhabited Arctica and may still haunt the interior."

Dawson leaned forward as if to climb out of the screen. "Who engaged you?" he demanded. "That Cullen woman? We were sorry for her, naturally, but she wasn't making sense, and when she got downright abusive—"

"Didn't her companions, reputable scientists, confirm her story?"

"No story to confirm. Look, they had the place ringed with detectors and alarms, and they kept mastiffs. Standard procedure in country where a hungry sauroid or whatever might happen by. Nothing could've entered unbeknownst."

"On the ground. How about a flyer landing in the middle of camp?"

"A man in a copter rig would've roused everybody."

"A winged being might be quieter."

"A living flyer that could lift a three-year-boy? Doesn't exist."

"Isn't in the scientific literature, you mean, Constable. Remember Graymantle; remember how little we know about Roland, a planet, an entire world. Such birds do exist on Beowulf—and on Rustum, I've read. I made a calculation from the local ratio of air density to gravity, and, yes, it's marginally possible here too. The child could have been carried off for a short distance before wing muscles were exhausted and the creature must descend."

Dawson snorted. "First it landed and walked into the tent where mother and boy were asleep.

Then it walked away, toting him, after it couldn't fly further. Does that sound like a bird of prey? And the victim didn't cry out, the dogs didn't bark!"

"As a matter of fact," Sherrinford said, "those inconsistencies are the most interesting and convincing features of the whole account. You're right, it's hard to see how a human kidnapper could get in undetected, and an eagle type of creature wouldn't operate in that fashion. But none of this applies to a winged intelligent being. The boy could have been drugged. Certainly the dogs showed signs of having been."

"The dogs showed signs of having overslept. Nothing had disturbed them. The kid wandering by wouldn't do so. We don't need to assume one damn thing except, first, that he got restless and, second, that the alarms were a bit sloppily rigged —seeing as how no danger was expected from inside camp—and let him pass out. And, third, I hate to speak this way, but we must assume the poor tyke starved or was killed."

Dawson paused before adding: "If we had more staff, we could have given the affair more time. And would have, of course. We did make an aerial sweep, which risked the lives of the pilots, using instruments which would've spotted the kid anywhere in a fifty-kilometer radius, unless he was dead. You know how sensitive thermal analyzers are. We drew a complete blank. We have more important jobs than to hunt for the scattered pieces of a corpse."

He finished brusquely. "If Mrs. Cullen's hired

you, my advice is you find an excuse to quit. Better for her, too. She's got to come to terms with reality."

Barbro checked a shout by biting her tongue.

"Oh, this is merely the latest disappearance of the series," Sherrinford said. She didn't understand how he could maintain his easy tone when Jimmy was lost. "More thoroughly recorded than any before, thus more suggestive. Usually an outwayer family has given a tearful but undetailed account of their child who vanished and must have been stolen by the Old Folk. Sometimes, years later, they'd tell about glimpses of what they swore must have been the grown child, not really human any longer, flitting past in murk or peering through a window or working mischief upon them. As you say, neither the authorities nor the scientists have had personnel or resources to mount a proper investigation. But as I say, the matter appears to be worth investigating. Maybe a private party like myself can contribute."

"Listen, most of us constables grew up in the outway. We don't just ride patrol and answer emergency calls; we go back there for holidays and reunions. If any gang of . . . of human sacrificers was around, we'd know."

"I realize that. I also realize that the people you came from have a widespread and deep-seated belief in nonhuman beings with supernatural powers. Many actually go through rites and make offerings to propitiate them."

"I know what you're leading up to," Dawson flared. "I've heard it before, from a hundred sensationalists. The aborigines are the Outlings. I thought better of you. Surely you've visited a museum or three, surely you've read literature from planets which do have natives—or damn and blast, haven't you ever applied that logic of yours?"

He wagged a finger. "Think," he said. "What have we in fact discovered? A few pieces of worked stone; a few megaliths that might be artificial; scratchings on rock that seem to show plants and animals, though not the way any human culture would ever have shown them; traces of fires and broken bones; other fragments of bone that seem as if they might've belonged to thinking creatures, as if they might've been inside fingers or around big brains. If so, however, the owners looked nothing like men. Or angels, for that matter. Nothing! The most anthropoid reconstruction I've seen shows a kind of two-legged crocagator.

"Wait, let me finish. The stories about the Outlings—oh, I've heard them too, plenty of them. I believed them when I was a kid—the stories tell how there're different kinds, some winged, some not, some half human, some completely human except maybe for being too handsome— It's fairyland from ancient Earth all over again. Isn't it? I got interested once and dug into the Heritage Library microfiles, and be damned if I didn't find almost the identical yarns, told by peasants centuries before spaceflight.

"None of it squares with the scanty relics we have, if they are relics, or with the fact that no area the size of Arctica could spawn a dozen different intelligent species, or . . . hellfire, man, with the way your common sense tells you aborigines would behave when humans arrived!"

Sherrinfold nodded. "Yes, yes," he said. "I'm less sure than you that the common sense of non-human beings is precisely like our own. I've seen so much variation within mankind. But, granted, your arguments are strong. Roland's too few scientists have more pressing tasks than tracking down the origins of what is, as you put it, a revived medieval superstition."

He cradled his pipe bowl in both hands and peered into the tiny hearth of it. "Perhaps what interests me most," he said softly, "is why—across that gap of centuries, across a barrier of machine civilization and its utterly antagonistic world view—no continuity of tradition whatsoever — why have hard-headed, technologically organized, reasonably well-educated colonists here brought back from its grave a belief in the Old Folk?"

"I suppose eventually, if the University ever does develop the psychology department they keep talking about, I suppose eventually somebody will get a thesis out of your question." Dawson spoke in a jagged voice, and he gulped when Sherrinford replied:

"I propose to begin now. In Commissioner Hauch Land, since that's where the latest incident occurred. Where can I rent a vehicle?"

"Uh, might be hard to do—"

"Come, come. Tenderfoot or not, I know better.

In an economy of scarcity, few people own heavy equipment. But since it's needed, it can always be rented. I want a camper bus with a ground-effect drive suitable for every kind of terrain. And I want certain equipment installed which I've brought along, and the top canopy section replaced by a gun turret controllable from the driver's seat. But I'll supply the weapons. Besides rifles and pistols of my own, I've arranged to borrow some artillery from Christmas Landing's police arsenal."

"Hoy? Are you genuinely intending to make ready for . . . a war . . . against a myth?"

"Let's say I'm taking out insurance, which isn't terribly expensive, against a remote possibility. Now, besides the bus, what about a light aircraft carried piggyback for use in surveys?"

"No." Dawson sounded more positive than hitherto. "That's asking for disaster. We can have you flown to a base camp in a large plane when the weather report's exactly right. But the pilot will have to fly back at once, before the weather turns wrong again. Meteorology's underdeveloped on Roland; the air's especially treacherous this time of year, and we're not tooled up to produce aircraft that can outlive every surprise." He drew breath. "Have you no idea of how fast a whirly-whirly can hit, or what size hailstones might strike from a clear sky, or—? Once you're there, man, you stick to the ground." He hesitated. "That's an important reason our information is so scanty about the outway, and its settlers are so isolated."

Sherrinford laughed ruefully. "Well, I suppose if details are what I'm after, I must creep along anyway."

"You'll waste a lot of time," Dawson said. "Not to mention your client's money. Listen, I can't forbid you to chase shadows, but—"

The discussion went on for almost an hour. When the screen finally blanked, Sherrinford rose, stretched, and walked toward Barbro. She noticed anew his peculiar gait. He had come from a planet with a fourth again of Earth's gravitational drag, to one where weight was less than half Terrestrial. She wondered if he had flying dreams.

"I apologize for shuffling you off like that," he said. "I didn't expect to reach him at once. He was quite truthful about how busy he is. But having made contact, I didn't want to remind him overmuch of you. He can dismiss my project as a futile fantasy which I'll soon give up. But he might have frozen completely, might even have put up obstacles before us, if he'd realized through you how determined we are."

"Why should he care?" she asked in her bitterness.

"Fear of consequences, the worse because it is unadmitted—fear of consequences, the more terrifying because they are unguessable." Sherrinford's gaze went to the screen, and thence out the window to the aurora pulsing in glacial blue and white immensely far overhead. "I suppose you saw I was talking to a frightened man. Down underneath his conventionality and scoffing, he believes in the Outlings—oh, yes, he believes."

The feet of Mistherd flew over yerba and outpaced wind-blown driftwood. Beside him, black and misshapen, hulked Nagrim the nicor, whose earthquake weight left a swath of crushed plants. Behind, luminous blossoms of a firethorn shone through the twining, trailing outlines of Morgarel the wraith.

Here Cloudmoor rose in a surf of hills and thickets. The air lay quiet, now and then carrying the distance-muted howl of a beast. It was darker than usual at winterbirth, the moons being down and aurora a wan flicker above mountains on the northern world-edge. But this made the stars keen, and their numbers crowded heaven, and Ghost Road shone among them as if it, like the leafage beneath, were paved with dew.

"Yonder!" bawled Nagrim. All four of his arms pointed. The party had topped a ridge. Far off glimmered a park. "Hoah, hoah! 'Ull we right off stamp dem flat, or pluck dem apart slow?"

We shall do nothing of the sort, bonebrain, Morgarel's answer slid through their heads. *Not unless they attack us, and they will not unless we make them aware of us, and her command is that we spy out their purposes.*

"Gr-r-rum-m-m. I know deir aim. Cut down trees, stick plows in land, sow deir cursed seed in de clods and in deir shes. 'Less we drive dem into de bitterwater, and soon, soon, dey'll wax too strong for us."

"Not too strong for the Queen!" Mistherd protested, shocked.

Yet they do have new powers, it seems, Morgarel reminded him. *Carefully must we probe them.*

"Den carefully can we step on dem?" asked Nagrim.

The question woke a grin out of Mistherd's own uneasiness. He slapped the scaly back. "Don't talk, you," he said. "It hurts my ears. Nor think; that hurts your head. Come, run!"

Ease yourself, Morgarel scolded. *You have too much life in you, human-born.*

Mistherd made a face at the wraith, but obeyed to the extent of slowing down and picking his way through what cover the country afforded. For he traveled on behalf of the Fairest, to learn what had brought a pair of mortals questing hither.

Did they seek that boy whom Ayoch stole? (He continued to weep for his mother, though less and less often as the marvels of Carheddin entered him.) Perhaps. A birdcraft had left them and their car at the now-abandoned campsite, from which they had followed an outward spiral. But when no trace of the cub had appeared inside a reasonable distance, they did not call to be flown home. And this wasn't because weather forbade the far-speaker waves to travel, as was frequently the case. No, instead the couple set off toward the mountains of Moonhorn. Their course would take them past a few outlying invader steadings and on into realms untrodden by their race.

So this was no ordinary survey. Then what was it?

Mistherd understood now why she who reigned had made her adopted mortal children learn, or retain, the clumsy language of their forebears. He had hated that drill, wholly foreign to Dweller ways. Of course, you obeyed her, and in time you saw how wise she had been. . . .

Presently he left Nagrim behind a rock—the

nicor would only be useful in a fight—and crawled
from bush to bush until he lay within man-lengths
of the humans. A rainplant drooped over him,
leaves soft on his bare skin, and clothed him in
darkness. Morgarel floated to the crown of a
shiverleaf, whose unrest would better conceal his
flimsy shape. He'd not be much help either. And
that was the most troublous, the almost appalling
thing here. Wraiths were among those who could
not just sense and send thought, but cast illusions.
Morgarel had reported that this time his power
seemed to rebound off an invisible cold wall
around the car.

Otherwise the male and female had set up no
guardian engines and kept no dogs. Belike they
supposed none would be needed, since they slept
in the long vehicle which bore them. But such con-
tempt of the Queen's strength could not be tol-
erated, could it?

Metal sheened faintly by the light of their campfire. They sat on either side, wrapped in coats
against a coolness that Mistherd, naked, found
mild. The male drank smoke. The female stared
past him into a dusk which her flame-dazzled eyes
must see as thick gloom. The dancing glow
brought her vividly forth. Yes, to judge from
Ayoch's tale, she was the dam of the new cub.

Ayoch had wanted to come too, but the Wonderful One forbade. Pooks couldn't hold still long
enough for such a mission.

The man sucked on his pipe. His cheeks thus
pulled into shadow while the light flickered across
nose and brow, he looked disquietingly like a
shearbill about to stoop on prey.

"—No, I tell you again, Barbro, I have no theories," he was saying. "When facts are insufficient, theorizing is ridiculous at best, misleading at worst."

"Still, you must have some idea of what you're doing," she said. It was plain that they had threshed this out often before. No Dweller could be as persistent as she or as patient as he. "That gear you packed—that generator you keep running—"

"I have a working hypothesis or two, which suggested what equipment I ought to take."

"Why won't you tell me what the hypotheses are?"

"They themselves indicate that that might be inadvisable at the present time. I'm still feeling my way into the labyrinth. And I haven't had a chance yet to hook everything up. In fact, we're really only protected against so-called telepathic influence—"

"What?" She started. "Do you mean . . . those legends about how they can read minds too—" Her words trailed off and her gaze sought the darkness beyond his shoulders.

He leaned forward. His tone lost its clipped rapidity, grew earnest and soft. "Barbro, you're racking yourself to pieces. Which is no help to Jimmy if he's alive, the more so when you may well be badly needed later on. We've a long trek before us, and you'd better settle into it."

She nodded jerkily and caught her lip between her teeth for a moment before she answered, "I'm trying."

He smiled around his pipe. "I expect you'll succeed. You don't strike me as a quitter or a whiner or an enjoyer of misery."

She dropped a hand to the pistol at her belt. Her voice changed; it came out of her throat like knife from sheath. "When we find them, they'll know what I am. What humans are."

"Put anger aside also," the man urged. "We can't afford emotions. If the Outlings are real, as I told you I'm provisionally assuming, they're fighting for their homes." After a short stillness he added: "I like to think that if the first explorers had found live natives, men would not have colonized Roland. But it's too late now. We can't go back if we wanted to. It's a bitter-end struggle, against an enemy so crafty that he's even hidden from us the fact that he is waging war."

"Is he? I mean, skulking, kidnapping an occasional child—"

"That's part of my hypothesis. I suspect those aren't harassments; they're tactics employed in a chillingly subtle strategy."

The fire sputtered and sparked. The man smoked awhile, brooding, until he went on:

"I didn't want to raise your hopes or excite you unduly while you had to wait on me, first in Christmas Landing, then in Portolondon. Afterward we were busy satisfying ourselves that Jimmy had been taken farther from camp than he could have wandered before collapsing. So I'm only now telling you how thoroughly I studied available material on the . . . Old Folk. Besides, at first I did it on the principle of eliminating every imaginable possibility, however absurd. I expected no result other than final disproof. But I went through everything, relics, analyses, histories, journalistic accounts, monographs; I talked to outwayers who happened to be in town and to what scientists we have who've taken any interest in the matter. I'm a quick study. I flatter myself I became as expert as anyone—though God knows there's little to be expert on. Furthermore, I, a comparative stranger to Roland, maybe looked on the problem with fresh eyes. And a pattern emerged for me.

"If the aborigines had become extinct, why hadn't they left more remnants? Arctica isn't enormous, and it's fertile for Rolandic life. It ought to have supported a population whose artifacts ought to have accumulated over millennia. I've read that on Earth, literally tens of thousands of paleolithic hand axes were found, more by chance than archeology.

"Very well. Suppose the relics and fossils were deliberately removed, between the time the last survey party left and the first colonizing ships arrived. I did find some support for that idea in the diaries of the original explorers. They were too preoccupied with checking the habitability of the planet to make catalogues of primitive monuments. However, the remarks they wrote down indicate they saw much more than later arrivals did. Suppose what we have found is just what the removers overlooked or didn't get around to.

"That argues a sophisticated mentality, thinking in long-range terms, doesn't it? Which in turn argues that the Old Folk were not mere hunters or neolithic farmers."

"But nobody ever saw buildings or machines or any such thing," Barbro objected.

"No. Most likely the natives didn't go through our kind of metallurgic-industrial evolution. I can conceive of other paths to take. Their full-fledged civilization might have begun, rather than ended, in biological science and technology. It might have developed potentialities of the nervous system, which might be greater in their species than in man. We have those abilities to some degree ourselves, you realize. A dowser, for instance, actually senses variations in the local magnetic field caused by a water table. However, in us, these talents are maddeningly rare and tricky. So we took our business elsewhere. Who needs to be a telepath, say, when he has a visiphone? The Old Folk may have seen it the other way around. The artifacts of their civilization may have been, may still be unrecognizable to men."

"They could have identified themselves to the men, though," Barbro said. "Why didn't they?"

"I can imagine any number of reasons. As, they could have had a bad experience with interstellar visitors earlier in their history. Ours is scarcely the sole race that has spaceships. However, I told you I don't theorize in advance of the facts. Let's say no more than the Old Folk, if they exist, are alien to us."

"For a rigorous thinker, you're spinning a mighty thin thread."

"I've admitted this is entirely provisional." He squinted at her through a roil of campfire smoke.

"You came to me, Barbro, insisting in the teeth of officialdom that your boy had been stolen, but your own talk about cultist kidnappers was ridiculous. Why are you reluctant to admit the reality of nonhumans?"

"In spite of the fact that Jimmy's being alive probably depends on it," she sighed. "I don't know."

A shudder. "Maybe I don't dare admit it."

"I've said nothing thus far that hasn't been speculated about in print," he told her. "A disreputable speculation, true. In a hundred years, nobody has found valid evidence for the Outlings being more than a superstition. Still, a few people have declared it's at least possible that intelligent natives are at large in the wilderness."

"I know," she repeated. "I'm not sure, though, what has made you, overnight, take those arguments seriously."

"Well, once you got me started thinking, it occurred to me that Roland's outwayers are not utterly isolated medieval crofters. They have books, telecommunications, power tools, motor vehicles; above all, they have a modern science-oriented education. Why *should* they turn superstitious? Something must be causing it." He stopped. "I'd better not continue. My ideas go further than this; but if they're correct, it's dangerous to speak them aloud."

Mistherd's belly muscles tensed. There was danger for fair, in that shearbill head. The Garland Bearer must be warned. For a minute he wondered about summoning Nagrim to kill these two. If the nicor jumped them fast, their firearms might avail them naught. But no. They might have left word at home, or— He came back to his ears. The talk had changed course. Barbro was murmuring, "—why you stayed on Roland."

The man smiled his gaunt smile. "Well, life on Beowulf held no challenge for me. Heorot is—or was; this was decades past, remember—Heorot was densely populated, smoothly organized, boringly uniform. That was partly due to the lowland frontier, a safety valve that bled off the dissatisfied. But I lack the carbon dioxide tolerance necessary to live healthily down there. An expedition was being readied to make a swing around a number of colony worlds, especially those which didn't have the equipment to keep in laser contact. You'll recall its announced purpose, to seek out new ideas in science, arts, sociology, philosophy, whatever might prove valuable. I'm afraid they found little on Roland relevant to Beowulf. But I, who had wangled a berth, I saw opportunities for myself and decided to make my home here."

"Were you a detective back there, too?"

"Yes, in the official police. We had a tradition of such work in our family. Some of that may have come from the Cherokee side of it, if the same means anything to you. However, we also claimed collateral descent from one of the first private inquiry agents on record, back on Earth before spaceflight. Regardless of how true that may be, I found him a useful model. You see, an archetype—"

The man broke off. Unease crossed his features.

"Best we go to sleep," he said. "We've a long distance to cover in the morning."

She looked outward. "Here is no morning."

They retired. Mistherd rose and cautiously flexed limberness back into his muscles. Before returning to the Sister of Lyrth, he risked a glance through a pane in the car. Bunks were made up, side by side, and the humans lay in them. Yet the man had not touched her, though hers was a bonny body, and nothing that had passed between them suggested he meant to do so.

Eldritch, humans. Cold and claylike. And they would overrun the beautiful wild world? Mistherd spat in disgust. It must not happen. It would not happen. She who reigned had vowed that.

The lands of William Irons were immense. But this was because a barony was required to support him, his kin and cattle, on native crops whose cultivation was still poorly understood. He raised some Terrestrial plants as well, by summerlight and in conservatories. However, these were a luxury. The true conquest of northern Arctica lay in yerba hay, in bathyrhiza wood, in pericoup and glycophyllon, and eventually, when the market had expanded with population and industry, in chalcanthemum for city florists and pelts of cage-bred rover for city furriers.

That was in a tomorrow Irons did not expect that he would live to see. Sherrinford wondered if the man really expected anyone ever would.

The room was warm and bright. Cheerfulness crackled in the fireplace. Light from fluoropanels

gleamed off hand-carven chests and chairs and
tables, off colorful draperies and shelved dishes.
The outwayer sat solid in his high seat, stoutly
clad, beard flowing down his chest. His wife and
daughters brought coffee, whose fragrance joined
the remnant odors of a hearty supper, to him, his
guests, and his sons.

But outside, wind hooted, lightning flared,
thunder bawled, rain crashed on roof and walls
and roared down to swirl among the courtyard
cobble_tones. Sheds and barns crouched against
hugeness beyond. Trees groaned, and did a wicked
undertone of laughter run beneath the lowing of a
frightened cow? A burst of hailstones hit the tiles
like knocking knuckles.

You could feel how distant your neighbors
were, Sherrinford thought. And nonetheless they
were the people whom you saw oftenest, did daily
business with by visiphone (when a solar storm
didn't make gibberish of their voices and chaos of
their faces) or in the flesh, partied with, gossiped
and intrigued with, intermarried with; in the end,
they were the people who would bury you. The
lights of the coastal towns were monstrously farther away.

William Irons was a strong man. Yet when now
he spoke, fear was in his tone. "You'd truly go
over Troll Scarp?"

"Do you mean Hanstein Palisades?" Sherrinford responded, more challenge than question.

"No outwayer calls it anything but Troll Scarp,"
Barbro said.

And how had a name like that been reborn, light-
years and centuries from Earth's Dark Ages?

"Hunters, trappers, prospectors—rangers, you call them—travel in those mountains," Sherrinford declared.

"In certain parts," Irons said. "That's allowed, by a pact once made 'tween a man and the Queen after he'd done well by a jack-o'-the-hill that a satan had hurt. Wherever the plumablanca grows, men may fare, if they leave man-goods on the altar boulders in payment for what they take out of the land. Elsewhere—" one fist clenched on a chair arm and went slack again—"'s not wise to go."

"It's been done, hasn't it?"

"Oh, yes. And some came back all right, or so they claimed, though I've heard they were never lucky afterward. And some didn't; they vanished. And some who returned babbled of wonders and horrors, and stayed witlings the rest of their lives. Not for a long time has anybody been rash enough to break the pact and overtread the bounds." Irons looked at Barbro almost entreatingly. His woman and children stared likewise, grown still. Wind hooted beyond the walls and rattled the storm shutters. "Don't you."

"I've reason to believe my son is there," she answered.

"Yes, yes, you've told and I'm sorry. Maybe something can be done. I don't know what, but I'd be glad to, oh, lay a double offering on Unvar's Barrow this midwinter, and a prayer drawn in the turf by a flint knife. Maybe they'll return him." Irons sighed. "They've not done such a thing in man's memory, though. And he could have a worse lot. I've glimpsed them myself, speeding madcap through twilight. They seem happier than we are.

Might be no kindness, sending your boy home again."

"Like in the Arvid song," said his wife.

Irons nodded. "M-hm. Or others, come to think of it."

"What's this?" Sherrinford asked. More sharply than before, he felt himself a stranger. He was a child of cities and technics, above all a child of the skeptical intelligence. This family *believed*. It was disquieting to see more than a touch of their acceptance in Barbro's slow nod.

"We have the same ballad in Olga Ivanoff Land," she told him, her voice less calm than the words. "It's one of the traditional ones—nobody knows who composed them—that are sung to set the measure of a ring-dance in a meadow."

"I noticed a multilyre in your baggage, Mrs. Cullen," said the wife of Irons. She was obviously eager to get off the explosive topic of a venture in defiance of the Old Folk. A songfest could help. "Would you like to entertain us?"

Barbro shook her head, white around the nostrils. The oldest boy said quickly, rather importantly, "Well, sure, I can, if our guests would like to hear."

"I'd enjoy that, thank you." Sherrinford leaned back in his seat and stoked his pipe. If this had not happened spontaneously, he would have guided the conversation toward a similar outcome.

In the past he had had no incentive to study the folklore of the outway, and not much chance to read the scanty references on it since Barbro brought him her trouble. Yet more and more he was becoming convinced that he must get an understanding—not an anthropological study, but a feel from the inside out—of the relationship between Roland's frontiersmen and those beings which haunted them.

A bustling followed, rearrangement, settling down to listen, coffee cups refilled and brandy offered on the side. The boy explained, "The last line is the chorus. Everybody join in, right?" Clearly he too hoped thus to bleed off some of the tension. Catharsis through music? Sherrinford wondered, and added to himself: No; exorcism.

A girl strummed a guitar. The boy sang, to a melody which beat across the storm noise:

> "It was the ranger Arvid
> rode homeward through the hills
> among the shadowy shiverleafs,
> along the chiming rills.
>   *The dance weaves under the firethorn.*

> "The night wind whispered around him
> with scent of brok and rue.
> Both moons rose high above him
> and hills aflash with dew.
>   *The dance weaves under the firethorn.*

> "And dreaming of that woman
> who waited in the sun,
> he stopped, amazed by starlight,
> and so he was undone.
>   *The dance weaves under the firethorn.*

"For there beneath a barrow
that bulked athwart a moon,
the Outling folk were dancing
in glass and golden shoon.
 The dance weaves under the firethorn.

"The Outling folk were dancing
like water, wind, and fire
to frosty-ringing harpstrings,
and never did they tire.
 The dance weaves under the firethorn.

"To Arvid came she striding
from whence she watched the dance,
the Queen of Air and Darkness,
with starlight in her glance.
 The dance weaves under the firethorn.

"With starlight, love, and terror
in her immortal eye,
the Queen of Air and Darkness—"

"No!" Barbro leaped from her chair. Her fists
were clenched and tears flogged her cheekbones.
"You can't—pretend that—about the things that
stole Jimmy!"

She fled from the chamber, upstairs to her guest
bedroom.

But she finished the song herself. That was
about seventy hours later, camped in the steeps
where rangers dared not fare.

She and Sherrinford had not said much to the
Irons family, after refusing repeated pleas to leave

the forbidden country alone. Nor had they exchanged many remarks at first as they drove north. Slowly, however, he began to draw her out about her own life. After a while she almost forgot to mourn, in her remembering of home and old neighbors. Somehow this led to discoveries—that he, beneath his professorial manner, was a gourmet and a lover of opera and appreciated her femaleness; that she could still laugh and find beauty in the wild land around her—and she realized, half guiltily, that life held more hopes than even the recovery of the son Tim gave her.

"I've convinced myself he's alive," the detective said. He scowled. "Frankly, it makes me regret having taken you along, I expected this would be only a fact-gathering trip, but it's turning out to be more. If we're dealing with real creatures who stole him, they can do real harm. I ought to turn back to the nearest garth and call for a plane to fetch you."

"Like bottommost hell you will, mister," she said. "You need somebody who knows outway conditions, and I'm a better shot than average."

"M-m-m . . . it would involve considerable delay too, wouldn't it? Besides the added distance, I can't put a signal through to any airport before this current burst of solar interference has calmed down."

Next "night" he broke out his remaining equipment and set it up. She recognized some of it, such as the thermal detector. Other items were strange to her, copied to his order from the advanced apparatus of his birthworld. He would tell her little about them. "I've explained my suspicion that the ones we're after have telepathic capabilities," he said in apology.

Her eyes widened. "You mean it could be true, the Queen and her people can read minds?"

"That's part of the dread which surrounds their legend, isn't it? Actually there's nothing spooky about the phenomenon. It was studied and fairly well defined centuries ago, on Earth. I dare say the facts are available in the scientific microfiles at Christmas Landing. You Rolanders have simply had no occasion to seek them out, any more than you've yet had occasion to look up how to build power-beamcasters or spacecraft."

"Well, how does telepathy work, then?"

Sherrinford recognized that her query asked for comfort as much as it did for facts, and he spoke with deliberate dryness: "The organism generates extremely long-wave radiation which can, in principle, be modulated by the nervous system. In practice, the feebleness of the signals and their low rate of information transmission make them elusive, hard to detect and measure. Our pre-human ancestors went in for more reliable senses, like vision and hearing. What telepathic trans-ceiving we do is marginal at best. But explorers have found extraterrestrial species that got an evolutionary advantage from developing the system further, in their particular environments. I imagine such species could include one which gets comparatively little direct sunlight—in fact, ap-pears to hide from broad day. It could even become so able in this regard that, at short range, it can pick up man's weak emissions and make man's primitive sensitivities resonate to its own strong sendings."

"That would account for a lot, wouldn't it?" Barbro said faintly.

"I've now screened our car by a jamming field," Sherrinford told her, "but it reaches only a few meters past the chassis. Beyond, a scout of theirs might get a warning from your thoughts, if you knew precisely what I'm trying to do. I have a well-trained subconscious which sees to it that I think about this in French when I'm outside. Communication has to be structured to be intelligible, you see, and that's a different enough structure from English. But English is the only human language on Roland, and surely the Old Folk have learned it."

She nodded. He had told her his general plan, which was too obvious to conceal. The problem was to make contact with the aliens, if they existed. Hitherto, they had only revealed themselves, at rare intervals, to one or a few backwoodsmen at a time. An ability to generate hallucinations would help them in that. They would stay clear of any large, perhaps unmanageable expedition which might pass through their territory. But two people, braving all prohibitions, shouldn't look too formidable to approach. And . . . this would be the first human team which not only worked on the assumption that the Outlings were real, but possessed the resources of modern, off-planet police technology.

Nothing happened at that camp. Sherrinford

said he hadn't expected it would. The Old Folk seemed cautious this near to any settlement. In their own lands they must be bolder.

And by the following "night," the vehicle had gone well into yonder country. When Sherrinford stopped the engine in a meadow and the car settled down, silence rolled in like a wave.

They stepped out. She cooked a meal on the glower while he gathered wood, that they might later cheer themselves with a campfire. Frequently he glanced at his wrist. It bore no watch—instead, a radio-controlled dial, to tell what the instruments in the bus might register.

Who needed a watch here? Slow constellations wheeled beyond glimmering aurora. The moon Alde stood above a snowpeak, turning it argent, though this place lay at a goodly height. The rest of the mountains were hidden by the forest that crowded around. Its trees were mostly shiverleaf and feathery white plumablanca, ghostly amidst their shadows. A few firethorns glowed, clustered dim lanterns, and the underbrush was heavy and smelled sweet. You could see surprisingly far through the blue dusk. Somewhere nearby, a brook sang and a bird fluted.

"Lovely here," Sherrinford said. They had risen from their supper and not yet sat down again or kindled their fire.

"But strange," Barbro answered as low. "I wonder if it's really meant for us. If we can really hope to possess it."

His pipestem gestured at the stars. "Man's gone to stranger places than this."

"Has he? I . . . oh, I suppose it's just something left over from my outway childhood, but do you know, when I'm under them I can't think of the stars as balls of gas, whose energies have been measured, whose planets have been walked on by prosaic feet. No, they're small and cold and magical; our lives are bound to them; after we die, they whisper to us in our graves." Barbro glanced downward. "I realize that's nonsense."

She could see in the twilight how his face grew tight. "Not at all," he said. "Emotionally, physics may be a worse nonsense. And in the end, you know, after a sufficient number of generations, thought follows feeling. Man is not at heart rational. He could stop believing the stories of science if those no longer felt right."

He paused. "That ballad which didn't get finished in the house," he said, not looking at her. "Why did it affect you so?"

"I couldn't stand hearing *them*, well, praised. Or that's how it seemed. Sorry for the fuss."

"I gather the ballad is typical of a large class."

"Well, I never thought to add them up. Cultural anthropology is something we don't have time for on Roland, or more likely it hasn't occurred to us, with everything else there is to do. But—now you mention it, yes, I'm surprised at how many songs and stories have the Arvid motif in them."

"Could you bear to recite it?"

She mustered the will to laugh. "Why, I can do better than that if you want. Let me get my multi-lyre and I'll perform."

She omitted the hypnotic chorus line, though,

when the notes rang out, except at the end. He watched her where she stood against moon and aurora.

"—the Queen of Air and Darkness
cried softly under sky:

"'Light down, you ranger Arvid,
and join the Outling folk.
You need no more be human,
which is a heavy yoke.'

"He dared to give her answer:
'I may do naught but run.
A maiden waits me, dreaming
in lands beneath the sun.

"'And likewise wait me comrades
and tasks I would not shirk,
for what is ranger Arvid
if he lays down his work?

"'So wreak your spells, you Outling,
and cast your wrath on me.
Though maybe you can slay me,
you'll not make me unfree.'

"The Queen of Air and Darkness
stood wrapped about with fear
and northlight-flares and beauty
he dared not look too near.

"Until she laughed like harpsong
and said to him in scorn:

'I do not need a magic
to make you always mourn.

"'I send you home with nothing
except your memory
of moonlight, Outling music,
night breezes, dew, and me.

"'And that will run behind you,
a shadow on the sun,
and that will lie beside you
when every day is done.

"'In work and play and friendship
your grief will strike you dumb
for thinking what you are—and—
what you might have become.

"'Your dull and foolish woman
treat kindly as you can.
Go home now, ranger Arvid,
set free to be a man!"

"In flickering and laughter
the Outling folk were gone.
He stood alone by moonlight
and wept until the dawn.
    The dance weaves under the firethorn."

She laid the lyre aside. A wind rustled leaves.
After a long quietness Sherrinford said, "And tales
of this kind are part of everyone's life in the outway?"

"Well, you could put it thus," Barbro replied.

"Though they're not all full of supernatural doings. Some are about love or heroism. Traditional themes."

"I don't think your particular tradition has arisen of itself." His tone was bleak. "In fact, I think many of your songs and stories were not composed by human beings."

He snapped his lips shut and would say no more on the subject. They went early to bed.

Hours later, an alarm roused them.

The buzzing was soft, but it brought them instantly alert. They slept in gripsuits, to be prepared for emergencies. Skyglow lit them through the canopy. Sherrinford swung out of his bunk, slipped shoes on feet, and clipped gun holster to belt. "Stay inside," he commanded.

"What's here?" Her pulse thuttered.

He squinted at the dials of his instruments and checked them against the luminous telltale on his wrist. "Three animals," he counted. "Not wild ones happening by. A large one, homeothermic, to judge from the infrared, holding still a short ways off. Another . . . hm, low temperature, diffuse and unstable emission, as if it were more like a . . . a swarm of cells coordinated somehow . . . pheromonally? . . . hovering, also at a distance. But the third's practically next to us, moving around in the brush; and that pattern looks human."

She saw him quiver with eagerness, no longer seeming a professor. "I'm going to try to make a capture," he said. "When we have a subject for interrogation—Stand ready to let me back in again fast. But don't risk yourself, whatever happens. And keep this cocked." He handed her a loaded big game rifle.

His tall frame poised by the door, opened it a crack. Air blew in, cool, damp, full of fragrances and murmurings. The moon Oliver was now also aloft, the radiance of both unreally brilliant, and the aurora seethed in whiteness and ice-blue.

Sherrinford peered afresh at his telltale. It must indicate the directions of the watchers, among those dappled leaves. Abruptly he sprang out. He sprinted past the ashes of the campfire and vanished under trees. Barbro's hand strained on the butt of her weapon.

Racket exploded. Two in combat burst onto the meadow. Sherrinford had clapped a grip on a smaller human figure. She could make out by streaming silver and rainbow flicker that the other was nude, male, long haired, lithe, and young. He fought demoniacally, seeking to use teeth and feet and raking nails, and meanwhile he ululated like a satan.

The identification shot through her: A changeling, stolen in babyhood and raised by the Old Folk. This creature was what they would make Jimmy into.

"Ha!" Sherrinford forced his opponent around and drove stiffened fingers into the solar plexus. The boy gasped and sagged. Sherrinford man-handled him toward the car.

Out from the woods came a giant. It might itself have been a tree, black and rugose, bearing four great gnarly boughs; but earth quivered and

boomed beneath its leg-roots, and its hoarse
bellowing filled sky and skulls.

Barbro shrieked. Sherrinford whirled. He
yanked out his pistol, fired and fired, flat whip-
cracks through the half-light. His free arm kept a
lock on the youth. The troll shape lurched under
those blows. It recovered and came on, more
slowly, more carefully, circling around to cut him
off from the bus. He couldn't move fast enough to
evade it unless he released his prisoner—who was
his sole possible guide to Jimmy—

Barbro leaped forth. "Don't!" Sherrinford
shouted. "For God's sake, stay inside!" The
monster rumbled and made snatching motions at
her. She pulled the trigger. Recoil slammed her in
the shoulder. The colossus rocked and fell. Somehow it got its feet back and lumbered toward her.
She retreated. Again she shot, and again. The creature snarled. Blood began to drip from it and
gleam oilily amidst dewdrops. It turned and went
off, breaking branches, into the darkness that
laired beneath the woods.

"Get to shelter!" Sherrinford yelled. "You're
out of the jammer field!"

A mistiness drifted by overhead. She barely
glimpsed it before she saw the new shape at the
meadow edge. "Jimmy!" tore from her.

"Mother." He held out his arms. Moonlight
coursed in his tears. She dropped her weapon and
ran to him.

Sherrinford plunged in pursuit. Jimmy flitted
away into the brush. Barbro crashed after,
through clawing twigs. Then she was seized and
borne away.

Standing over his captive, Sherrinford strengthened the fluoro output until vision of the wilderness was blocked off from within the bus. The boy squirmed beneath that colorless glare.

"You are going to talk," the man said. Despite the haggardness in his features, he spoke quietly.

The boy glared through tangled locks. A bruise was purpling on his jaw. He'd almost recovered ability to flee while Sherrinford chased and lost the woman. Returning, the detective had barely caught him. Time was lacking to be gentle, when Outling reinforcements might arrive at any moment, Sherrinford had knocked him out and dragged him inside. He sat lashed into a swivel seat.

He spat. "Talk to you, manclod?" But sweat stood on his skin, and his eyes flickered unceasingly around the metal which caged him.

"Give me a name to call you by."

"And have you work a spell on me?"

"Mine's Eric. If you don't give me another choice, I'll have to call you . . . m-m-m . . . Wuddikins."

"What?" However eldritch, the bound one remained a human adolescent. "Mistherd, then." The lilting accent of his English somehow emphasized its sullenness. "That's not the sound, only what it means. Anyway, it's my spoken name, naught else."

"Ah, you keep a secret name you consider to be real?"

"She does. I don't know myself what it is. She knows the real names of everybody."

Sherrinford raised his brows. "She?"

"Who reigns. May she forgive me, I can't make the reverent sign when my arms are tied. Some invaders call her the Queen of Air and Darkness."

"So." Sherrinford got pipe and tobacco. He let silence wax while he started the fire. At length he said:

"I'll confess the Old Folk took me by surprise. I didn't expect so formidable a member of your gang. Everything I could learn had seemed to show they work on my race—and yours, lad—by stealth, trickery, and illusion."

Mistherd jerked a truculent nod. "She created the first nicors not long ago. Don't think she has naught but dazzlements at her beck."

"I don't. However, a steel-jacketed bullet works pretty well too, doesn't it?"

Sherrinford talked on, softly, mostly to himself: "I do still believe the, ah, nicors—all your half-humanlike breeds—are intended in the main to be seen, not used. The power of projecting mirages must surely be quite limited in range and scope as well as the number of individuals who possess it. Otherwise she wouldn't have needed to work as slowly and craftily as she has. Even outside our mindshield, Barbro—my companion—could have resisted, could have remained aware that whatever she saw was unreal . . . if she'd been less shaken, less frantic, less driven by need."

Sherrinford wreathed his head in smoke. "Never mind what I experienced," he said. "It couldn't have been the same as for her. I think the command was simply given us. 'You will see what you most desire in the world, running away from you into the forest.' Of course, she didn't travel many meters before the nicor waylaid her. I'd no hope of trailing them; I'm no Arctican woodsman, and besides, it'd have been too easy to ambush me. I came back to you." Grimly: "You're my link to your overlady."

"You think I'll guide you to Starhaven or Carheddin? Try making me, clod-man."

"I want to bargain."

"I s'pect you intend more'n that." Mistherd's answer held surprising shrewdness. "What'll you tell after you come home?"

"Yes, that does pose a problem, doesn't it? Barbro Cullen and I are not terrified outwayers. We're of the city. We brought recording instruments. We'd be the first of our kind to report an encounter with the Old Folk, and that report would be detailed and plausible. It would produce action."

"So you see I'm not afraid to die," Mistherd declared, though his lips trembled a bit. "If I let you come in and do your manthings to my people, I'd have naught left worth living for."

"Have no immediate fears," Sherrinford said. 'You're merely bait." He sat down and regarded the boy through a visor of calm. (Within, it wept in him: *Barbro, Barbro!*) "Consider. Your Queen can't very well let me go back, bringing my prisoner and telling about hers. She has to stop that somehow. I could try fighting my way through—this car is better armed than you know—but that wouldn't free anybody. Instead, I'm staying put. New forces of hers will get here as fast as they can. I assume they won't blindly throw themselves against a machine gun, a howitzer, a fulgurator. They'll parley first, whether their intentions are honest or not. Thus I make the contact I'm after."

"What d' you plan?" The mumble held anguish.

"First, this, as a sort of invitation." Sherrinford reached out to flick a switch. "There. I've lowered my shield against mind-reading and shape-casting. I daresay the leaders, at least, will be able to sense that it's gone. That should give them confidence."

"And next?"

"Next we wait. Would you like something to eat or drink?"

During the time which followed, Sherrinford tried to jolly Mistherd along, find out something of his life. What answers he got were curt. He dimmed the interior lights and settled down to peer outward. That was a long few hours.

They ended at a shout of gladness, half a sob, from the boy. Out of the woods came a band of the Old Folk.

Some of them stood forth more clearly than moons and stars and northlights should have caused. He in the van rode a white crownbuck whose horns were garlanded. His form was manlike but unearthly beautiful, silver blond hair falling from beneath the antlered helmet, around the proud cold face. The cloak fluttered off his back like living wings. His frost-colored mail rang as he fared.

Behind him, to right and left, rode two who bore swords whereon small flames gleamed and flick-

ered. Above, a flying flock laughed and trilled and
tumbled in the breezes. Near them drifted a half-
transparent mistiness. Those others who passed
among trees after their chieftain were harder to
make out. But they moved in quicksilver grace and
as it were to a sound of harps and trumpets.

"Lord Luighaid." Glory overflowed in Mistherd's tone. "Her master Knower—himself."

Sherrinford had never done a harder thing than
to sit at the main control panel, finger near the
button of the shield generator, and not touch it.
He rolled down a section of canopy to let voices
travel. A gust of wind struck him in the face, bearing odors of the roses in his mother's garden. At
his back, in the main body of the vehicle, Mistherd
strained against his bonds till he could see the on-
coming troop.

"Call to them," Sherrinford said. "Ask if they
will talk with me."

Unknown, flutingly sweet words flew back and
forth. "Yes," the boy interpreted. "He will, the
Lord Luighaid. But I can tell you, you'll never be
let go. Don't fight them. Yield. Come away. You
don't know what 'tis to be alive till you've dwelt in
Carheddin under the mountain."

The Outlings drew nigh.

Jimmy glimmered and was gone. Barbro lay in
strong arms, against a broad breast, and felt the
horse move beneath her. It had to be a horse,
though only a few were kept any longer on the
steadings, and they only for special uses or love.
She could feel the rippling beneath its hide, hear a

rush of parted leafage and the thud when a hoof struck stone; warmth and living scent welled up around her through the darkness.

He who carried her said mildly, "Don't be afraid, darling. It was a vision. But he's waiting for us, and we're bound for him."

She was aware in a vague way that she ought to feel terror or despair or something. But her memories lay behind her—she wasn't sure just how she had come to be here—she was borne along in a knowledge of being loved. At peace, at peace, rest in the calm expectation of joy . . .

After a while the forest opened. They crossed a lea where boulders stood gray-white under the moons, their shadows shifting in the dim hues which the aurora threw across them. Flitteries danced, tiny comets, above the flowers between. Ahead gleamed a peak whose top was crowned in clouds.

Barbro's eyes happened to be turned forward. She saw the horse's head and thought, with quiet surprise: Why, this is Sambo, who was mine when I was a girl. She looked upward at the man. He wore a black tunic and a cowled cape, which made his face hard to see. She could not cry aloud, here. "Tim," she whispered.

"Yes, Barbro."

"I buried you—"

His smile was endlessly tender. "Did you think we're no more than what's laid back into the ground? Poor torn sweetheart. She who's called us is the All Healer. Now rest and dream."

"Dream," she said, and for a space she struggled

to rouse herself. But the effort was weak. Why should she believe ashen tales about . . . atoms and energies, nothing else to fill a gape of emptiness . . . tales she could not bring to mind . . . when Tim and the horse her father gave her carried her on to Jimmy? Had the other thing not been the evil dream, and this her first drowsy awakening from it?

As if he heard her thoughts, he murmured, "They have a song in Outling lands. The Song of the Men:

"The world sails
to an unseen wind.
Light swirls by the bows.
The wake is night.

But the Dwellers have no such sadness."

"I don't understand," she said.

He nodded. "There's much you'll have to understand, darling, and I can't see you again until you've learned those truths. But meanwhile you'll be with our son."

She tried to lift her head and kiss him. He held her down. "Not yet," he said. "You've not been received among the Queen's people. I shouldn't have come for you, except that she was too merciful to forbid. Lie back, lie back."

Time blew past. The horse galloped tireless, never stumbling, up the mountain. Once she glimpsed a troop riding down it and thought they were bound for a last weird battle in the west against . . . who? . . . one who lay cased in iron and

sorrow—Later she would ask herself the name of
him who had brought her into the land of the Old
Truth.

Finally spires lifted splendid among the stars,
which are small and magical and whose whisper-
ings comfort us after we are dead. They rode into a
courtyard where candles burned unwavering,
fountains splashed and birds sang. The air bore
fragrance of brok and pericoup, of rue and roses,
for not everything that man brought was horrible.
The Dwellers waited in beauty to welcome her.
Beyond their stateliness, pooks cavorted through
the gloaming; among the trees darted children;
merriment caroled across music more solemn.

"We have come—" Tim's voice was suddenly,
inexplicably, a croak. Barbro was not sure how he
dismounted, bearing her. She stood before him
and saw him sway on his feet.

Fear caught her. "Are you well?" She seized
both his hands. They felt cold and rough. Where
had Sambo gone? Her eyes searched beneath the
cowl. In this brighter illumination, she ought to
have seen her man's face clearly. But it was
blurred, it kept changing. "What's wrong, oh,
what's happened?"

He smiled. Was that the smile she had
cherished? She couldn't completely remember. "I,
I must go," he stammered, so low she could
scarcely hear. "Our time is not ready." He drew
free of her grasp and leaned on a robed form
which had appeared at his side. A haziness swirled
over both their heads. "Don't watch me go . . .
back into the earth," he pleaded. "That's death for

you. Till our time returns—There, our son!"

She had to fling her gaze around. Kneeling, she spread wide her arms. Jimmy struck her like a warm, solid cannonball. She rumpled his hair; she kissed the hollow of his neck; she laughed and wept and babbled foolishness; and this was no ghost, no memory that had stolen off when she wasn't looking. Now and again, as she turned her attention to yet another hurt which might have come upon him—hunger, sickness, fear—and found none, she would glimpse their surroundings. The gardens were gone. It didn't matter.

"I missed you so, Mother. Stay?"

"I'll take you home, dearest."

"Stay. Here's fun. I'll show. But you stay."

A sighing went through the twilight. Barbro rose. Jimmy clung to her hand. They confronted the Queen.

Very tall she was in her robes woven of north-lights, and her starry crown and her garlands of kiss-me-never. Her countenance recalled Aphrodite of Milos, whose picture Barbro had often seen in the realms of men, save that the Queen's was more fair and more majesty dwelt upon it and in the night-blue eyes. Around her the gardens woke to new reality, the court of the Dwellers and the heaven-climbing spires.

"Be welcome," she spoke, her speaking a song, "forever."

Against the awe of her, Barbro said, "Moon-mother, let us go home."

"That may not be."

"To our world, little and beloved," Barbro

dreamed she begged, "which we build for our-selves and cherish for our children."

"To prison days, angry nights, works that crumble in the fingers, loves that turn to rot or stone or driftweed, loss, grief, and the only sure-ness that of the final nothingness. No. You too, Wanderfoot who is to be, will jubilate when the banners of the Outworld come flying into the last of the cities and man is made wholly alive. Now go with those who will teach you."

The Queen of Air and Darkness lifted an arm in summons. It halted, and none came to answer.

For over the fountains and melodies lifted a gruesome growling. Fires leaped, thunders crashed. Her hosts scattered screaming before the steel thing which boomed up the mountainside. The pooks were gone in a whirl of frightened wings. The nicors flung their bodies against the unalive invader and were consumed, until their Mother cried to them to retreat.

Barbro cast Jimmy down and herself over him. Towers wavered and smoked away. The mountain stood bare under icy moons, save for rocks, crags, and farther off a glacier in whose depths the auroral light pulsed blue. A cave mouth darkened a cliff. Thither folk streamed, seeking refuge underground. Some were human of blood, some grotesques like the pooks and nicors and wraiths; but most were lean, scaly, long-tailed, long-beaked, not remotely men or Outlings.

For an instant, even as Jimmy wailed at her breast—perhaps as much because the enchant-ment had been wrecked as because he was afraid

—Barbro pitied the Queen who stood alone
in her nakedness. Then that one also had fled, and
Barbro's world shivered apart.

The guns fell silent; the vehicle whirred to a
halt. From it sprang a boy who called wildly,
"Shadow-of-a-Dream, where are you? It's me,
Mistherd, oh, come, come!"—before he remembered that the language they had been raised in
was not man's. He shouted in that until a girl crept
out of a thicket where she had hidden. They stared
at each other through dust, smoke, and moonglow.
She ran to him.

A new voice barked from the car, "Barbro,
hurry!"

Christmas Landing knew day; short at this time
of year, but sunlight, blue skies, white clouds,
glittering water, salt breezes in busy streets, and
the sane disorder of Eric Sherrinford's living
room.

He crossed and uncrossed his legs where he sat,
puffed on his pipe as if to make a veil, and said,
"Are you certain you're recovered? You mustn't
risk overstrain."

"I'm fine," Barbro Cullen replied, though her
tone was flat. "Still tired, yes, and showing it, no
doubt. One doesn't go through such an experience
and bounce back in a week. But I'm up and about.
And to be frank, I must know what's happened,
what's going on, before I can settle down to regain
my full strength. Not a word of news anywhere."

"Have you spoken to others about the matter?"

"No. I've simply told visitors I was too

exhausted to talk. Not much of a lie. I assumed there's a reason for censorship."

Sherrinford looked relieved. "Good girl. It's at my urging. You can imagine the sensation when this is made public. The authorities agreed they need time to study the facts, think and debate in a calm atmosphere, have a decent policy ready to offer voters who're bound to become rather hysterical at first." His mouth quirked slightly upward. "Furthermore, your nerves and Jimmy's get their chance to heal before the journalistic storm breaks over you. How is he?"

"Quite well. He continues pestering me for leave to go play with his friends in the Wonderful Place. But at his age, he'll recover—he'll forget."

"He may meet them later anyhow."

"What? We didn't—" Barbro shifted in her chair. "I've forgotten too. I hardly recall a thing from our last hours. Did you bring back any kidnapped humans?"

"No. The shock was savage as it was, without throwing them straight into an . . . an institution. Mistherd, who's basically a sensible young fellow, assured me they'd get along, at any rate as regards survival necessities, till arrangements can be made." Sherrinford hesitated. "I'm not sure what the arrangements will be. Nobody is, at our present stage. But obviously they include those people—or many of them, especially those who aren't fullgrown—rejoining the human race. Though they may never feel at home in civilization. Perhaps in a way that's best, since we will need some kind of mutually acceptable liaison with the Dwellers."

His impersonality soothed them both. Barbro became able to say, "Was I too big a fool? I do remember how I yowled and beat my head on the floor."

"Why, no." He considered the big woman and her pride for a few seconds before he rose, walked over and laid a hand on her shoulder. "You'd been lured and trapped by a skillful play on your deepest instincts, at a moment of sheer nightmare. Afterward, as that wounded monster carried you off, evidently another type of being came along, one that could saturate you with close-range neuropsychic forces. On top of this, my arrival, the sudden brutal abolishment of every hallucination, must have been shattering. No wonder if you cried out in pain. Before you did, you competently got Jimmy and yourself into the bus, and you never interfered with me."

"What did you do?"

"Why, I drove off as fast as possible. After several hours, the atmospherics let up sufficiently for me to call Portolondon and insist on an emergency airlift. Not that that was vital. What chance had the enemy to stop us? They didn't even try—But quick transportation was certainly helpful."

"I figured that's what must have gone on." Barbro caught his glance. "No, what I meant was, how did you find us in the backlands?"

Sherrinford moved a little off from her. "My prisoner was my guide. I don't think I actually killed any of the Dwellers who'd come to deal with me. I hope not. The car simply broke through them, after a couple of warning shots, and after-

ward outpaced them. Steel and fuel against flesh
wasn't really fair. At the cave entrance, I did have
to shoot down a few of those troll creatures. I'm
not proud of it."

He stood silent. Presently: "But you were a captive," he said. "I couldn't be sure what they might
do to you, who had first claim on me." After
another pause: "I don't look for any more
violence."

"How did you make . . . the boy . . . co-operate?"

Sherrinford paced from her to the window,
where he stood staring out at the Boreal Ocean. "I
turned off the mindshield," he said. "I let their
band get close, in full splendor of illusion. Then I
turned the shield back on, and we both saw them
in their true shapes. As we went northward, I explained to Mistherd how he and his kind had been
hoodwinked, used, made to live in a world that
was never really there. I asked him if he wanted
himself and whomever he cared about to go on till
they died as domestic animals—yes, running in
limited freedom on solid hills, but always called
back to the dream-kennel." His pipe fumed
furiously. "May I never see such bitterness again.
He had been taught to believe he was free."

Quiet returned, above the hectic traffic. Charlemagne drew nearer to setting; already the east
darkened.

Finally Barbro asked, "Do you know why?"

"Why children were taken and raised like that?
Partly because it was in the pattern the Dwellers
were creating; partly in order to study and experi-
ment on members of our species—minds, that is,

not bodies; partly because humans have special strengths which are helpful, like being able to endure full daylight."

"But what was the final purpose of it all?"

Sherrinford paced the floor. "Well," he said, "of course the ultimate motives of the aborigines are obscure. We can't do more than guess at how they think, let alone how they feel. But our ideas do seem to fit the data.

"Why did they hide from man? I suspect they, or rather their ancestors—for they aren't glittering elves, you know; they're mortal and fallible too—I suspect the natives were only being cautious at first, more cautious than human primitives, though certain of those on Earth were also slow to reveal themselves to strangers. Spying, mentally eavesdropping, Roland's Dwellers must have picked up enough language to get some idea of how different man was from them, and how powerful; and they gathered that more ships would be arriving, bringing settlers. It didn't occur to them that they might be conceded the right to keep their lands. Perhaps they're still more fiercely territorial than we. They determined to fight, in their own way. I dare say, once we begin to get insight into that mentality, our psychological science will go through its Copernican revolution."

Enthusiasm kindled in him. "That's not the sole thing we'll learn, either," he went on. "They must have science of their own, a nonhuman science born on a planet that isn't Earth. Because they did observe us as profoundly as we've ever observed

ourselves; they did mount a plan against us, one
that would have taken another century or more to
complete. Well, what else do they know? How do
they support their civilization without visible agriculture or aboveground buildings or mines or anything? How can they breed whole new intelligent
species to order? A million questions, ten million
answers!''

"*Can* we learn from them?" Barbro asked softly.
"Or can we only overrun them as you say they
fear?"

Sherrinford halted, leaned elbow on mantel,
hugged his pipe and replied, "I hope we'll show
more charity than that to a defeated enemy. It's
what they are. They tried to conquer us and failed,
and now in a sense we are bound to conquer them,
since they'll have to make their peace with the
civilization of the machine rather than see it rust
away as they strove for. Still, they never did us any
harm as atrocious as what we've inflicted on our
fellow men in the past. And I repeat, they could
teach us marvelous things; and we could teach
them, too, once they've learned to be less in-
tolerant of a different way of life."

"I suppose we can give them a reservation," she
said, and didn't know why he grimaced and
answered so roughly:

"Let's leave them the honor they've earned!
They fought to save the world they'd always
known from that—" he made a chopping gesture
at the city—"and just possibly we'd be better off
ourselves with less of it."

He sagged a trifle and sighed, "However, I suppose if Elfland had won, man on Roland would at last—peacefully, even happily—have died away. We live with our archetypes but can we live in them?"

Barbro shook her head. "Sorry, I don't understand."

"What?" He looked at her in a surprise that drove out melancholy. After a laugh: "Stupid of me. I've explained this to so many politicians and scientists and commissioners and Lord knows what, these past days, I forgot I'd never explained to you. It was a rather vague idea of mine, most of the time we were traveling, and I don't like to discuss ideas prematurely. Now that we've met the Outlings and watched how they work, I do feel sure."

He tamped down his tobacco. "In limited measure," he said, "I've used an archetype throughout my own working life. The rational detective. It hasn't been a conscious pose—much—it's simply been an image which fitted my personality and professional style. But it draws an appropriate response from most people, whether or not they've ever heard of the original. The phenomenon is not uncommon. We meet persons who, in varying degrees, suggest Christ or Buddha or the Earth Mother, or say, on a less exalted plane, Hamlet or d'Artagnan. Historical, fictional, and mythical, such figures crystallize basic aspects of the human psyche, and when we meet them in our real experience, our reaction goes deeper than consciousness."

He grew grave again: "Man also creates archetypes that are not individuals. The Anima, the Shadow—and, it seems, the Outworld. The world of magic, or glamour—which originally mean enchantment—of half-human beings, some like Ariel and some like Caliban, but each free of mortal frailties and sorrows—therefore, perhaps, a little carelessly cruel, more than a little tricksy; dwellers in dusk and moonlight, not truly gods but obedient to rulers who are enigmatic and powerful enough to be—Yes, our Queen of Air and Darkness knew well what sights to let lonely people see, what illusions to spin around them from time to time, what songs and legends to set going among them. I wonder how much she and her underlings gleaned from human fairy tales, how much they made up themselves, and how much men created all over again, all unwittingly, as the sense of living on the edge of the world entered them."

Shadows stole across the room. It grew cooler and the traffic noises dwindled. Barbro asked mutedly, "But what could this do?"

"In many ways," Sherrinford answered, "the outwayer *is* back in the Dark Ages. He has few neighbors, hears scanty news from beyond his horizon, toils to survive in a land he only partly understands, that may any night raise unforeseeable disasters against him, and is bounded by enormous wildernesses. The machine civilization which brought his ancestors here is frail at best. He could lose it as the Dark Ages nations had lost Greece and Rome, as the whole of Earth seems to have lost it. Let him be worked on, long, strongly, cunningly, by the archetypical Outworld, until he has come to believe in his bones that the magic of the Queen of Air and Darkness is greater than the energy of engines; and first his faith, finally his deeds will follow her. Oh, it wouldn't happen fast. Ideally, it would happen too slowly to be noticed, especially by self-satisfied city people. But when in the end a hinterland gone back to the ancient way turned from them, how could they keep alive?"

Barbro breathed, "She said to me, when their banners flew in the last of our cities, we would rejoice."

"I think we would have, by then," Sherrinford admitted. "Nevertheless, I believe in choosing one's destiny."

He shook himself, as if casting off a burden. He knocked the dottle from his pipe and stretched, muscle by muscle. "Well," he said, "it isn't going to happen."

She looked straight at him. "Thanks to you."

A flush went up his thin cheeks. "In time, I'm sure, somebody else would have—What matters is what we do next, and that's too big a decision for one individual or one generation to make."

She rose. "Unless the decision is personal, Eric," she suggested, feeling heat in her own face.

It was curious to see him shy. "I was hoping we might meet again."

"We will."

Ayoch sat on Wolund's Barrow. Aurora shuddered so brilliant, in such vast sheaves of light, as almost to hide the waning moons. Firethorn blooms had fallen; a few still glowed around the tree roots, amidst dry brok which crackled underfoot and smelled like woodsmoke. The air remained warm, but no gleam was left on the sunset horizon.

"Farewell, fare lucky," the pook called. Mistherd and Shadow-of-a-Dream never looked back. It was as if they didn't dare. They trudged on out of sight, toward the human camp whose lights made a harsh new star in the south.

Ayoch lingered. He felt he should also offer good-bye to her who had lately joined him that slept in the dolmen. Likely none would meet here again for loving or magic. But he could only think of one old verse that might do. He stood and trilled:

"Out of her breast
a blossom ascended.
The summer burned it.
The song is ended."

Then he spread his wings for the long flight away.

HOME

Like a bullet, but one that hunted its own target, the ferry left the mother ship and curved down from orbit. Stars crowded darkness, unwinking and wintry. Yakov Kahn's gaze went out the viewpoint over the pilot board, across thirty-three light-years to the spark which was Sol. Almost convulsively, he looked away again, sought the clotted silver of the Milky Way and the sprawl of Sagittarius. There, behind dust clouds where new suns were being born, lay the galaxy's heart.

Once he had dreamed of seeking thither himself. But he was a boy then, who stood on a rooftop and peered through city sky-glow and city haze, wanting only to be yonder. Afterward the dream struck facts of distance, energy, and economics. The wreck had not gone under in an instant. His sons, his grandsons—

No. Probably no man ever would.

Beside him, Bill Redfeather's craggy features scowled at instruments. "All systems check," he reported.

Kahn's mouth twitched slightly upward. "I should hope so."

Redfeather looked irritated. It was the pilot's, not the co-pilot's, responsibility to be sure they wouldn't burn as a meteorite in the atmosphere of the planet.

Its night side swelled before them, a monstrous darkness when you remembered the lights of Earth, but rimmed to dayward with blue and rosy red. An ocean sheened, polished metal scutcheoned with a hurricane; and that was alien too, no pelagicultural cover, no floating towns or crisscrossing transport webs. As he watched how Kahn regarded the sight, Redfeather's mood turned gentle.

"You think too damn much, Jake," he said.

"Well—" Kahn shrugged. "My last space trip."

"Nonsense. They'll need men yet on the Lunar run."

"A nice, safe shuttle." Kahn's Israeli accent harshened his English. "No, thank you. I will make a clean break and stay groundside. High time I began raising a family anyway."

If I can find a girl. Almost seventy years will have passed since we started out. And even then I was an anachronism, too many missions to too many stars. . . . Cut that! No self-pity allowed.

"I wonder what they've become like," Redfeather said.

"Eh?" Kahn pulled himself out of his thoughts. "Who?"

"The people, of course. A century here, cut off from the rest of the human race. That must have done things to them."

Thus far the crew had talked little about what they would find. Too depressing. But evasion had to end. "They will probably seem more familiar to you than to me," Kahn said, "being drawn from North America. Their radio reports haven't suggested any more social change than one would expect in a scientific base. A certain primitivism, I imagine; nothing else."

"Even among nonhumans?"

"They don't appear to have been significantly influenced by their neighbors. Or vice versa, for that matter. Too large a difference. I should think the primary effect on them was due to Mithras itself."

"How?"

"Room to move around. Wilderness. Horizons. But we will see."

The ferry was coming into daylight now. Groombridge 1830 rose blindingly over the curve of its innermost planet. Clouds drifted gold across plains and great wrinkled mountains.

"Think we can get in some hunting and such?" Redfeather asked eagerly. "I mean the real thing, not popping loose at a robot in an amusement park."

"No doubt," Kahn said. "We will have time. They can't pack up and leave on no more notice than our call after we entered orbit."

"Damned shame, to end the project," Redfeather said. "I hope they solved the rotation problems, anyhow."

"Which?"

"You know. With the tidal action this sun must exert, why does Mithras have only a sixty-hour day?"

"Oh, that. That was answered in the first decade the base was here. I have read old reports. A smaller liquid core makes for less isostatic friction. Other factors enter in, too, like the absence of a satellite. Trivial, compared to what they have been learning since. Imagine a biochemistry like Earth's, but with its own evolution, natives as intelligent as we are but not human, an entire *world*."

Kahn's fist smote the arm of his chair. He bounced a little in his harness, under the low deceleration pressure. "The Directorate is governed by idiots," he said roughly. "Terminating the whole interstellar program just because some cost accountant machine says population has grown so large and resources so low that we can't afford to keep on learning. My God, we can't afford not to! Without new knowledge, what hope have we for changing matters?"

"Could be the Directors had that in mind also," Redfeather grunted.

Kahn gave the co-pilot a sharp glance. Sometimes Redfeather surprised him.

The houseboat came down the Benison River, past Riptide Straits, and there lay the Bay of

Desire. The sun was westering, a huge red-gold ball that struck fire off the waters. Kilometers distant, on the opposite shore, the Princess reared her blue peak high over the clustered, climbing roofs of Withylet village; closer at hand, the sails of boats shone white as the wings of the sea whistlers cruising above them. The air was still warm, but through an open window David Thrailkill sensed a coolness in the breeze, and a smell of salt, off the Weatherwomb Ocean beyond the Door.

"Want to take the helm, dear?" he asked Leonie.

"Sure, if you'll mind Vivian," said his wife.

Thrailkill went aft across the cabin to get a bottle of beer from the cooler. The engine throb was louder there, and didn't sound quite right. Well, an overhaul was overdue, after so long a time upriver. He walked forward again, with his seven-year-old daughter in tow. (That would have been three years on Earth, an enchanting age, though already he could see that she would have her mother's blond good looks and a touch of his own studiousness.) Leonie chuckled at them as they went by.

Strongtail was on the porch, to savor the view. They were following the eastern bayshore. It rose as steeply as the other side, in hills that were green from winter rains but had begun to show a tinge of summer's tawniness. Flameflowers shouted color among pseudograsses and scattered boskets. Thrailkill lowered his lanky form into a chair, cocked feet on rail, and tilted the bottle. Cold pungency gurgled past his lips, like water cloven by the twin bows. "Ahhh!" he said. "I'm almost sorry to come home."

Vivian flitted in Strongtail's direction, several balls clutched to her chest. "Juggle?" she begged.

"Indeed," said the Mithran. The girl laughed for joy, and bounced around as much as the balls. Strongtail had uncommon skill in keeping things aloft and awhirl. His build helped, of course. The first expedition had compared the autochthons to kangaroos with bird heads and arms as long as a gibbon's. But a man who had spent his life among them needed no chimeras. To Thrailkill, his friend's nude, brown-furred small form was a unity, more graceful and in a way more beautiful than any human.

The slender beak remained open while Strongtail juggled, uttering those trills which men could not imitate without a vocalizer. "Yes, a pleasant adventure," he said. "Fortune is that we have ample excuse to repeat it."

"We sure do." Thrailkill's gaunt face cracked in a grin. "This is going to rock them back on their heels in Treequad. For nigh on two hundred and fifty years, we've been skiting across the world, and never dreamed about an altogether fantastic culture right up the Benison. *Won't* Painted Jaguar be surprised?"

He spoke English. After an Earth century of contact, the Mithrans around the Bay understood even if they were not able to voice the language. And naturally every human kid knew what the flutings of his playmates meant. You couldn't travel far, though, before you met strangeness; not surprising, on a planet whose most advanced

civilization was pre-industrial and whose natives
were nowhere given to exploration or empire
building.

Sometimes Thrailkill got a bit exasperated with
them. They were too damned gentle. Not that they
weren't vigorous, merry, et cetera. You couldn't
ask for a better companion than Strongtail. But he
lacked ambition. He'd helped build this boat, and
gone xenologizing on it, for fun and to oblige his
buddy. When the mores of the riparian tribes
became evident in all their dazzling complexities,
he had not seen why the humans got so excited; to
him, it was merely an occasion for amusement.

Thrailkill dismissed that recollection. *Mithras is
their planet,* he reminded himself, not for the first
time. *We're here simply because their ancestors
let us establish a base. If they seldom take any of the
machines and ideas we offer, if they refuse chance
after chance to really accomplish something, that's
their own affair. Maybe I just envy their attitude.*

"I do not grasp your last reference," said
Strongtail.

"Hm? Painted Jaguar? An old story among my
people." Thrailkill looked toward the sun, where it
touched the haze around the Princess with amber.
Earth's sun he had watched only on film, little and
fierce and hasty in heaven. "I'm not sure I understand it myself, quite."

Point Desire hove in view, the closest thing to a
city that the region possessed, several hundred
houses with adobe walls and red tile roofs on a
headland above the docks. A dozen or so boats
were in, mainly trading ketches from the southern

arm of the Bay.

"Anxious though I am to see my kindred," the Mithran said, "I think we would do wrong not to dine with Rich-in-Peace."

Thrailkill laughed. "Come off it, you hypocrite. You know damn well you want some of her cooking." He rubbed his chin. "As a matter of fact, so do I."

The houseboat strode on. When it passed another craft, Strongtail exchanged cheerful whistles. That the blocky structure moved without sails or oars was no longer a cause of wonder, and never had been very much. The people took for granted that humans made curious things.

"Indeed this has been a delightful journey," Strongtail mused. "Morning mists rolling still and white, islands hidden among waterstalks, a fish line to trail aft, and at night our jesting in our own snug world. . . . I would like a houseboat for myself."

"Why, you can use this one any time," Thrailkill said.

"I know. But so many kin and friends would wish to come with me, years must pass before they have each shared my pleasure. There should be at least one other houseboat."

"So make one. I'll help whenever I get a chance, and you can have a motor built in Treequad."

"For what fair value in exchange? I would have to work hard, to gather food or timber or whatever else the builder might wish." Strongtail relaxed. "No, too many other joys wait, ranging Hermit Woods, lazing on Broadstrands, making

music under the stars. Or playing with your cub."
He sent the balls through a series of leaps that
made Vivian squeal.

The boat eased into a berth. There followed the
routine of making fast, getting shipshape, packing
the stuff which must go ashore. That went quickly,
because several Mithrans stopped their dockside
fishing in order to help. They seemed agitated
about something, but wouldn't say what. Presently everyone walked to the landward end of
the dock. Planks boomed underfoot.

Rich-in-Peace's inn was not large, even by local
standards, and few customers were present. Those
sat on their tails at the counter, which had been
split from a single scarletwood log, and talked
with more excitement than usual. Leonie let the
door screen fold behind her. "Hello," she called.
"We're back for some of your delicious chowder."

"And beer," Strongtail reminded. "Never forget
beer."

Rich-in-Peace bustled around the counter. Her
big amber eyes glistened. The house fell silent;
this was her place, she was entitled to break the
news.

"You have not heard?" she caroled.

"No, our radio went out on the way back."
Thrailkill replied. "What's happened?"

She spread her hands. They had three fingers
apiece, at right angles to each other. "But so
wonderful!" she exclaimed. "A ship has come
from your country. They say you can go home." As
if the implications had suddenly broken on her,
she stopped. After a moment: "I hope you will

want to come back and visit us."

She doesn't realize, flashed through the stupefaction in Thrailkill. He was only dimly aware of Leonie's tight grasp on his arm. *That's a one-way trip.*

Sunset smoldered away in bronze and gold. From the heights above Treequad, Kahn and Thrailkill could look past the now purple hills that flanked the Door, out to a glimpse of the Weatherwomb Ocean. The xenologist sighed. "I always wanted to build a real seagoing schooner and take her there," he said. "Coasting down to Gate-of-the-South—what a trip!"

"I am surprised that the natives have not done so," Kahn said. "They appear to have the capability, and it would be better for trade than those toilsome overland routes you mentioned."

"I suggested that, and my father before me," Thrailkill answered. "But none of them cared to make the initial effort. Once we thought about doing it ourselves, to set an example. But we had a lot of other work, and too few of us."

"Well, if the natives are so shiftless, why do you care about improving their lot?"

Thrailkill bristled at the insult to his Mithrans, until he remembered that Kahn could not be expected to understand. "'Shiftless' is the wrong word," he said. "They work as hard as necessary. Their arts make everything of ours look sick. Let's just call them less adventurous than humans." His smile was wry. "Probably the real reason we've done so much here, and wanted to do so much more. Not for altruism, just for the hell of it."

The mirth departed from him. He looked from the Door, past the twinkling lanterns of Goodwort and Withylet which guarded it, back across the mercury sheet of the Bay, to Treequad at his feet.

"So, I'm not going to build that schooner," he said. Roughly: "Come on, we'd better return."

They started downhill, over a trail which wound among groves of tall sweet-scented sheathbud trees. Leaves rustled in the twilight, a flock of marsh birds winged homeward with remote trumpetings, insects chirred from the pseudograsses. Below, Treequad was a darkness filling the flatlands between hills and Bay. Lights could be seen from windows, and the Center tower was etched slim against the waters; but the whole impression was of openness and peace, with some underlying mystery to which men could not quite put a name.

"Why did you establish yourselves here, rather than at the town farther north?" Kahn asked. His voice seemed flat and loud, and the way he jumped from subject to subject was also an offense to serenity. Thrailkill didn't mind, though. He had recognized his own sort of man in the dark, moody captain, which was why he had invited Kahn to stay with him and had taken his guest on this ramble.

Good Lord, what can he do but grab blindly at whatever he notices? He left Earth a generation ago, and even if he read everything we sent up till then, why, we never could transmit more than a fraction of what we saw and heard and did. He's got two and a half—well, an Earth century's worth of questions to ask.

Thrailkill glanced around. The eastern sky had turned plum color, where the first few stars trod forth. *We ourselves,* he thought, *have a thousand years' worth; ten thousand years'. But of course now those questions will never be asked.*

"Why Treequad?" he said slowly. "Well, they already had a College of Poets and Ceremonialists here—call it the equivalent of an intellectual community, though in human terms it isn't very. They made useful go-betweens for us, in dealing with less well-educated natives. And then, uh, Point Desire is a trading center, therefore especially worth studying. We didn't want to disturb conditions by plumping our own breed down right there."

"I see. That is also why you haven't expanded your numbers?"

"Partly. We'd like to. This continent, this whole planet, is so underpopulated that— But a scientific base can't afford to grow. How would everyone be brought home again when it's terminated?"

Fiercely: "Damn you on Earth! You're terminating us too soon!"

"I agree," Kahn said. "If it makes any consolation, all the others are being ended too. They don't mind so greatly. This is the sole world we have found where men can live without carrying around an environmental shell."

"What? There must be more."

"Indeed. But how far have we ranged? Less than fifty light-years. And never visited half the stars in that radius. You don't know what a gigantic project it is, to push a ship close to the speed of light. Too gigantic. The whole effort is coming to an end, as Earth grows poor and weary. I doubt if it will ever be revived."

Thrailkill felt a chill. The idea hadn't occurred to him before, in the excitement of meeting the ferriers, but— "What can we do when we get there?" he demanded. "We're not fitted for . . . for city life."

"Have no fears," Kahn said. "Universities, foundations, vision programs, any number of institutions will be delighted to have you. At least, that was so when I left, and society appears to have gotten static. And you should have party conversation for the rest of your lives, about your adventures on Mithras."

"M-m-m, I s'pose." Thrailkill rehearsed some fragments of his personal years.

Adventure enough. When he and Tom Jackson and Gleam-of-Wings climbed the Snowtooths, white starkness overhead and the wind awhistle below them, the thunder and plumes of an avalanche across a valley, the huge furry beast that came from a cave and must be slain before it slew them. Or shooting the rapids on a river that tumbled down the Goldstream Hills, landing wet and cold at Volcano to boast over their liquor in the smoky-raftered taproom of Monstersbane Inn. Prowling the alleys and passing the lean temples of the Fivedom; standing off a horde of the natives' half-intelligent, insensately ferocious cousins, in the stockade at Tearwort; following the caravans through the Desolations, down to Gate-of-the-

South, while drums beat unseen from dry hills; or simply this last trip, along the Benison through fogs and waterstalks, to those lands where the dwellers gave their lives to nothing but rites that made no sense and one dared not laugh—Indeed Earth offered nothing like that, and the vision-screen people would pay well for a taste of it to spice their fantasies.

Though Thrailkill remembered quieter times more clearly, and did not see how they could be told. The Inn of the Poetess, small and snug beneath the stormcloud mass of Demon Mountain, firelight, songs, comradeship; shadows and sun-flecks and silence in Hermit Woods; sailing out to Fish Hound Island with Leonie on their wedding night, that the sunrise might find them alone on its crags (how very bright the stars had been—even little Sol was a beacon for them); afterward, building sand castles with Vivian on Broadstrands, while the surf rolled in from ten thousand kilometers of ocean. They used to end such a day by finding some odd eating place in Kings Point Station or Goodwort, and Vivian would fall asleep to the creak of the sweeps as their ferry trudged home across the water.

Well, those were private memories anyway.

He realized they had been walking for quite some time in silence. Only their footfalls on the cobbles, now that they were back in town, or an occasional trill from the houses that bulked on either side, could be heard. Courtesy insisted he should make conversation with the vaguely visible shape on his right. "What will you do?" he asked.

"After we return, I mean."

"I don't know," Kahn said. "Teach, perhaps."

"Something technical, no doubt."

"I could, if need be. Science and technology no longer change from generation to generation. But I would prefer history. I have had considerable time to read history, in space."

"Really? I mean, the temporal contraction effect—"

"You forget that at one gravity acceleration, a ship needs a year to reach near-light speed, and another year to brake at the end. Your passengers will be in suspended animation, but we of the crew must stand watch."

Kahn lit a cigaret. Earlier, Thrailkill had experimented with one, but tobacco made him ill, he found. He wondered for a moment if Earth's food had the savor of Mithran. *Funny. I never appreciated kernelkraut or sour nuts or filet of crackler till now, when I'm about to lose them.*

The cigaret end brightened and faded, brightened and faded, like a tiny red watchlight in the gloaming. "After all," Kahn said, "I have seen many human events. I was born before the Directorate came to power. My father was a radiation technician in the Solar War. And, too, mine are an old people, who spent most of their existence on the receiving end of history. It is natural that I should be interested. You have been more fortunate."

"And the Mithrans are luckier yet, eh?"

"I don't know. Thus far, they are essentially a historyless race. Or are they? How can you tell?

We look through our own eyes. To us, accomplishment equals exploitation of the world. Our purest science and art remain a sort of conquest. What might the Mithrans do yet, in Mithran terms?"

"Let us keep up the base," Thrailkill said, "and we'll keep on reporting what they do."

"That would be splendid," Kahn told him, "except that there will be no ships to take your descendants home. You have maintained yourselves an enclave of a few hundred people for a century. You cannot do so forever. If nothing else, genetic drift in that low a population would destroy you."

They walked on unspeaking, till they reached the Center. It was a village within the village, clustered around the tower. Thence had sprung the maser beams, up through the sky to the relay satellite, and so to those on Earth who wondered what the universe was like. *No more*, Thrailkill thought. *Dust will gather, nightcats will nest in corroding instruments, legends will be muttered about the tall strangers who built and departed, and one century an earthquake will bring down the tower which talked across space, and the very myths will die.*

On the far side of the Mall, close to the clear plash of Louis' Fountain, they stopped. There lay Thrailkill's house, long and solid, made to endure. His grandfather had begun it, his father had completed it, he himself had wanted to add rooms but had no reason to when he would only be allowed two children. The windows were aglow, and he heard a symphony of Mithran voices.

"What the devil!" he said. "We've got company." He opened the door.

The fireplace danced with flames, against the evening cold. Their light shimmered off the beautiful grain of wainscots, glowed on patterned rugs and the copper statue which owned one corner, and sheened along the fur of his friends. The room was full of them: Strongtail, Gleam-of-Wings, Nightstar, Gift-of-God, Dreamer, Elf-in-the-Forest, and more and more, all he had loved who could get here quickly enough. They sat grave on their tails, balancing cups of herb tea in their hands, while Leonie attended to the duties of a hostess.

She stopped when Thrailkill and Kahn entered. "How late you are!" she said. "I was growing worried."

"No need," Thrailkill replied, largely for Kahn's benefit. "The last prowltiger hereabouts was shot five years ago." *I did that. Another adventure— hai, what a stalk through the folded hills! (The Mithrans didn't like it. They attached some kind of significance to the ugly brutes. But prowltigers never took a Mithran. When the Harris boy was killed, we stopped listening to objections. Our friends forgave us eventually.)* He looked around. "You honor this roof," he said with due formalism. "Be welcome in good cheer."

Strongtail's music was a dirge. "Is the story true that you can never return?"

"Yes, I'm afraid so," Thrailkill said. Aside to Kahn: "They want us to stay. I'm not sure why. We haven't done anything in particular for them."

"But you tried," said Nightstar. "That was a large plenty, that you should care."

"And you were something to wonder at," Elf-in-the-Forest added.

"We have enjoyed you," Strongtail said. "Why must you go?"

"We took council," sang Gift-of-God, "and came hither to ask from house to house that you remain."

"But we can't!" Leonie's words cracked over.

"Why can you not?" responded Dreamer.

It burst upon Thrailkill. He stood in the home of his fathers and shouted: "Why not? We can!"

The long night drew toward a close. Having slept, Kahn borrowed one of the flitters that had been manufactured here and went after Bill Redfeather, who'd gone on a jaunt with one of the autochthons.

He hummed across the Bay under constellations not so different from those on Earth. Thirty-three light-years were hardly significant in the galaxy. But the humans no longer used human names; those were the Boat, the Garden of Healing, the Fourfold, that wheeled and glittered around another pole star. *I suppose there are more native influences*, he thought. *Not too many, but some. I wonder what kind of civilization they would build. They could hardly help but do better than Earth, on a rich and uncrowded planet. In time they would be able to launch starships of their own.*

The unrolling map guided him toward Starkbeam, and when the hamlet came into sight he detected the emissions from Redfeather's portable transceiver and homed on them. They led him to a peak that loomed over the peninsular hills and the soaring scarletwood forest. He must come down vertically on a meadow.

Dew soaked his breeches as he stepped out. The eastern sky had paled, but most light still came from the stars, and from the campfire that fluttered before a tent. Redfeather and Strongtail squatted there, half seen in shadows. A pot on a framework of sticks bubbled above, merrily competing with the first sleepy bird-chirps. The air was raw, and Kahn shivered and felt glad to settle down with hands held near the coals.

Strongtail murmured some notes. "I think that means 'welcome,' " Redfeather said. Strongtail nodded. "Breakfast will be ready soon. Or lunch or something. Hard to get used to his diurnal period. What do the base people do?"

"About twenty hours awake, ten asleep, around the clock," Kahn said. "Have you had a good outing?"

"Lord, yes. Strongtail's a mighty fine guide, even if he can't talk to me. Very kind of you to take me." Strongtail trilled in pleasure. "I do wish I could hunt, but my pal here doesn't quite approve. Oh, well, I'm glad to get out in the woods anyway." Redfeather stirred the pot. "I suppose you're joining us?"

"No, that wasn't why I called." Kahn lit a cigaret and smoked in short, hard puffs. "Business. Regrets, but you will have to come directly back with me."

"Huh? What's the rush? I mean, unless the people changed their minds about staying."

"No, they haven't. They have been threshing the matter this whole night. Hardly any of them wish to leave with us. I argued, but I might as well have talked to those trees."

"Why bother, Jake? We don't have positive orders to bring them back." Redfeather smiled. "Give me a few days here, and I could well decide to stay myself."

"What?" Kahn stared at the firelit face. "Yes, I see. I am not personally one for the bucolic life—"

"No need to be. Having made the final decision, we . . . they'll want mines, factories, sawmills, everything you can name."

Kahn glanced at Strongtail. "What do you say to that?" he asked. "Do you wish these things done?"

The Mithran nodded slowly. A qualified "Yes," Kahn assumed; he didn't like the idea, but various regions could be given the humans and there was plenty of room elsewhere. If, indeed, anything that formal was contemplated. Thrailkill had remarked that the autochthons had no concept of real estate as property.

Kahn finished his cigaret, ground out the stub with a vicious gesture, and rose. "Excuse me, Strongtail," he said. "We have private affairs to discuss. Come into the flitter, Bill."

Privacy was another notion, incomprehensible, with which Strongtail cooperated to oblige. He tended the pot, drank in its odors and the green scent of the awakening forest, was briefly saddened by the trouble he had sensed, and then turned his mind to more easy and pleasurable thoughts. Once he started, Kahn's yell pierced the flitter canopy. "God damn you, I am the captain and you will obey orders!" He knew that humans often submitted themselves, however reluctantly, to the will of someone else. The fact that Mithrans left a job whenever they got bored had occasioned friction in the early days. Later generations solved the problem by rarely employing Mithrans.

Well-a-day, they made up for their peculiarities by such things as houseboats. It would be amusing, no, wonderful to see what they did when they really felt themselves part of the land.

Unless—No, while the prowltiger episode, and certain others, had been unfortunate, limits were not exceeded. Should that ever happen, Strongtail would be forced to kill. But he would continue to love as he did.

The canopy slid back and the Earthmen returned. Kahn looked grim, Redfeather was quiet and shaken. Sweat filled his brows. "I'm sorry," he told the Mithran, "I must go to the spaceship."

The meeting hall in Treequad was so big that the entire human population could gather within. Mounting the stage, Kahn looked beyond gaily muraled walls to the faces. The very graybeards, he thought, had an air of youth which did not exist for any age on Earth. Sun and wind had embraced them throughout their lives. They had had a planet to wander in, as men had not owned since Columbus.

He turned to Thrailkill, who had accompanied him. Normally an elected speaker presided over these sessions, but today they listened to him and naturally his host went along. "Is everybody here?" he asked.

Thrailkill's gaze swept the room. Sunlight streamed in the windows, to touch women's hair and men's eyes with ruddiness. A quiet had fallen, underscored by rustlings and shufflings. Somewhere a baby cried, but was quickly soothed.

"Yes," he said. "The last field expedition came in two hours ago, from the Icefloe Dwellers." He scowled at Kahn. "I don't know why you want this assembly. Our minds are made up."

The spaceman consulted his watch. He had to stall for a bit. His men wouldn't get down from orbit for some minutes yet, and then they must walk here. "I told you," he said. "I want to make a final appeal."

"We've heard your arguments," Thrailkill said.

"Not formally."

"Oh, all right." Thrailkill advanced to the lectern. The PA boomed his words forth under the rafters.

"The meeting will please come to order," he said. "As you know, we're met for the purpose of officially ratifying the decision that we have reached. I daresay Captain Kahn will need such a recorded vote. First he'd like to address you." He bowed slightly to his guests and took a chair. Leonie was in the front row with Vivian; he winked at them.

Kahn leaned on the stand. His body felt heavy and tired. "Ladies and gentlemen," he said, "you have spent many hours this past night talking things over in private groups. Quite an exciting night, no? I have asked you to come here after sleeping on the question, because your choice should be made in a calmer mood, it being irrevocable.

"Hardly any of you have agreed to leave with us. I wonder if the majority have considered what their own desires mean. As was said long ago, 'Il faut vouloir les consequences de ce que l'on veut.' " Blankness met him, driving home how far these people had drifted from Earth. "I mean you must want the results of what you want. You are too few to maintain a culture at the modern level. True, your ancestors brought along the means to produce certain amenities, and you have a lot of information on microtape. But there are only so many heads among you, and each head can hold only so much. You are simply not going to have enough engineers, medical specialists, psychopediatricians, geneticists . . . every trained type necessary to operate a civilization, as opposed to a mere scientific base. Some of your children will die from causes that could have been prevented. Those who survive will mature ignorant of Earth's high heritage.

"A smiliar thing happened before, on the American frontier. But America was close to Europe. The new barbarism ended in a few generations, as contact strengthened. You will be alone, but no more than one thin thread of radio, a lifetime passing between message and answer. Do you want to sink back into a dark age?"

Someone called, "We've done okay so far." Others added remarks. Kahn was content to let them wrangle; thus he gained time, without drawing on his own exhausted resources. But Thrailkill shushed them and said:

"I believe we're aware of that problem, Captain.

In fact, we've lived with it during the whole existence of this . . . colony." *There*, Kahn thought. *He spoke the word*. "We haven't really been bothered. From what we hear about Earth, we've gained more than we've lost." Applause. "And now that you've made us realize this is our home, this is where we belong, why, we won't stay small. For purely genetic reasons we'll have to expand our population as fast as possible. My wife and I always did want a houseful of kids. Now we can have them." Cheering began. His reserve broke apart. "We'll build our own civilization! And someday we'll come back to you, as visitors. You're giving up the stars. We're not!"

They rose from their chairs and shouted.

Kahn let the noise surf around him, while he stood slumped. *Soon*, he begged. *Let it be soon*. Seeing that he remained where he was, the crowd grew gradually still. He waited till the last one had finished talking to his neighbor. Then the silence was so deep that he could hear the songbirds outside.

"Very well," he said in a dull tone. "But what is to become of the Mithrans?"

Thrailkill, who had also stayed on his feet, said rapidly, "You mentioned that to me before, Captain. I told you then and I tell you now, the planet has room for both races. We aren't going to turn on our friends."

"My mate Bill Redfeather is an Amerind," Kahn said. "Quite a few of his ancestors were friends to the white man. It didn't help them in the long run. I am a Jew myself, if you know what that means.

My people spent the better part of two thousand years being alien. We remember in our bones how that was. Finally some started a country of their own. The Arabs who were there objected, and lived out the rest of their lives in refugee camps. Ask Muthaswamy, my chief engineer, to explain the history of Moslem and Hindu in India. Ask his assistant Ngola to tell you what happened when Europe entered Africa. And, as far as that goes, what happened when Europe left again. You cannot intermingle two cultures. One of them will devour the other. And already, this minute, yours is the more powerful."

They mumbled, down in the hall, and stared at him and did not understand. He sucked air into his lungs and tried anew:

"Yes, you don't intend to harm the Mithrans. Thus far there has been little conflict. But when your numbers grow, when you begin to rape the land for all the resources this hungry civilization needs, when mutual exasperation escalates into battle—can you speak for your children? Your grandchildren? Their grandchildren, to the end of time? The people of Bach and Goethe brought forth Hitler. No, you don't know what I am talking about, do you?

"Well, let us suppose that man on this planet reverses his entire previous record and gives the natives some fairly decent reservations and does not take them away again. Still, how much hope have they of becoming anything but parasites? They cannot become one with you. The surviving Amerinds could be assimilated, but they were human. Mithrans are not. They do not and cannot think like humans. But don't they have the right to live in their world as they wish, make their own works, hope their own hopes?

"You call this planet underpopulated. By your standards, that is correct. But not by the natives'. How many individuals per hectare do you expect an economy like theirs to support? Take away part of a continent, and you murder that many unborn sentient beings. But you won't stop there. You will take the world, and so murder an entire way of existence. How do you know that way isn't better than ours? Certainly you have no right to deny the universe the chance that it is better."

They seethed and buzzed at his feet. Thrailkill advanced, fists clenched, and said flatly, "Have you so little pride in being a man?"

"On the contrary," Kahn answered, "I have so much pride that I will not see my race guilty of the ultimate crime. We are not going to make anyone else pay for our mistakes. We are going home and see if we cannot amend them ourselves."

"So you say!" Thrailkill spat.

O God of mercy, send my men. Kahn looked into the eyes of the one whose salt he had eaten, and knew they would watch him for what remained of his life. And behind would gleam the Bay of Desire, and the Princess' peak holy against a smokeless heaven, and the Weatherwomb waiting for ships to sail west. "You will be heroes on Earth," he said. "And you will at least have memories. I—"

The communicator in his pocket buzzed

"Ready." He slapped it once: "Go ahead."

Thunder crashed on the roof, shaking walls. A deeptoned whistle followed. Kahn sagged back against the lectern. That would be the warboat, with guns and nuclear bombs.

The door flew open. Redfeather entered, and a squad of armed men. The rest had surrounded the hall.

Kahn straightened. His voice was a stranger's, lost in the yells and cries: "You are still citizens of the Directorate. As master of an official ship, I have discretionary police authority. Will or no, you shall come back with me."

He saw Leonie clutch her child to her. He ducked Thrailkill's roundhouse swing and stumbled off the stage, along the aisle toward his men. Hands grabbed at him. Redfeather fired a warning burst, and thereafter he walked alone. He breathed hard, but kept his face motionless. It wouldn't do for him to weep. Not yet.

And so end these chronicles of the folk who took the long road to the stars. And long it is, not at all like those here, nor the highways of other fictional universes. It is unlike them in another way, too. It is a road that is always open. It is real . . .

OUR MANY ROADS
TO THE STARS

There are countless varieties of science fiction these days, and I would be the last to want any of them restricted in any way. Nevertheless, what first drew me to this literature and, after more years than I like to add up, still holds me, is its dealing with the marvels of the universe. To look aloft at the stars on a clear night and think that someday, somehow we might actually get out among them, rouses the thrill anew, and I become young again. After all, we made it to the Moon didn't we? Meanwile, only science fiction of the old and truly kind takes the imagination forth on that journey. Therefore I put up with its frequent flaws; and so does many another dreamer.

But are we mere dreamers, telling ourselves stories of voyages yonder as our ancestors told of voyages to Avalon and Cibola? Those never existed, and the stars do; but, realistically, does any possibility of reaching them?

The case against interstellar travel traditionally begins with the sheer distances. While Pioneer 10 and 11, the Jupiter flybys, will leave the Solar System, they won't get as far as Alpha Centauri, the nearest neighbor sun, for more than 40,000 years. (They aren't actually bound in that direction.) At five times their speed, or 100 miles per second, which we are nowhere close to reaching today, the trip would take longer than recorded history goes back. And the average separation of stars in this galactic vicinity is twice as great.

If we could go very much faster—

At almost the speed of light, we'd reach Alpha Centauri in about four and a third years. But as most of you know, we who were faring would experience a shorter journey. Both the theory of relativity and experimental physics show that time passes "faster" for a fast-moving object. The closer the speed of light, the greater the difference, until at that velocity itself, a spaceman would make the trip in no time at all. However, the girl he left behind him would measure his transit as taking the same number of years as a light ray does; and he'd take equally long in coming back to her.

In reality, the velocity of light *in vacuo*, usually symbolized by *c*, cannot be attained by any material body. From a physical viewpoint, the reason lies in Einstein's famous equation $E = mc^2$. Mass and energy are equivalent. The faster a body moves, the more energy it has, and hence the more mass. This rises steeply as velocity gets close to c, and at that speed would become infinite, an obvious impossibility.

Mass increases by the same factor as time (and length) shrink. An appendix to this essay defines the terms more precisely than here. A table there gives some representative values of the factor for different values of velocity, v compared to c. At $v = 7c$, that is, at a speed of 70% light's, time aboard ship equals distance covered in light-years. Thus, a journey of 10 light-years at $0.7c$ would occupy 10 years of the crew's lives, although to people on Earth or on the target planet, it would take about 14.

There's a catch here. We have quietly been supposing that the whole voyage is made at exactly this rate. In practice, the ship would have to get up to speed first, and brake as it neared the goal. Both these maneuvers take time; and most of this time is spent at low velocities where the relativistic effects aren't noticeable.

Let's imagine that we accelerate at one gravity, increasing our speed by 32 feet per second each second and thus providing ourselves with a comfortable Earth-normal weight inboard. It will take us approximately a year (a shade less) to come near c, during which period we will have covered almost half a light-year, and during most of which period our time rate won't be significantly different from that of the outside cosmos. In fact, not until the eleventh month would the factor get as low as 0.5, though from then on it would start a really steepening nosedive. Similar considerations apply at journey's end, while we slow down. Therefore a trip under these conditions would never take less than two years as far as we are concerned; if the distance covered is 10 light-years, the time required is 11 years as far as the girl (or boy) friend left behind is concerned.

At the "equalizing" v of 0.7 c, these figures become 10.7 years for the crew and 14.4 years for the stay-at-homes. This illustrates the dramatic gains that the former, if not the latter, can make by pushing c quite closely. But let's stay with that value of 0.7 c for the time being, since it happens to be the one chosen by Bernard Oliver for his argument against the feasibility of star travel.

Now, Dr. Oliver, vice president for research and development at Hewlett-Packard, is definitely not unimaginative, nor hostile to the idea as such. Rather, he is intensely interested in contacting extraterrestrial intelligence, and was the guiding genius of Project Cyclops, which explored the means of doing so by radio. The design which his group came up with could, if built, detect anybody who's using radio energy like us today within 100 light-years. Or it could receive beacon signals of reasonable strength within 1000 light-years: a sphere which encloses a million suns akin to Sol and half a billion which are different.

Still, he does not fudge the facts. Making the most favorable assumption, a matter-antimatter annihilation system which expels radiation itself, he has calculated the minimum requirement for a round trip with a stopover at the destination star, at a peak speed of 0.7c. Assuming 1000 tons of ship plus payload, which is certainly modest, he found that it must convert some 33,000 tons of fuel into energy—sufficient to supply the United States, at present levels of use, for half a million years. On first starting off from orbit, the ship would spend 10 times the power that the Sun gives to our entire Earth. Shielding requirements alone, against stray gamma rays, make this an absurdity, not to speak of a thousand square miles of radiating surface to cool the vessel if as little as one one-millionth of the energy reaches it in the form of waste heat.

Though we can reduce these figures a good deal if we assume it can refuel at the other end for its return home, the scheme looks impractical regardless. Moreover, Dr. Oliver, no doubt deliberately, has not mentioned that space is not empty. Between local stars, it contains about one hydrogen atom per cubic centimeter, plus smaller amounts of other materials. This is a harder vacuum than any we can achieve artificially. But a vessel ramming through it at $0.7c$ would release X-radiation at the rate of some 50 million roentgen units per hour. It takes less than 1000 to kill a human being. No material shielding could protect the crew for long, if at all.

Not every scientist is this pessimistic about the rocket to the stars, that is, a craft which carries its own energy source and reaction mass. Some hope for smaller, unmanned probes, perhaps moving at considerably lower speeds. But given the mass required for their life support and equipment, men who went by such a vehicle would have to reckon on voyages lasting generations or centuries.

This is not impossible, of course. Maybe they could pass the time in suspended animation. Naturally radioactive atoms in the body set an upper limit to that, since they destroy tissue which would then not be replaced. But Carl Sagan, astronomer and exobiologist at Cornell University, estimates that a spore can survive up to a million years. This suggests to me that humans should be good for anyway several thousand.

Or maybe, in a huge ship with a complete ecology, an expedition could beget and raise children to carry their mission on. Calculations by Gerard K. O'Neill, professor of physics at Harvard, strongly indicate that this is quite feasible. His work has actually dealt with the possibility of establishing permanent, self-sustaining colonies in orbit, pleasanter to live in than most of Earth and capable of producing more worldlets like themselves from extraterrestrial resources. He concludes that we can start on it *now*, with existing technology and at startlingly low cost, and have the first operational by the late 1980's. Not long afterward, somebody could put a motor on one of these.

The hardened science fiction reader may think such ideas are old hat. And so they are, in fiction. But to me the fact is infinitely more exciting than any story—that the accomplishment can actually be made, that sober studies by reputable professionals are confirming the dream.

True, I'd prefer to believe that men and women can get out there faster, more easily, so that the people who sent them off will still be alive when word arrives of what they have discovered. Is this wishful thinking? We've written off the rocket as a means of ultra-fast travel, but may there be other ways?

Yes, probably there are. Even within the framework of conventional physics, where you can never surpass c, we already have more than one well-reasoned proposal. If not yet as detailed and mathematical as Oberth's keystone work on interplanetary travel of 1929, the best of them seem equivalent to Tsiolkovsky's cornerstone work of 1911. If the time scale is the same for future as for past developments, then the first manned Alpha Centauri expedition should leave about the year 2010. . . .

That's counting from R. W. Bussard's original paper on the interstellar ramjet, which appeared in 1960. Chances are that a flat historical parallel is silly. But the engineering ideas positively are not. They make a great deal of sense.

Since the ramjet has been in a fair number of stories already, I'll describe the principle rather briefly. We've seen that at high speeds, a vessel must somehow protect its crew from the atoms and ions in space. Lead or other material shielding is out of the question. Hopelessly too much would be required, it would give off secondary radiation of its own, and ablation would wear it down, incidentally producing a lot of heat, less readily dissipated in space than in an atmosphere. Since the gas must be controlled anyway, why not put it to work?

Once the ship has reached a speed which turns out to be reasonable for a thermonuclear rocket—and we're on the verge of that technology today—a scoop can collect the interstellar gas and funnel it into a reaction chamber. There, chosen parts can be fusion-burned for energy to throw the rest out backward, thus propelling the vessel forward. Ramjet aircraft use the same principle, except that they must supply fuel to combine with the oxygen they collect. The ramjet starcraft takes everything it needs from its surroundings. Living off the country, it faces none of the mass-ratio problems of a rocket, and might be able to crowd c very closely.

Needless to say, even at the present stage of pure theory, things aren't that simple. For openers, how large an apparatus do we need? For a ship-plus-payload mass of 1000 tons, accelerating at one gravity and using proton-proton fusion for power, Bussard and Sagan have both calculated a scoop radius of 2000 kilometers. Now we have no idea as yet how to make that particular reaction go. We are near the point of fusing deuterons, or deuterons and tritons (hydrogen nuclei with one and two neutrons respectively), to get a net energy release. But these isotopes are far less common than ordinary hydrgen, and thus would require correspondingly larger intakes. Obviously, we can't use collectors made of metal.

But then, we need nonmaterial shielding anyway. Electromagnetic fields exert force on charged particles. A steady laser barrage emitted by the ship can ionize all neutral atoms within a safety zone, and so make them controllable, as well as vaporizing rare bits of dust and gravel which would otherwise be a hazard. (I suspect, myself, that this won't be necessary. Neutral atoms have electrical asymmetries which offer a possible grip to the forcefields of a more advanced technolgoy than ours. I also feel sure we will master the proton-proton reaction, and eventually matter-antimatter annihilation. But for now, let's play close to our vests). A force-field scoop, which being massless can be of enormous size, will catch these ions, funnel them down paths which are well clear of the crew section and into a fusion chamber, cause the chosen nuclei to burn, and expel everything aft to drive the vessel forward, faster and faster.

To generate such fields, A.J. Fennelly of Yeshiva University and G.L. Matloff of the Polytechnic Institute of New York propose a copper cylinder coated with a super-conducting layer of niobium-tin alloy. The size is not excessive, 400 meters in length and 200 in diameter. As for braking, they suggest a drogue made of boron, for its high melting point, ten kilometers across. This would necessarily work rather slowly. But then, these authors are cautious in their assumptions; for instance, they derive a peak velocity of just $0.12c$. The system could reach Alpha Centauri in about 53 years, Tau Ceti in 115.

By adding wings, however, they approximately halve these travel times. The wings are two great superconducting batteries, each a kilometer square. Cutting the lines of the galactic magnetic

field, they generate voltages which can be tapped
for exhaust acceleration, for magnetic bottle con-
tainers for the power reaction, and for inboard
electricity. With thrust shut off, they act as auxil-
iary brakes, much shortening the deceleration
period. When power is drawn at different rates on
either side, they provide maneuverability—majes-
tically slow, but sufficient—almost as if they were
huge oars.

All in all, it appears that a vessel of this general
type can bring explorers to the nearest stars while
they are still young enough to carry out the exploration—and the preliminary colonization?—themselves. Civilization at home will start receiving a
flood of beamed information, fascinating, no
doubt often revolutionary in unforeseeable ways,
within a few years of their arrival. Given only
a slight lengthening of human life expectancy,
they might well spend a generation out yonder and
get home alive, still hale. Certainly their children
can.

Robert L. Forward, a leading physicist at
Hughes Research Laboratories, has also interested himself in the use of the galactic magnetic field. As he points out, the ion density in interstellar space is so low that a probe could easily
maintain a substantial voltage across itself. Properly adjusted, the interaction forces produced by
this will allow mid-course corrections and ter-
minal maneuvers at small extra energy cost. Thus
we could investigate more than one star with a
single probe, and eventually bring it home again.

Indeed, the price of research in deep space is

rather small. Even the cost of manned vessels is estimated by several careful thinkers as no more than ten billion dollars each—starting with today's technology. That's about 50 dollars per American, much less than we spend every year on cigarettes and booze, enormously less than goes for wars, bureaucrats, subsidies to inefficient businesses, or the servicing of the national debt. For mankind as a whole, a starship would run about $2.50 per head. The benefits it would return in the way of knowledge, and thus of improved capability, are immeasurably great.

But to continue with those manned craft. Mention of using interstellar magnetism for maneuvering raises the thought of using it for propulsion. That is, by employing electromagnetic forces which interact with that field, a ship could ideally accelerate itself without having to expel any mass backward. This would represent a huge saving over what the rocket demands.

The trouble is, the galactic field is very weak, and no doubt very variable from region to region. Though it can be valuable in ways that we have seen, there appears to be no hope of using it for a powerful drive.

Might we invent other devices? For instance, if we could somehow establish a negative gravity force, this might let our ship react against the mass of the universe as a whole, and thus need no jets. Unfortunately, nobody today knows how to do any such thing, and most physicists take for granted it's impossible. Not all agree: because antigravity-type forces do occur in relativity theory, under special conditions.

Physics does offer one way of reaching extremely high speeds free, the Einsteinian catapult. Later I shall have more to say about the weird things that happen when large, ultra-dense masses spin very fast. But among these is their generation of a force different from Newtonian gravity, which has a mighty accelerating effect of its own. Two neutron stars, orbiting nearly in contact, could kick almost to light velocity a ship which approached them on the right orbit.

Alas, no such pair seems to exist anywhere near the Solar System. Besides, we'd presumably want something similar in the neighborhood of our destination, with exactly the characteristics necessary to slow us down. The technique looks rather implausible. What is likely, though, is that closer study of phenomena like these may give us clues to the method of constructing a field drive.

Yet do we really need it? Won't the Bussard ramjet serve? Since it picks up everything it requires as it goes, why can't it keep on accelerating indefinitely, until it comes as close to c as the captain desires? The Fennelly-Matloff vehicle is not intended to do this. But why can't a more advanced model?

Quite possibly it can!

Before taking us off on such a voyage, maybe I'd better answer a question or two. If the ship, accelerating at one gravity, is near c in a year, and if c is the ultimate speed which nature allows, how can the ship keep on accelerating just as hard, for just as long as the flight plan says?

The reason lies in the relativistic contraction of space and time, when these are measured by a fast-moving observer. Suppose we, at rest with respect to the stars, track a vessel for 10 light-years at its steady speed of $0.9c$. To us, the passage takes 11 years. To the crew, it takes 4.4 years: because the distance crossed is proportionately less. They never experience faster-than-light travel either. What they do experience, when they turn their instruments outward, is a cosmos strangely flattened in the direction of their motion, where the stars (and their unseen friends at home) age strangely fast.

The nearer they come to c, the more rapidly these effects increase. Thus as they speed up, they perceive themselves as accelerating at a steady rate through a constantly shrinking universe. Observers on a planet would perceive them as accelerating at an ever lower rate through an unchanged universe. At last, perhaps, millions of light-years might be traversed and millions of years pass by outside while a man inboard draws a breath.

By the way, those authors are wrong who have described the phenomenon in terms of "subjective" versus "objective" time. One set of measurements is as valid an another.

The "twin paradox" does not arise. This old chestnut says, "Look, suppose we're twins, and you stay home while I go traveling at high speed. Now I could equally well claim I'm stationary and you're in motion—therefore that you're the one flattened out and living at a slower rate, not me.

So what happens when we get back together
again? How can each of us be younger than his
twin?''

It overlooks the fact that the traveler does come
home. The situation would indeed be symmetrical
if the spaceman moved forever at a fixed velocity.
But then he and his brother, by definition, never
would meet to compare notes. His accelerations
(which include slowdowns and changes of course)
take the whole problem out of special and into
general relativity. Against the background of the
stars, the traveler has moved in a variable fashion;
forces have acted on him.

Long before time and space measurements
aboard ship differ bizarrely much from those on
Earth, navigational problems will arise. They are
the result of two factors, aberration and Doppler
effect.

Aberration is the apparent displacement of an
object in the visual field of a moving observer. It
results from combining his velocity with the
velocity of light. (Analogously, if we are out in the
rain and, standing still, feel it falling straight
down, we will feel it hitting us at a slant when we
start walking. The change in angle will be larger if
we run.) At the comparatively small orbital speed
of Earth, sensitive instruments can detect the
aberration of the stars. At speeds close to c, it will
be huge. Stars will seem to crawl across the sky as
we accelerate, bunching in its forward half and
thinning out aft.

Doppler effect, perhaps more widely familiar, is
the shift in observed wavelength from an emitting

object, when the observer's velocity changes. If we move away from a star, we see its light reddened; if we move toward a star, we see its light turned more blue. Again, these changes become extremely marked as we approach c.

Eventually our relativistic astronaut sees most of the stars gathered in a ring ahead of him, though a few sparsely strewn individuals remain visible elsewhere. The ring itself, which Frederik Pohl has dubbed the "starbow," centers on a circle which is mainly dark, because nearly all light from there has been blue-shifted out of the frequencies we can see. The leading or inner edge of the ring is bluish white, its trailing or outer edge reddish; in between is a gradation of colors, akin to what we normally observe. Fred Hollander, a chemist at Brookhaven National Laboratories, has calculated the starbow's exact appearance for different v. It gets narrower and moves farther forward, the bull's eye dead ahead gets smaller and blacker, the faster we go—until, for instance, at $0.9999c$ we perceive a starbow about ten degrees of arc in width, centered on a totally black circle of about the same diameter, and little or nothing shows anywhere else in the sky.

At that speed, $0.9999c$, we'd cross 100 light-years in 20 months of our personal lifetimes. So it's worth trying for; but we'll have to figure out some means of knowing where we are! Though difficult, the problem does not look unsolvable in principle.

It may become so beyond a certain velocity. If we travel under acceleration the whole way, speeding up continuously to the half-way point, thereafter braking at the same rate until we reach our goal: then over considerable distances we get truly staggering relativity factors. The longer a voyage, the less difference it makes to us precisely how long it is.

Thus, Dr. Sagan points out that explorers faring in this wise at one gravity will reach the nearer stars within a few years, Earth time, and slightly less, crew time. But they will cross the approximately 650 light-years to Deneb in 12 or 13 years of their own lifespans; the 30,000 light-years to the center of our galaxy in 21 ship years; the two million light-years to the Andromeda galaxy in 29 ship years; or the 10 million light-years to the Virgo cluster of galaxies in 31 ship years. If they can stand higher accelerations, or have some way to counteract the drag on their bodies, they can cross these gulfs in less of their own time; the mathematical formula governing this is in the appendix.

But will the starbow become too thin and dim for navigation? Or will they encounter some other practical limit? For instance, when matter is accelerated, it radiates energy in the form of gravity waves. The larger the mass, the stronger this radiation; and of course the mass of our spaceship will be increasing by leaps and bounds and pole-vaults. Eventually it may reach a condition where it is radiating away as much energy as it can take in, and thus be unable to go any faster.

However, the real practical limit is likelier to arise from the fact that we have enough stars near home to keep us interested for millennia to come. Colonies planted on worlds around some of these can, in due course, serve as nuclei for human expansion ever further into the universe.

Because many atoms swept through its force-fields are bound to give off light, a ramjet under weigh must be an awesome spectacle. At a safe distance, probably the hull where the crew lives is too small for the naked eye. Instead, against the constellations one sees a translucent shell of multicolored glow, broad in front, tapering aft to a fiery point where the nuclear reaction is going on. (Since this must be contained by force-fields anyway, there is no obvious reason for the fusion chamber to be a metal room.) Thence the exhaust streams backward, at first invisible or nearly so, where its particles are closely controlled, but becoming brilliant further off as they begin to collide, until finally a nebula-like chaos fades away into the spatial night.

It's not only premature, it's pointless to worry about limitations. Conventional physics appears to tell us that, although nature has placed an eternal bound on the speed of our traveling, the stars can still be ours . . . if we really want them.

Yet we would like to reach them more swiftly, with less effort. Have we any realistic chance whatsoever of finding a way around the light-velocity barrier?

Until quite recently, every sensible physicist would have replied with a resounding "No." Most continue to do so. They point to a vast mass of experimental data; for instance, if subatomic particles did not precisely obey Einsteinian laws, our big accelerators wouldn't work. The conservatives

ask where there is the slightest empirical evidence
for phenomena which don't fit into the basic
scheme of relativity. And they maintain that, if
ever we did send anything faster than light, it
would violate causality.

I don't buy that last argument, myself. It seems
to me that, mathematically and logically, it pre-
supposes part of what it sets out to prove. But this
gets a bit too technical for the present essay,
especially since many highly intelligent persons
disagree with me. Those whom I mentioned are
not conservatives in the sense of having stick-in-
the-mud minds. They are among the very people
whose genius and imagination make science the
supremely exciting, creative endeavor which it is
these days.

Nevertheless we do have a minority of equally
qualified pioneers who have lately been advancing
new suggestions.

I suppose the best known idea comes from
Gerald Feinberg, professor of physics at Columbia
University. He has noted that the Einsteinian
equations do not actually forbid material particles
which move faster than light—if these have a mass
that can be described by an imaginary number
(that is, an ordinary number multiplied by the
square root of minus one. Imaginary quantities
are common, e.g., in the theory of electromagnet-
ism). Such "tachyons," as he calls them, would
travel faster and faster the *less* energy they have; it
would take infinite energy to slow them down to c,
which is thus a barrier for them too.

Will it forever separate us, who are composed of

"tardyons," from the tachyon part of the cosmos? Perhaps—but not totally. It is meaningless to speak of anything which we cannot, in principle, detect if it exists. If tachyons do, there must be some way by which we can find experimental evidence for them, no matter how indirect. This implies some kind of interaction (via photons?) with tardyons. But interaction, in turn, implies a possibility of modulation. That is, if they can affect us, we can affect them.

And . . . in principle, if you can modulate, you can do anything. Maybe it won't ever be feasible to use tachyons to beam a man across space; but might we, for instance, use them to communicate faster than light?

Needless to say, first we have to catch them, i.e. show that they exist. This has not yet been done, and maybe it never can be done because in fact there aren't any. Still, one dares hope. A very few suggestive data are beginning to come out of certain laboratories—

Besides, we have other places to look. Hyperspace turns out to be more than a hoary science fiction catchphrase. Geometrodynamics now allows a transit from point to point, without crossing the space between, via a warp going "outside" that space—often called a wormhole. Most wormholes are exceedingly small, of subatomic dimensions; and a trip through one is no faster than a trip through normal space. Nevertheless, the idea opens up a whole new field of research, which may yield startling discoveries.

Black holes have been much in the news, and in

science fiction, these past several years. They are masses so dense, with gravity fields so strong, that light iself cannot escape. Theory has predicted for more than 40 years that all stars above a particular size must eventually collapse into the black hole state. Today astronomers think they have located some, as in Cygnus X-1. And we see hypotheses about black holes of less than stellar mass, which we might be able to find floating in space and utilize.

For our purposes here, the most interesting trait of a black hole is its apparent violation of a whole series of conservation laws so fundamental to physics that they are well-nigh Holy Writ. Thus many an issue, not long ago considered thoroughly settled, is again up for grabs. The possibility of entering a black hole and coming out "instantly" at the far end of a space warp is being seriously discussed. Granted, astronauts probably couldn't survive a close approach to such an object. But knowledge of these space warp phenomena and their laws, if they do occur in reality, might well enable us to build machines which—because they don't employ velocity—can circumvent the c barrier.

Black holes aren't the sole things which play curious tricks on space and time. An ultra-dense toroid, spinning very rapidly in smoke ring fashion, should theoretically create what is called a Kerr metric space warp, opening a way to hyperspace.

The most breathtaking recent development of relativity that I know of is by F.J. Tipler, a physicist at the University of Maryland. According to his calculations, not just near-instantaneous crossings of space should be possible, but time travel should be! A cylinder of ultra-dense matter, rotating extremely fast (velocity at the circumference greater than $0.5c$) produces a region of multiple periodic spacetime. A particle entering this can, depending on its exact track, reach any event in the universe during which the cylinder exists.

The work was accepted for publication in *Physical Review*, which is about as respectable as science can get. Whether it will survive criticism remains to be seen. But if nothing else, it has probably knocked the foundation out from under the causality argument against faster-than-light travel: by forcing us to rethink our whole concept of causality.

The foregoing ideas lie within the realm of accepted physics, or at least on its debatable borders. Dr. Forward has listed several others which are beyond the frontier . . . but only barely, and only by date. Closer study could show, in our near future, that one or more of them refer to something real.

For instance, we don't know what inertia "is." It seems to be a basic property of matter; but why? Could it be an inductive effect of gravitation, as Mach's Principle suggests? If so, could we find ways to modify it, and would we then be held back by the increase of mass with velocity?

Could we discover, or produce, negative mass? This would gravitationally repel the usual positive kind. Two equal masses, positive and negative, linked together, would make each other accelerate in a particular direction without any change in momentum or energy. Could they therefore transcend c?

A solution of Einstein's field equations in five dimensions for charged particles gives an electron velocity of a billion trillion c. What then of a spaceship, if the continuum should turn out to have five rather than four dimensions?

Conventional physics limits the speed of mass-energy. But information is neither; from a physical standpoint, it represents negative entropy. So can information outrun light, perhaps without requiring any medium for its transmission? If you can send information, in principle you can send anything.

Magnificent and invaluable though the structure of relativity is, does it hold the entire truth? There are certain contradictions in its basic assumptions which have never been resolved and perhaps never can be. Or relativity could be just a special case, applying only to local conditions.

Once we are well and truly out into space, we may find the signs of a structure immensely more ample.

These speculations have taken us quite far beyond known science. But they help to show us how little known that science really is, even the parts which have long felt comfortingly, or confiningly, familiar. We can almost certainly reach the stars. Very possibly, we can reach them easily.

If we have the will.

Appendix

Readers who shudder at sight of an equation can skip this part, though they may like to see the promised table. For different velocities, it gives the values of the factors "tau" and "gamma." These are simply the inverses of each other. A little explanation of them may be in order.

Suppose we have two observers, A and B, who have *constant* velocities. We can consider either one as being stationary, the other as moving at velocity v. A will measure the length of a yardstick B carries, in the direction of motion, and the interval between two readings of a clock B carries, as if these quantities were multiplied by tau. For example, if v is 0.9 c, then B's yardstick is merely 0.44 times as long in A's eyes as if B were motionless; and an hour, registered on B's clock, corresponds to merely 0.44 hour on A's. On the other hand, mass is multiplied by gamma. That is, when B moves at 0.9c, his mass according to A is 2.26 times what it was when B was motionless.

B in turn, observes himself as normal, but A and A's environs as having suffered exactly the same changes. Both observers are right.

v	Tau	Gamma
$0.1c$	0.995	1.005
$0.5c$	0.87	1.15
$0.7c$	0.72	1.39
$0.9c$	0.44	2.26
$0.99c$	0.14	7.10
$0.9999c$	0.017	58.6

The formula for tau is $(1 - v^2/c^2)^{1/2}$ where the exponent "$1/2$" indictes a square root. Gamma equals one divided by tau, or $(1 - v^2/c^2)^{1/2}$.

As for relativistic acceleration, if this has a constant value a up to midpoint, then a negative (braking) value $-a$ to destination, the time to cover a distance S equals $(2c/a)$ arc cos $(1 - aS^{1/2}2c^2)$. For long distances, this reduces to $(2c/a)$ ln $(aS/c^2$ where "ln" means "natural logarithm." The maximum velocity, reached at midpoint, is $c [1 - (1 + aS/2c^2)^{-2}]^{1/2}$.

Postscript

Since this essay first appeared, in 1975, much further thought and study have been going on. The likelihood of the "starbow" has been questioned; so has the practicality of the Bussard ramjet. These matters are still controversial, though. Meanwhile, the idea of a matter-antimatter rocket is looking more hopeful than it formerly did. The whole field of interstellar astronautics remains lively, exciting, and infinitely promising.

But mankind will never see that promise fulfilled unless we, today, continue pioneering in those parts of space that we can already reach.

Poul Anderson

Five-time Hugo Winner
Three-time Nebula Winner

☐	48-507-7	**Winners**	**$2.75**
☐	48-545-X	**Maurai & Kith**	**$2.75**
☐	48-515-8	**Fantasy**	**$2.50**
☐	48-579-4	**The Guardians of Time**	**$2.95**
☐	48-553-0	**New America**	**$2.95**
☐	48-517-4	**Explorations**	**$2.50**
☐	48-550-6	**The Gods Laughed**	**$2.95**
☐	48-561-1	**Twilight World** *March 83*	**$2.75**

The Psychotechnic League Series

☐	48-512-6	**The Psychotechnic League**	**$2.50**
☐	48-527-1	**Cold Victory**	**$2.75**
☐	48-533-6	**Starship**	**$2.75**